A SHOCKING DISCOVERY

I stepped down the stairs and pushed on the door. Why did this feel familiar? I put my shoulder to the wood, pressed as hard as I could, and managed to gain a few inches more, but not enough for easy access. Could I squeeze through the narrow opening? I pushed my arm and shoulder through first, forced my knee in, then my hips. My head was last, and there was a panicky moment when I thought I might get stuck there permanently, with my body half in the cabin and my head wedged between the frame and the door.

Once inside, I groped along the wall for a light switch but found none. After the brilliant sunshine of the deck above, it took more than a moment before my eyes became accustomed to the dim light in the small, fusty cabin. But once they had, I was not happy with what I saw. The long, dark shape I'd made out peering through the cabin portholes from above was now discernible. A man was lying diagonally across the berth that filled the triangular space of the small cabin. His head was thrown back, and his mouth gaped open; a trickle of blood had dribbled from the corner of his mouth down his cheek and pooled in the creases of his neck. He was dead.

OTHER BOOKS IN THE *Murder, She Wrote* SERIES

THE MAINE MUTINY

A *Murder, She Wrote* Mystery

A Novel by Jessica Fletcher
and Donald Bain
based on the
Universal television series
created by Peter S. Fischer,
Richard Levinson & William Link

A SIGNET BOOK

SIGNET
Published by New American Library, a division of
Penguin Group (USA) Inc., 375 Hudson Street,
New York, New York 10014, USA
Penguin Group (Canada), 10 Alcorn Avenue, Toronto,
Ontario M4V 3B2, Canada (a division of Pearson Penguin Canada Inc.)
Penguin Books Ltd., 80 Strand, London WC2R 0RL, England
Penguin Ireland, 25 St. Stephen's Green, Dublin 2,
Ireland (a division of Penguin Books Ltd.)
Penguin Group (Australia), 250 Camberwell Road, Camberwell, Victoria 3124,
Australia (a division of Pearson Australia Group Pty. Ltd.)
Penguin Books India Pvt. Ltd., 11 Community Centre, Panchsheel Park,
New Delhi - 110 017, India
Penguin Group (NZ), cnr Airborne and Rosedale Roads, Albany,
Auckland 1310, New Zealand (a division of Pearson New Zealand Ltd.)
Penguin Books (South Africa) (Pty.) Ltd., 24 Sturdee Avenue,
Rosebank, Johannesburg 2196, South Africa

Penguin Books Ltd., Registered Offices:
80 Strand, London WC2R 0RL, England

First published by Signet, an imprint of New American Library,
a division of Penguin Group (USA) Inc.

First Printing, April 2005
10 9 8 7 6 5 4 3 2 1

PUBLISHER'S NOTE
This is a work of fiction. Names, characters, places, and incidents either are
the product of the author's imagination or are used fictitiously, and any resem-
blance to actual persons, living or dead, business establishments, events, or
locales is entirely coincidental.

To all the honest and hardworking men and women of Maine who bring in the lobsters, with admiration and fondness.

Prologue

I think it was the smell that woke me.

I've lived near the ocean my entire life, not counting the time I moved to Indiana for a semester to teach at Schoolman College, nor the time I lived in New York City as a part-time professor at Manhattan University. Even then, I'd come home to Cabot Cove on the weekends. And I don't mind the smell of fish. If you live in a coastal village in Maine, you get used to it. When Ethan Cragg and I used to go fishing, his boat was pretty aromatic, especially when he was cleaning our catch at the end of the day. So I know the smell of a working boat, and a lobster boat definitely falls into that category.

But this was different.

I cracked my eyes open. The sun was beating down on my head. I love the mornings when its rays slant through my east-facing windows. I like to pause, turn my back to the panes, close my eyes, and luxuriate in the sun's warm embrace, just for a moment, before the day's work pulls me away. Had I left the shades open last night? I didn't remember.

I'd been dreaming about a lobster boat on the water. I shut my eyes again and tried to recapture the vision. It had to do with the upcoming lobster festival.

And Spencer Durkee was there. He's something of a town eccentric, when he isn't cuddling up to a bottle down at the beach. A lobsterman for sixty-five of his more than eighty years, he regales youngsters and oldsters alike with his colorful accounts of rumrunners during Prohibition. I suspect he's spinning tales he's heard but never really experienced. All the same, everyone loves to hear him tell the stories. Yes, Spencer was in my dream. What was he doing there? We were on a boat, weren't we? I struggled to remember, but the details were fading away, the sun bleaching them out of my consciousness. Even so, I could still hear the quiet lapping of the sea on the hull, and feel the gentle rocking when the boat bobbed in the water.

What a vivid dream, I thought.

Sometime during the night I must have kicked off my covers. A breeze was fluttering fabric against my legs. I felt it move across my body. I tried to turn over to escape the blinding light, but my bed was all lumpy and hard.

This isn't my bed!

The shock of recognition made me bolt up quickly. I cringed at the pain and reached out to steady myself, my hand pressing against a hard surface. My heart was sounding a tattoo in my chest. I tried, but couldn't take a deep breath, settling instead for shallow panting. Dizzy. Why was I so dizzy? And where was I?

I held perfectly still and squinted against the brilliant light. Gradually, my surroundings came into focus. Outside. I was outside; that's why the sun was so intense. I shaded my eyes with a trembling hand and looked down. I was sitting on a pile of rope. *My lumpy bed,* I thought, grasping a coil of the line and holding on as if it would keep me from tumbling overboard.

Overboard! You're on a boat, a lobster boat.

Across the beam of the boat, a white buoy painted in stripes of yellow and purple—Spencer Durkee's colors—leaned against the corner where the rail meets the washboard, a ledge that runs along the back of the boat. Two wire-and-wood lobster traps sat nearby, empty except for the three bricks in the bottom that kept them from floating along the ocean floor when the current was strong. Above me dangled the pulley of the hydraulic pot hauler, a winch used to pull lobster traps up to the surface. It was attached to the purple roof of the wheelhouse, a Spencer Durkee trademark. "Never have no trouble pickin' out my boat in the float."

I'm on Spencer's boat, the Done For. *How did I get here?*

My head ached, and I squeezed my eyes closed against the throbbing. Maintaining a hold on the rope with my right hand, I gingerly probed the left side of my head, discovering a good-sized egg that was tender to the touch. I opened my eyes again and looked up. Had I hit my head against the pulley?

You'd better find out what's going on, Jessica, I told myself. *It doesn't matter if you're in pain. Something is terribly wrong. Get moving.*

Every muscle in my body complained as I tried to pull myself up to a standing position. I rolled over onto my knees, but was unable to balance on the uneven surface of the rope. I crawled off the coils to the smoother planks of the platform, and slipped off my shoes. They were not appropriate for standing on a deck. *And a dress. I'd never have worn a dress if I'd known I would be on a boat.* Slowly I raised myself till I was standing, legs apart, knees flexed, and bent forward, the only way I could maintain my equilibrium. I took a few breaths and straightened up. Carefully I moved to the middle of the deck, sliding in my stocking feet. I untied the sleeves of a cotton sweater that was looped around my shoulders—how did it get so dirty? I pulled it over my head and pushed my arms through. I wasn't cold. But the sun was high and would burn my skin to a crisp, if it hadn't already.

Now upright, I gazed around. Like all lobster boats, Spencer's sat low in the water, the rail not much more than knee height. Heavy seas would slap easily over the transom and the sides. Fortunately it was relatively calm, with a breeze raising only a slight chop, the small waves and delicate whitecaps extending as far as I could see. Alone. No land in sight, not even the slim dark blue silhouette on the horizon that indicated a terrestrial body. No. Only a straight line of water stretching away to where it met the sky. I staggered to the rail and looked toward the bow of the boat. The seascape was the same. Water. No land. But a bank of dark clouds was heading my way.

Well, Jessica. You've been in fixes before. What do we do now?

My mind raced. I'd never piloted a boat of any size other than a rowboat. Could I serve as master of this vessel? Could I find my way home? That was assuming, of course, that I could get the boat started. Had we run out of gas? The events leading up to my presence on the boat were lost in the fog of memory. I'd heard a bump on the head could cause amnesia. Was

I one of its victims? I knew who I was. But I had no recollection of how I'd gotten here.

I swallowed convulsively and realized my throat was parched. *What I'd give for a glass of water. How ironic,* I thought. The lines from *The Rime of the Ancient Mariner* by Samuel Taylor Coleridge sprang immediately to mind. How many times had I taught that poem?

> *Water, water, everywhere,*
> *And all the boards did shrink;*
> *Water, water, everywhere,*
> *Nor any drop to drink.*

I took a deep breath and straightened my shoulders. The first thing to do was to look around and see what was available. Lobster boats had radios, didn't they? That would be a place to start.

Having a purpose gave me some energy. Perhaps there was some water on board. Maybe even something to eat. I sighed. Well, the day wasn't lost altogether. Spencer practically lived on his boat. There must be some supplies or emergency gear, like a flare. And if I could figure out how to operate the radio, help might be just a call away. *The first thing to do is to get out of the sun,* I told myself. *Then everything will fall into place.*

A lobster boat has a wheelhouse, a standing shelter from which the vessel is piloted. The *Done For*'s shelter had a roof and one long side for protection from the elements. An old-fashioned ring life preserver hung from a hook next to a small red fire extinguisher. In the corner, Spencer's yellow rubber overalls and slicker had been hung on a peg, the bulky gear stretched and stiff, looking as if they could stand by themselves.

The opposite wall was shorter, the open area behind it accommodating the pot hauler. Sliding my feet along the deck, I sought refuge in the wheelhouse and examined the equipment fastened to the bulkhead. Spencer's boat lacked the advanced technology most lobstermen rely on these days.

"I lived my whole life lobsterin'," he once told me. "What do I need with radar or a chart plotter? Those dubs can't find their way out of the bay, with the pier on their left and the rocks on their right, without spendin' fifty thousand dollars on a machine to point them to where the water is."

I pulled on the wheel; it was locked, the key to the engine missing. Of the three round gauges above it, only the compass was moving, its quivering needle pointing southeast. I tapped the gas gauge. The indicator was buried below empty, but I hoped it was only because the engine was off.

Okay, so there's no radar or chart plotter, not even a depth finder—or Fathometer, as the lobstermen call it. But there is a radio.

It was battered and black, bolted to the top of the bulkhead, with numbered dials and two silver switches. I flipped the switches and twisted the dials, hoping for the sound of static to signify it was working. But the only noise was the squeak of the pot hauler's pulley as it swung back and forth in time with the rocking boat. I fiddled with the radio dials for a long time, moving from what I guessed would be one channel to another, my ear against the speaker straining to hear something. I checked the back and squinted at the bottom to see if the wires were frayed, but they were threaded through a hole in the bulkhead, out of my line of sight.

To the left of the wheel was a big wooden box probably used as a seat. I found a latch holding the top down, unlocked it, and was rewarded when it opened to reveal a jumble of fishing paraphernalia, a nail clipper, wire, a cracked coffee cup, a box of plastic sandwich bags, some of which had been used for screws, rubber washers, and other hardware. Dropping to my knees, I dug through the box, careful to set aside anything sharp, making piles of similar items on the deck, and hoping for something, anything, that would help me cope with my precarious predicament. I found a hammer, screwdriver, matches, fishing cap with a bent peak, and odd pieces, the uses for which mystified me. There was a small pad of paper, its corners all curled from the humid air, and a stub of a pencil with no eraser. In the bottom was a spool of lightweight fishing line, but no hooks. It didn't look as if I'd be able to catch my lunch. I replaced the contents that lay scattered about me, secured the top, and sat on the box. *Don't panic now. You're safe. You're dry,* I told myself. *It's summer. There are lots of fishermen and pleasure craft on the water. I'm bound to come across another boat if I'm not too many miles from shore, if I'm still in the Gulf of Maine, if I haven't been caught and carried in an east-flowing current to be lost at sea.*

Despite the warmth of the day, I shivered. *Goodness!* Where had that thought come from? *Lost at sea?*

I tried desperately to remember where I'd been,

what I'd done before I woke up aboard the *Done For*. Was the name of the boat prophetic for me? Was *I* done for? Had I interfered one too many times? Was someone I'd investigated taking revenge? Had I been involved in a case and come too close to the solution, too close for someone's comfort? But who? And why?

My head ached, but the answers, if they were there, floated somewhere beyond my consciousness. I could almost grasp them. But they slipped away, leaving me frustrated and tired.

I leaned back against the bulkhead and closed my eyes. It would be so easy to sleep, so easy to fade into blankness and escape the frightening reality of my situation. My eyes popped open.

"That is not an option, Jessica," I said out loud, my voice hoarse to my ears. My lips were dry and chapped.

I pushed out of my seat. There was a bit more of this boat to explore, but first I had to ensure my safety. I removed my stockings. Bare feet would hold better on the slippery deck. I tucked up the skirt of my dress into my belt so it wouldn't trip me, opened the box again, and picked out the fishing cap. It was dirty but it would shield my face from the glare of the sun. Bending over and holding on to the rail, I inched my way to the back of the boat. On the top of the washboard was a series of strips spaced eight inches apart.

I could hear Spencer's voice in my head. "Gotta have somethin' to keep the pots from sliding all over the washboard. Makes a nice seat, too, if you don't mind the ridges."

I knelt on the hot deck, pushed the lobster traps

aside, and peered beneath the shelf, reaching a hand under to feel for what I couldn't see. I pulled out a red metal can shaped like a muffin with a spout on top. I shook it and heard some fluid slap against the side. I unscrewed the spout and inhaled the distinct odor of gasoline. But there wasn't a bait barrel or a bin to hold lobsters, nothing to catch water if I was aboard long enough for it to rain. I stood and took some ungainly steps back toward the wheelhouse. *I don't have my sea legs yet*, I thought, lurching a bit, *but I don't have time to wait for them to develop.*

At the short wall of the wheelhouse, I gripped a metal upright, took a deep breath, raised one knee, and placed a foot on the railing. I needed to see what was forward of the wheelhouse. The boat had a trunk cabin, a small space for storage below, the top of which jutted out on the foredeck. Through the windshield I could see there was a hatch on the roof, but the only way to reach it was to climb on the railing and make my way along the narrow ledge to the bow. One false step and I could end up in the water. If that happened, I wasn't sure I could clamber back into the boat without assistance.

Praying not to trip, and holding my breath, I climbed up onto the ledge, clinging to the edge of the purple roof and the radio antenna as I sidestepped my way toward the forward deck. My weight caused the boat to dip, and my feet skidded on the narrow decking, one slipping down toward the sea. For a second I thought my worst fears were about to come true and I would topple off the side. I dug my fingernails into the roof molding and hung on; my toes reached for the deck and curled around the raised rail. I let out a big breath and rested my head on my arms till my heartbeat slowed and I could move again.

Where the shelter ended, the cabin roof, a low platform, rose from the deck, and I gratefully climbed on top and sat with my back against the wheelhouse windshield, bracing my feet on the hatch. *Whew!* My sweater clung to my dress, damp from perspiration and sea spray. I'd lost Spencer's hat when I'd stumbled, but I felt the thrill of a dangerous feat successfully achieved. I forced away the thought of the return trip and drew a deep breath, smiling as I let it out. Ahead of me the water was flat, the earlier chop smoothed out. A light breeze ruffled my hair. A flock of seabirds—gannets, maybe?—flew just above the surface of the ocean, dropping down to dip their beaks into the water. It was beautiful and peaceful.

My tranquil feeling was short-lived, however. I needed to get into the cabin. Perhaps I could find something to help me understand how I got here. At worst, it might contain provisions. Wouldn't it be wonderful if there was a bottle of water? Reluctantly, I crawled forward and knelt over the hatch, hooking my fingers over the edge and pulling up as hard as I could. It wouldn't budge. *My luck that it opens only from the inside.* I tried again, but was no closer to lifting the lid of the hatch. *There must be a door I've overlooked.* Vaguely, I remembered seeing a door. I thought I'd given the wheelhouse a thorough inspection, but I could have missed something. I leaned over the side of the cabin roof and noticed two oval portholes. They didn't open but allowed light into the tiny cabin. Stretching out on the cabin roof, I slid my body slightly over the edge and, shading my eyes, tried to peer into the cabin through the scratched glass of the porthole. I could barely make out what was inside. Something long and dark—perhaps a berth—but the details were lost in glass that had been etched by years of salt water and scrubbing. Both portholes on the port side and the pair on the starboard side were equally impenetrable, and the only option left was to hunt for the access.

Having conquered the narrow rail once allowed me to negotiate it easily on the return trip. This time I was prepared for the dip when my weight tilted the vessel as I retraced my steps, edging along the railing toward the rear of the boat. But the joy of success was no less sweet when I jumped down to the aft deck from the railing.

I examined the bulkhead minutely, using all my strength to push the heavy wooden box out of the way to see what was behind it. Nothing. But I had missed the low door that squatted in back of Spencer's overalls and slicker. The rubber apparel had flared out, concealing the line of the closed door and the recessed steps that gave access to the cabin below. I wrapped my arms around Spencer's foul-weather gear, lifted it off its peg, and laid it on the deck out of the way. I went back to the door, leaned over, and pressed on the panel. It swung inward a few inches, but something kept it from opening completely.

I stepped down the stairs and pushed on the door. Why did this feel familiar? I put my shoulder to the wood, pressed as hard as I could, and managed to gain a few inches more, but not enough for easy access. Could I squeeze through the narrow opening? I pushed my arm and shoulder through first, forced my knee in, then my hips. My head was last, and there was a panicky moment when I thought I might get stuck there permanently, with my body half in the cabin and my head wedged between the frame and the door.

Once inside, I groped along the wall for a light switch but found none. After the brilliant sunshine of the deck above, it took more than a moment before my eyes became accustomed to the dim light in the small, fusty cabin. But once they had, I was not happy with what I saw. The long, dark shape I'd made out peering through the cabin portholes from above was now discernible. A man was lying diagonally across the berth that filled the triangular space of the small cabin. His head was thrown back, and his mouth gaped open; a trickle of blood had dribbled from the corner of his mouth down his cheek and pooled in the creases of his neck. He was dead.

Chapter One

You'd never know that Mara's had a beautiful view. The windows that overlooked the waterfront from the luncheonette's favorable location on the docks in Cabot Cove were spattered with rain, the mist off the bay obscuring even the tall masts that tilted back and forth on the choppy surface of the harbor.

Gwen Anissina, body bent forward, arms folded on the table just behind her empty coffee cup, dropped her head and wailed. "Please, somebody, tell me it's not going to rain the Saturday after next."

Barnaby Longshoot swiveled toward Gwen from his seat at the counter. "Don't know why not. Been rainin' every weekend since Memorial Day. Wettest summah I ever see."

"Shut up, Barnaby. Gwen's miserable enough as it is. More coffee, hon?" Mara filled Gwen's cup from one of the two pots she was holding and leaned over to check the milk level in the stainless-steel pitcher on the table. "I gave you decaf this time. It's your third cup."

Mara turned to me. "What about you, Jessica? Like a refill?"

"Not for me, thanks, Mara," I said, passing my hand

over the top of my cup. "I've had my quota for the day."

Mara moved on to the next booth, where Mayor Jim Shevlin and two colleagues were huddled over a map of the town, trying to figure out how to accommodate all the tourists if the upcoming lobster festival were rained out.

Cabot Cove had its share of tourists every summer, but the town's attractions were typical of Maine—quaint houses, many of them Victorian, like mine, and a busy harbor with two charter-boat stations offering, depending upon the season, fishing, island exploring, whale watching, sea kayaking, and scuba diving at a sunken wreck down the coast. Visitors usually made a beeline to the docks, or to one of our seaside restaurants, driving right past the downtown. For years, the merchants had been trying to convince the town fathers that something was needed to bring out-of-towners to Main Street, but their pleas had been, if not exactly ignored, tabled. Finally, they took matters into their own hands. The chamber of commerce prevailed upon the *Cabot Cove Gazette* to conduct a survey, soliciting suggestions for ways to draw tourists to the village center. The newspaper promised to publish the most interesting proposals in a weekly feature on the front page.

Submissions had poured in, and the mayor, with elections not far off, succumbed to the pressure and agreed to judge the proposals with an eye toward implementing the best ideas. One wag advocated a wet-T-shirt contest, which was rejected immediately, although just the thought caused consternation among the members of the Ladies' Auxiliary, who had in mind something less raucous, like a crafts fair.

After sifting through a pile of letters, the mayor's office had decided against a permanent installation, turning down proposals for an amusement park, a petting zoo, and a maritime museum, and instead settled on a temporary event, one that could start off small and grow as success allowed. The final decision, outlined in a poster exhibit in the village library, gathered a number of the suggestions into the first annual Cabot Cove lobster festival, to be held in late August so as not to compete with the long-standing lobster festival in Rockland earlier in the month.

To start, plans called for a parade through the center of town; the crowning of a Miss Cabot Cove Lobsterfest, each candidate to be sponsored by a local business; a Ladies' Auxiliary crafts fair; an arts competition among local schoolchildren for the best expression of "What Cabot Cove Means to Me," the entries to be displayed in shops along Main Street; and all culminating in a community lobster dinner under a tent in the village center, the success of which relied heavily on Cabot Cove's lobstermen supplying the centerpiece of the meal.

"How many can you seat inside, Mara?" asked Roger Cherry. He was a retired accountant and former president of the chamber, who'd volunteered to help the town with the event. Mayor Shevlin was relying on him to come up with foul-weather plans.

"Fifty-four at tables and in the booths. Eight at the counter," Mara said, filling the men's coffee cups. "If we let the awning down, and the wind's not too bad, we can probably fit another fifteen outside on the dock. If the weather's fair, I can push that up to thirty."

"Fair weather's no problem," Roger said. "We just want to make sure the tourists have places to go and things to do if it rains."

"I'll help put out the chairs, won't I, Mara?" Barnaby called from his stool at the end of the counter. In his thirties, Barnaby was a slow learner who'd left school early and made his living doing odd jobs for the town merchants. Mara employed him every summer to work in her restaurant.

"How many people do you figure you'll get?" she asked.

"No way to know," Roger replied. "We could get anywhere from a couple hundred to several thousand over the festival's three days, but, of course, a good portion of them will be local citizens."

"Won't hurt to remind them of what they can find in Cabot Cove. We're not a mall, but we've got a lot to offer, all the same." The speaker was David Ranieri, who, with his brother, Jim, owned Charles Department Store, which had been a mainstay of downtown commerce for decades. It was the first place I looked for anything I needed, from sewing notions to small appliances to shoes, and, remarkably, they always seemed to have it in stock.

Gwen opened her bag and pulled out an electronic organizer. She drew a slender stylus from its side and tapped the screen. "How am I ever going to get everything done in the next fourteen days?"

"What do you have to do?" I asked.

"Well, I've already sent press releases to every local

paper up and down the coast, and I've used an online service to send notices to travel editors across the country. I sent the local PBS stations a tape of the mayor talking about the festival. I'm hoping they'll bite for an interview. If they don't, we can run it ourselves on public access, but it doesn't reach as wide an audience. The radio station will do a remote broadcast from the village square during the festival, and they're doing a promotion starting next week, giving away tickets."

"Sounds like you're doing very well," I said, impressed with her industry.

Gwen nodded and again tapped the screen. "It's a start, but I still have to do the final schedule for the Web site, and write up a story on Cabot Cove lobstermen for the *Gazette*. And they're not being terribly cooperative."

"Who's not being cooperative?"

"The lobstermen, not the *Gazette*. The paper's been wonderful. Even so, I'm swamped." She put down the organizer and counted off on her fingers. "I have to talk to the photographer about his schedule, and the shuttle-bus company about theirs. We don't have enough street parking, so we're going to run a bus from the high school parking lot to downtown. The barbershop quartet wants to go on at the same time as the Dixieland band, and the leaders are not talking to each other. I also have the children's art exhibit to coordinate. All the drawings have to be mounted on boards and distributed to the merchants to hang in their windows. And we have to pick up the evening gowns from the rental place in Bangor, make sure they fit, and have rehearsals for the beauty pageant, not to mention that I still have to round up the final judges to choose Miss Cabot Cove Lobsterfest." Gwen stopped counting and looked up at me. "I don't suppose you'd agree to be a judge, would you?"

"I'm sure you can find someone infinitely more qualified for that task than I," I said, smiling to soften the refusal. "But perhaps I can help you with the Web site or with the article for the *Gazette*. I'm between book projects right now, and it won't hurt to exercise my writing muscles a bit."

"Oh, Mrs. Fletcher, if you would take the *Gazette* article off my hands, I would be eternally grateful. I've been chasing Linc Williams for a week, but he won't give me the time of day. I can't decide if it's because I'm a woman, or because I'm from away, but he just won't talk to me."

Lincoln Williams was the head of the local lobstermen's association, a man of great importance, both in his own eyes and in those of his colleagues. He traced his family ties to Cabot Cove going back close to two centuries. All the men had been fishermen, but those in the last few generations had gone out for lobster, and each had led the association, passing the presidency down from father to son as if the position were a royal throne. None of the members of his association, I knew, would consent to an interview without Linc's say-so. And getting to Linc, as Gwen had found out, was not easily accomplished, unless you were a lobsterman. I doubted Linc would condescend to talk to me, either, but I knew another way to reach him.

"What kind of story were you looking for?"

"It's for the festival edition of the *Gazette*, the one that'll be handed out for free the first day. The new editor, Evelyn Phillips, wants kind of a 'day in the life of a lobsterman' story. She's doing her own piece on the history of Cabot Cove and has someone else doing an article on how to eat a lobster."

"Okay."

"Do you think you can do it?"

"I'm pretty sure I can," I said, hoping it was true. "Mary Carver is on the Friends of the Library committee with me. Her husband, Levi, is a lobsterman. I'll ask Mary to ask Levi to ask Linc if I can trail along for a day on one of the boats."

Gwen's eyes shone. "That would be perfect, Mrs. Fletcher. Thank you. Thank you. Thank you. I am in your debt forever."

"Don't thank me yet," I said, smiling. "Now that I've volunteered, I hope I don't let you down."

"You could never let me down. You've done so much already. I don't know where I'd be without the Friends of the Library and the Ladies' Auxiliary. That old saying, 'If you want something done, ask a busy woman,' is absolutely true. The Cabot Cove Lobsterfest could never come off if it weren't for the women in this town."

"Well, we're all excited about this event, and hope it will give the downtown economy the boost it deserves."

"It will, if history is any guide," she said. "The festival over in Rockland has raised a ton of money for community programs there. I'm sure the Cabot Cove version will be just as successful. You'll see."

"I'm sure it will, too," I said. "Just look who we have working for us."

She pumped her fist into the air. "Yeah, Gwendolyn Anissina, girl genius."

"What was that?" Barnaby called over from the counter.

We laughed.

"Well, I'd better get going," Gwen said. "No sense in sitting and complaining; that won't get it done. Thank you again, Mrs. Fletcher."

"Please, it's Jessica."

"Okay. It's Jessica." She gathered her windbreaker and handbag, paid Mara at the register, and, with a " 'Bye, all," made her exit, holding the door open for Seth Hazlitt, who was coming in, before she went out into the rain.

"Where's she off to in this weather?" Seth asked, sliding onto the bench Gwen had just vacated, and dragging a plastic shopping bag in with him.

"More places than I can keep track of," I said to Cabot Cove's favorite physician, and my oldest and dearest friend.

"Mornin', Doc," Mara said, clearing away Gwen's dishes. "Can I get you a cup of coffee?"

"Ayuh. You can."

"Anything else?"

Seth looked over to the counter, where Mara had a cake plate piled with Danish and doughnuts under a plastic cover. "Happen to have any of that peach cobbler left over from yesterday?" he asked.

"Made some fresh this morning. I'll bring it right over."

"Gwen was just giving us a rundown of her schedule for the next two weeks," I said. "She's going to need some help."

"You volunteerin'?" Seth asked.

"As a matter of fact I did," I said. "I'm going to write an article for her for the paper."

"That's nice. You let me know if you need my assistance," he said.

"There is something you could help her out with," I said.

"What's that?"

"She's looking for judges for the Miss Cabot Cove Lobsterfest Contest."

"The beauty pageant?"

"Now, don't dismiss it out of hand."

"You'd make a great judge, Doc," Mara said, as she slid a cup of coffee and a dish of warm cobbler in front of Seth.

"I'm not going to ogle a bunch of girls walking around in bathing suits. It's undignified," he said, taking up a heaping forkful of the sweet dessert to which Mara had added a scoop of vanilla ice cream.

"That's only a small part of it," I said. "There's a talent contest and current-events questions. You'd be good at judging that. Besides, it's all in fun, and for the benefit of Cabot Cove."

"Mmm-hmm," he said around the mouthful of cobbler.

"I wouldn't mind spendin' time lookin' at beautiful girls," Barnaby put in, "but no one asked me."

"And no one will," Mara said. "You'd vote for the first one to flirt with you."

"I would," Barnaby agreed.

"Don't you have something to do in the kitchen?" Mara asked him.

"Nope. I'm on my break," he said, quickly turning back to his coffee.

"Think about it," I said to Seth. "Gwen's working so hard. We should all help her out."

"That one's a driver, all right," Roger said. He turned to the mayor. "Where'd you find her?"

"Put an ad for a festival coordinator in the Bangor paper."

"Not the *Gazette*?" Seth asked.

"Shh." The mayor looked around to see who was nearby. "Don't tell Matilda Watson, please; she'll skin me alive. But I wanted someone with event-planning experience, and we don't have anyone in town who fits that description."

Matilda Watson was the longtime owner of the *Cabot Cove Gazette*. She was not known for her patience, and had been through a succession of editors, firing them for minor infractions as fast as she hired them. She kept the publisher title for herself and was not above browbeating people in town into advertising in her paper. Some people thought she—and not the chamber of commerce—was behind the original idea of a survey to bring traffic to the downtown stores, using the project as a way to solicit more ads.

"What experience does Gwen have?" Mara asked. "She looks like she's barely out of school."

"That's true," Mayor Shevlin said. "She graduated in June from the New England School of Communications. She's young but she's full of energy and ideas. She volunteered at Rockland's lobster festival for the past three years, and was even one of the contestants in their Sea Goddess pageant before that. Didn't capture the crown but got a lot of experience. She knows how a good festival runs. We could do a lot worse than to emulate Rockland's success. So I hired her."

"Plus, she must work cheap," Barnaby called from his stool, setting off a wave of laughter.

Mayor Shevlin's cheeks turned pink. "Well, there is that," he admitted.

I kept Seth company while he finished his breakfast, then gathered up my things. "You'll have to excuse me," I said. "Doesn't look as if the weather's improving, and I have errands to run."

"Wait," he said. "Got something for you."

"What's that?"

He reached into the shopping bag he'd placed on the seat beside him and pulled out a small green folding umbrella. "Patient dropped these off this morning," he said. "Gave me two of them. Here, you take this one. I don't need so many umbrellas. Just end up losin' 'em anyway."

"Thank you," I said. "As it happens, I left my umbrella at home. Your timing is perfect."

He grinned. "Glad to be of service."

"I'll call you later," I said. "Think about being a judge. You'll get to sit on the podium. It has the best view of the parade. And all the girls' mothers will likely ply you with cakes and pies to try to gain your favor."

I pulled on my slicker and went to pay for my coffee and English muffin.

"All taken care of," Mara said when I approached the register. "Gwen treated you to breakfast."

"That's very nice," I said, closing my wallet, "but don't let her do it again."

"Why not?"

"You heard the mayor. She's not getting paid very much. I'd like to see her stay in town after the festival, if she can find work here. It's refreshing to meet someone of her energy and enthusiasm. How is she doing?"

"Gwen's a nice girl, but you know how the old-timers are. They're not very welcoming to newcomers. I never can understand that. It's like if you're not related to half the town and can't point to your grandmother's house, you're still considered to be from away. They're polite, just not really friendly. It'll always be that way, too, unless she marries a local boy."

I nodded. "It's a shame. A town needs new blood and new ideas to prosper."

I pulled up my hood, waved good-bye, and stepped out into the wet. Slipping my new umbrella out of its green sleeve, I pushed the button and it flew open. Immediately a gust of wind blew it inside out. I managed to get the umbrella right side out again, only to have it reverse itself once more. I struggled to close the umbrella and dropped it into my shoulder bag. Head bent against the blustery weather, I walked up the dock toward town. I had debated taking out my bicycle this morning, but decided to walk instead, on the theory that the bike was rustier than I. Of course, it had been a gentle rain when I'd left home. It was coming on a gale now.

I understood why the mayor was worried. If we had this kind of weather for the festival, we'd be hard-pressed to keep up a cheerful atmosphere, much less attract a big crowd. Money had been spent in expectation not only of making it back but of reaching a profit. The mayor's reelection campaign was scheduled to kick off the day after the festival, and the lobstermen were going to build up the supply of lobsters by holding their catch out of the market to ensure that there would be enough to serve all the attendees. If those visitors didn't materialize, the lobstermen stood to lose a lot of money when they flooded the market with the crustaceans. There was a lot hinging on the success of this event. So much could go wrong.

Chapter Two

Mary Carver was hanging wash on the line behind her house the next day when I walked around to the backyard.

"Good morning, Mary."

"Hi, there, Jessica," she said, reaching into her straw basket for a blue T-shirt, which she draped over the line. "Hope you don't mind if I keep on workin'. Got to take advantage of the weather while I can. Sun's been so stingy this summah, and my cellar's damp enough to begin with. We haven't worn dry clothes in over a month."

"No need to stop on my account," I said. "As I said on the phone, I can talk and you can listen just as easily with busy hands as idle ones."

"Levi's been urgin' me to get another of those electric dryers ever since ours went on the fritz." She paused in her task, propped her hands on her hips, and looked up at me. "But I'm stubborn, I guess. My mother always hung her wash outside, and I like the smell of clothes dried in the sun." She resumed her chore. "Of course, the constant rain these past months has been givin' me second thoughts." She eyed the lowering clouds.

"I love the smell of clothes dried on the line, too,"

I said, "but I also love the convenience of a dryer, especially when I'm in a hurry, which I always seem to be."

"If we get another week of this rain, I'll be running to the appliance store," she said. "Hand me some of those, would you please, Jessica?"

I pulled out a handful of clothespins from a bucket next to the basket and passed them to her two at a time as she pegged up the laundry. As Mary worked, I explained my predicament, having offered to write a story, but not sure how to approach the lobstermen's association with the request to observe the work by riding along on one of the boats for a day.

"I was hoping you could advise me," I said.

"You know, some of the men might be superstitious about havin' a female on their boat," Mary said, taking the clothespin I held out.

"One or two of the old-timers might," I said, reaching into the bucket for another. "But I can't believe they'd all feel that way."

Mary laughed. "Even if they did, they wouldn't dare say it."

"Don't some of the wives work on the boats with their husbands?"

"Some do, especially in the busy season. More often the ones starting out. I used to go out with Levi before the children came. Later on, when the kids were little, he'd take on a man every summah to help out as sternman."

"Sternman?"

"The one who stands at the stern, pulls up the pots, empties them, throws them back. Levi used to do it all himself, pilot the boat and be his own sternman, but as soon as we were able to put by a little extra money, he got himself a helper. Most of the men these days—leastwise the ones with bigger boats and hundreds of traps—have a helper. I have to warn you: It's very busy on board. There wouldn't be a lot of room. And you'd have to sign on for the whole day. It would cost them time and money if they had to come back to the dock to let you off."

"I'd never ask that," I said. "I'll try to be as inconspicuous as possible, stay out of the way, observe, and ask questions only when they're not in the middle of work."

"You know, Jessica, if it were still Gwen asking, she might never get the chance to go."

"Why not?"

"She's way too young and pretty for any of the wives to trust their husbands to."

I laughed. "Well, there's no danger here," I said.

Mary reddened. "I didn't mean any offense, Jessica."

"None taken, Mary. I'm long past the need to fish for compliments."

Mary lifted the empty laundry basket and rested it on her hip. She started toward the house, and waved me to join her. "Come have some coffee. I've got a Bundt cake I baked this morning. Should be about cool by now."

I followed Mary into her pretty yellow, black, and white kitchen. It had recently been renovated, and she was pleased with the gleaming granite countertop and elegant maple cabinets, inspired by a picture she'd found in a decorating magazine. Many a Friends of the Library meeting convened around her large oval table, where details of the project of the moment could be argued without disturbing the peace of the library's reading room.

"Don't trip on Anna's sneakers," she said, pointing out a pair of red-and-white high-tops that had been left on the kitchen floor. "I purposely didn't put them away because I want her to pick up after herself. That's a lesson she's havin' a hard time learnin'."

"Many youngsters are like that, I'm sure," I said.

"Maybe so, but her father will give her what-for if he finds them when he gets home. I'm letting her take the consequences this time, if she doesn't put them away."

While Mary stowed her laundry basket and turned the cake out of its pan onto a plate, I walked to the wrought-iron baker's rack against the wall where black-framed photographs of the Carver family were arrayed on a shelf. Images of Mary and Levi when they were young marrieds sat next to pictures of their three children through the years. The eldest, Ginny, was married now, with a child of her own on the way. I'd met her only once or twice. I was more familiar with her "baby sister," twelve-year-old Anna, she of the offending sneakers. A whirligig of a girl, constantly on the move, she would fly in and out of the kitchen during our meetings, working her charm on her mother for privileges she'd never have gotten if the library's Friends had not been in attendance. A school photograph showed an impish, grinning face under curly hair that hadn't seen a brush that day.

Mary came up behind me. "That's Evan," she said, referring to a photo I had picked up to examine. It was of a young man on a boat.

"He must be about seventeen now," I said, looking at the handsome teenager with his mother's blue eyes and his father's sturdy build. I replaced the photo on the shelf.

"Eighteen come January," his mother replied. "He's been helping out his father this summah. Keeps him busy, and he's too tired at day's end to go girlin' with his friends."

She pulled a teapot off another shelf. "I seem to remember you prefer tea," she said.

"Only if it's no bother."

"It's no bother at all," she said. "I've got one of those instant hot spigots. Audrey Williams bragged about getting one in her new kitchen, and I figured if it's good enough for her, it's good enough for me."

Audrey Williams, wife of Linc, was a proud woman; proud of her house, proud of her children, and proud of her husband, the president of the lobstermen's association. She was on the Friends of the Library committee with us, but was not a favorite among the other wives, according to comments I'd heard passed from time to time at Loretta's hair salon.

Mary fixed cups of Earl Grey tea and sliced two pieces of cake, which she set on the table.

"Evan's got his eye on the Brown girl, Abigail. Know her?"

"Is she the one Charles Department Store is sponsoring in the beauty pageant?" I asked, pulling out a chair and sitting.

"That's the one. She works there part-time."

"I've seen her picture in the store window. Very pretty."

"And smart, too," Mary said, putting a pitcher of

milk on the table and joining me. "She was in Evan's class. She's goin' away to Colby College this fall."

Mary looked off into space. Her eyes were sad, as if she were wrestling with some difficulty. She broke off a piece of cake, chewed thoughtfully, and took a sip of tea. I wondered what was occupying her, when she said, "He's had a crush on her since sixth grade."

"Abigail Brown?"

"Yes."

"It worries you?"

She sighed, staring into her cup. "Evan told me he wants to marry her." She looked up at me. "He's too young to make such a commitment. I want him to see a little of the world before he settles down. Levi and I got married so young. We were high school sweethearts. Ginny and Pete, too. I was hoping Evan wouldn't follow quite so closely in our footsteps."

"Does Abigail want to marry him? I thought you said she plans to go to college."

"I'm not sure Abby knows how serious he is. They've been in the same group of friends a long time. She's been teasing Evan lately, urging him to apply to Colby, too."

"It doesn't sound as if they're about to elope," I said, smiling.

"Gorry, Jess. I certainly hope not."

"Don't you like her?"

"It's not a matter of liking or not liking, although I do like her. She's a nice girl from a good family. My mother and her grandmother were second cousins. It's just that Evan is so young, and he's a stubborn son of a gun, just like his father."

"And his mother, to hear you tell it."

Mary laughed. "I guess I'm caught in my own words."

"Anyway, young people often have a change of heart, don't they?" I said. "I seem to remember when I was teaching, the students in my classes played musical chairs all year, according to who had a girlfriend—or boyfriend—at the time."

"That's true," she admitted. "And if Abby wins the Miss Lobsterfest crown, she's likely to attract a lot of potential beaus." She stopped, a piece of cake halfway to her mouth. Shaking her head, she put it down. "That's the mother's dilemma. I don't want him to be too serious about her, but I also don't want her to reject him."

I smiled. "How many young women entered the competition?"

"There are eight altogether. Rockland had twenty in the Sea Goddess pageant, but their winner represents the state's lobster industry for the comin' year. We can't offer that, so we wanted to keep ours small. The winner holds the crown till next summer, but we'll have to think up some events for her to participate in or we won't get any girls willin' to compete again."

"You sound as if you don't think we can do that."

"I'll tell you, Jessica, this project has really taxed my patience. Oh, I'm sure we'll think of something—even if it's only the launching of the back-to-school sales days. That's the easy part, but there have been a lot of tough parts, too. And I'm really worried how it's going to turn out."

"An event as ambitious as this is going to go through growing pains before we get all the elements of it worked out," I said. "We all knew that. But at our last meeting, I got the impression that everything was under control. Isn't it?"

Mary's brows lifted and she studied the ceiling for a moment. "Not exactly. At least from what I hear."

"What is it you're hearing, Mary? And from whom?"

"It's the guys; they're grumbling a lot."

"What guys?"

"The lobstermen."

"What are they unhappy about?"

"Well, you know the men have been asked to hold off selling their catch to the market so we have enough in the pound to serve all the tourists during the festival."

"The lobstermen's association agreed to that when we first started planning the event. Are they changing their minds now?"

"It's not that they're changin' their minds, but they feel they're gettin' . . . well, cheated."

"Cheated! How?"

Mary looked uncomfortable. "I don't know if I should say anything. It's just stuff I hear." She fiddled with the edge of her napkin, her lips pressed into a line. Finally she looked at me. "You've been working hard on this project, as much as the rest of us. You got a right to know."

I nodded to encourage her. "If it's something confidential—" I started to say.

"No, it's nothin' like that. It's just that the price of lobster has been going up recently. All the rain and fog cut back on fishing days up and down the coast. Not just us. That, plus the catches are off last season's mark. Don't know where those critters go in the rain.

Seems to me it's wet all the time for lobsters. But, fact is, if the supply goes down—and it has—the prices go up. Restaurants in Boston and New York still want their lobster."

"That's good for the lobstermen, isn't it?"

"If they sell now, it would be. They could get top dollar. But if they hold their catch for the festival, which they promised they would, the prices could drop by then. If they do, the men stand to lose a lot of money. This is what we live on, Jessica. We don't want to gamble with our income."

"I thought the dealer had agreed to pay the going price for the lobsters we're holding for the festival."

"Henry Pettie? He's a slippery one. He may have agreed in March when we were making plans. But now he sees a way to boost his profit. He's offering thirty cents a pound less than what the market is going for now. The men are torn. They want to support the festival, but they don't want Pettie to take advantage of their goodwill."

"I don't blame them. Has anyone spoken to him?"

"It's complicated. Pettie holds the notes on a lot of the men's boats."

"You mean he lends them money and uses the boats as collateral?"

"Well, the banks won't," she said, sounding defensive.

"Why not?"

"They say the business is too precarious. The men never know how much they're goin' to make. And that's true. You're lucky if you have a house, but they won't give a dime for a boat. Or for the equipment.

Those Fathometers and radios and satellite boxes, they cost a fortune. There's not a lobsterman in town doesn't owe Pettie money. And he makes 'em sign for it. Keeps a little black book in his back pocket. Threatens to collect whenever someone goes up against 'im.''

"Even so, there must be some recourse when he's paying below the market rate.''

"Levi says their hands are tied. The festival committee negotiated with the dealer, and the association had a man on the committee, representin' the lobstermen. He signed the contract.''

"Oh, dear. Didn't he show it to others in the association first?''

Mary shook her head. "You can't really blame him. No one thought Pettie would exploit the situation for his own gain. But Spencer's an old man. Maybe he was the wrong one to put on the committee, but no else volunteered.''

"Spencer Durkee?''

"Yes. There are a bunch of Monday-morning quarterbacks now heapin' abuse on him, carryin' on about how they would never have signed that contract. There's lots of resentment. The other morning Spencer went out and found his lines cut; he lost all his traps. Then, when he went into town to try to scare up new ones, someone poured a pile of rotten bait on the *Done For*'s deck.''

"How awful.''

"It was in the *Gazette*. I'm surprised you didn't see it.''

"I get behind in my reading when I'm finishing up

a book," I said. "I have a pile of magazines and news-
papers at home to look through before I recycle
them."

"I can't imagine why they put something like that
in the paper. We were all embarrassed. Levi helped
Spencer clean it up, and he came home stinkin' worse
than I've ever smelled him. And that's saying something. Some of the men can be very mean when they're
provoked. But what's the point of poundin' up an old
man? And who knows if one of these young highliners
would've been any better at reading the contract?
They didn't raise their hands when asked to serve on
the committee, so they've only themselves to blame."

"Is there anything the committee can do now?" I
asked.

"I think it's too late. The lobstermen's association
is meeting tonight."

"Oh, dear," I said. "You don't think they'd do anything to jeopardize the festival, do you?"

"I can't promise you that."

"Where are they meeting?"

"Down at Nudd's Bait and Tackle, on the other end
of the docks from Mara's."

"I know the place."

"I wouldn't get in the middle of this, Jessica."

"No. No," I said. "They should work it out
themselves."

"I'm sure they will," she said, pouring me another
cup of tea. "When Levi gets home, I'll talk to·him
about your request. I'm sure he won't mind passing it
along to Linc. The lobstermen can use a positive story
in the press. The paper covers our dirty laundry fast
enough."

I thought about what Mary had told me as I rode my bicycle home. The lobstermen were a community within a community. They were like a closed club, with their own rules and punishments for those who broke them. But they were quick to take care of their own when someone needed help. And they prided themselves on contributing to the wider community as well. Cabot Cove was counting on that. The lobstermen were represented on every charitable and civic organization in town. I hoped their goodwill would prevail when it came to the lobster festival. We would be sunk without them.

Chapter Three

"It was the days of Prohibition, see. And the rumrunners'ud bring down the whiskey from Canada and drop anchor just beyond the three-mile limit."

Spencer Durkee sat on a folding metal chair outside Nudd's Bait & Tackle, his fishing cap pushed up high on his forehead and his gnarled fingers working to loosen a knot in a length of twine. A half dozen children lingered nearby, the braver ones crowding close, the more timid hanging back. But all eyes, and certainly all ears, were focused on the old man, who entertained the youngsters while their fathers milled about inside Nudd's, waiting for the meeting to start.

Seth Hazlitt had given me a lift into town. He was on his way to the hospital; one of his patients had stepped on the blade of a hoe, opening a sizable gash in her head when the handle rose up to smite her. Seth had dropped me at the dock, extracting a promise that I would call him if I couldn't find a ride home from among the fishermen attending the meeting. I'd walked down to Nudd's to find Spencer regaling the youngsters with stories of the days of rumrunners off the Maine coast.

"Why'd they call them 'rumrunners' if they was carrying whiskey? Why wasn't it 'whiskey runners'?" The speaker was Levi and Mary's daughter Anna, her dark, curly hair shoved under a Red Sox cap with the peak turned to the back. Attired in a green T-shirt and faded overalls with one shoulder strap hanging loose, she bounced on the toes of her untied sneakers, the laces gray and spotted from having been dragged along the ground.

"You know the answer to that, girl."

"I don't remember."

Spencer leaned forward and lowered his voice to just above a whisper, drawing the children closer. "The smugglers started out in the Caribbean, see. That's where they make rum. They'd sail north along the coast from Florida all the way up heah, sellin' crates of rum. When the cargo bay was empty, they'd take a run up to Saint John's, pick up a supply of Canadian whiskey, an' sell it on the way back south."

"But they still could've been called 'whiskey runners.'"

Spencer frowned at Anna. "Mebbe. But 'rumrunner' had a nice ring to it, so it stuck," he said.

"Why'd they anchor so far out?" asked a boy of about ten who had kept his distance from the storyteller.

"Well, see, that was so the coast guard couldn't come fer them. At that time, if you went beyond three miles from shore, you'da been in international waters. Later they made it twelve miles, but the distance didn't stop the rum-runnin'. The guard only had jurisdiction in U.S. territory, and they had a lot of water to cover."

"But they knew the rumrunners were there, didn't they?" asked Anna.

"Sometimes they did and sometimes they didn't," Spencer said, freeing the knot, rolling the twine into a ball, and tucking it in his shirt pocket. "But even when they did, they had a hard time catching the little boats that went out to pick up the bottles."

"Why?"

"Why? Well, because a good many of them were lobstermen, and lobstermen are the cleverest breed of fishermen there are."

Anna grinned at the familiar line. She'd heard the story many times before but never tired of Spencer's telling. She knew all the places he would pause and wait for the children's questions, and she jumped in to hurry him along. "How'd they fool the guard?"

"They didn't always—the coast guard's a sharp bunch, and their cutters were wicked fast. The captain, he figures they're in heavy water, and, with the lobster boats weighted down with bottles, they should be an easy catch. But the lobstermen knew a trick or two. They'd frog around in international waters, waitin' for the ebb tide. Then, just before low water, they'd make their escape." Spencer's eyes cut from one child to another. "As the tide goes out, what happens?"

"The water goes down and you can see the sandbars that connect the islands," Anna said, triumphant.

"That's right. Those cutters come after our men, but the lobster boats give 'em the slip. They'd cross over the shoal slicker'n a smelt, just before the water receded. The big coast guard cutter couldn't follow or the rocks'ud stove up the hull." He sat back with a satisfied smile on his face.

"What happened then?" the ten year old asked. He had been inching closer to Cabot Cove's pied piper.

"Their captain was some ugly about losing his quarry, but by the time the tide switched, the lobstermen had emptied their boats, sold off the goods, and were sittin' down to breakfast."

Levi stuck his head out the door of Nunn's. "You fillin' them youngsters with that bilge again?"

"Bilge, my foot," Spencer replied. "That's history I'm givin' them."

Levi wasn't a tall man, probably my height, broad-shouldered and thickset. His hair was sun-bleached a sandy color, somewhere between red and blond, and his face, neck, and forearms were heavily sprinkled with freckles. "We're about to start, Spencer. Come on in." He nodded at me. "How do, Jessica? Got your item on the agenda. Sorry we can't invite you for the whole meetin'."

"I understand," I said. "I'll wait to hear your decision."

"Anna, scooch down and tie your shoes," he said, pointing at his daughter's sneakers.

She knelt to fiddle with her laces.

Spencer put his hands on his knees and pushed to his feet. "Got to go in now," he said.

"Wait, wait," Anna cried, jumping up and pulling on his sleeve. "You didn't tell us where the bottles went."

Spencer tugged at the waistband of his trousers and pulled them up so high that his gray socks, which were puddled at his ankles, were visible. "Allst I know is this," he said, winking at me as he shuffled to the door. "Maine had been dry a long time, so most of the booty probably got drunk in Massachusetts, mebbe even New York. Though I hear tell a few bottles found their way into the cellar of what was then the local inn. That's the library building these days." He turned to eye his fans—"Might still be a few bottles down there, if you care to take a look"—and went inside.

I envisioned our librarian besieged by an army of Cabot Cove's schoolchildren wanting to visit the basement, where, it just happened, the children's book department was located.

A few youngsters followed Spencer inside to sit with their fathers during the discussions, while the older ones wandered off to play till the meeting ended. I took the chair Spencer had vacated and watched Anna and her friends pull pebbles from their pockets and skip the stones across the water. I noticed she wasn't the only one with untied sneakers. It must be a trend these days, I thought, hoping none of them landed facedown on the dock from tripping on their laces.

Mary had telephoned me that afternoon to let me know that Levi had agreed to raise my request with the lobstermen. I imagined it was a hard sell, but she would never let on that her husband had been anything but helpful. Would I mind sticking around in the event they had any questions? she'd asked. Grateful to have my petition given a hearing so quickly, I agreed to stay outside until I was called, or rather on the chance I might be called.

I didn't mind waiting. It was a balmy evening. The sun had peeked between the clouds to cheer the town's spirits. It had another hour to go before it set. I took a deep breath, enjoying the briny air. The water was chockablock with boats at anchor, lines flapping against masts, setting off melodious, if dissonant, notes. Tourists wandered on the dock, admiring the boats and ogling the occasional yacht that sat at anchor in the bay. A high-pitched squeak floated across the wharf from where Mara stood cranking up the awning in front of her luncheonette. The children's voices competed with the cries of the gulls, echoing back from the far end of the dock, where a pelican with a gullet full of fish launched himself into the air, hoping to evade them both—the gulls and the children. The sounds of the harbor were music to me. They represented home, as much as my treasured house on Candlewood Lane. Although my fishing days were limited by my busy travel and work schedule, my affection for the waterfront was undiminished. No matter where in the world I roamed, nothing could touch my heart more than the beauty of Cabot Cove's bay, the charm of the village, the friendship of the colorful and generous people who drew their living from the sea and from the industries that sprang up to serve the fishing community.

I closed my eyes and sighed, enjoying my private concert, only to have a voice intrude on my reverie.

"They meetin' yet?"

I glanced up to see a sturdy woman about my age with short-cropped gray hair; perched on her nose were half-glasses attached to a gold cord. She wore a flowered green housedress and a loose linen jacket with patch pockets of the same fabric as the dress. A large, heavy-looking tote bag pressed down on one shoulder, making her tilt to the right.

"Yes," I said. "I believe they've just started. You probably haven't missed much."

"Oh, they'd never let me in," she said, grinning. "Guess you're not a lobsterman, either."

"No, I'm not," I said, returning her smile.

"I'll wait," she said. "Name's Evelyn Phillips." She stuck out her hand.

"Oh, yes, the new editor of the *Gazette*," I said, taking her hand. "I'm Jessica Fletcher. I'm sorry there's not another chair."

"That's no problem." She reached into her bag and pulled out a bundle of short black bars tied up with a bungee cord. She released the hooks, snapped the bars together to form a tripod, set a small padded leather disk on top to create a stool, and settled herself on the tiny seat.

"I certainly know your name," she said, setting the considerably lightened tote bag on the dock. "You're probably Cabot Cove's most famous citizen."

"I don't know about that," I said, embarrassed.

"Read one of your mysteries last winter. Liked it a lot."

"That's very kind of you to say."

"Not kind. Just true."

"Well, welcome to town. I heard you're originally from Bangor; is that so?"

"Right in one," she replied. "Guess that makes me a city girl. In any case, like all Matilda Watson's editors, I'm from away. She must've run out of local applicants a long time ago."

"She does seem to go through editors at a rapid clip," I agreed. "I hope you break the pattern."

"Thanks very much. I hope so, too. I have a chance at a longer run, since she's so wrapped up in the pageant for the festival."

"Miss Lobsterfest? I hadn't heard that."

"Just happened today. I'm hoping it's because she

thinks the paper is in competent hands. Named herself pageant coordinator and is already poking her fingers into all parts of the pie. Gwen Anissina, bless her heart, is so grateful for help, she'll take it wherever it comes from.''

I shook my head. "It's hard to believe that Matilda would involve herself with a beauty contest," I said, thinking of the publisher who was often described as an aggressive, hard-nosed businesswoman.

"It's a stretch," Evelyn said. "Must be living vicariously; maybe she wanted to enter a pageant when she was young and never had the chance, although she doesn't seem the pageant type."

"My view precisely," I said.

"By the by, why are you hanging out outside the lobstermen's association?"

"I believe I'm here for you," I said.

"For me?" Her eyes twinkled. "Well, that's news I haven't heard."

"Gwen asked me to substitute for her on the day-in-the-life-of-a-lobsterman article. She said you wanted it for the festival edition. I assumed she'd informed you. I hope you don't mind the switch in authors."

"Mind? I'm absolutely tickled. And so will our readers be. Not every day they get to read a piece by a celebrity on the pages of the *Gazette*. Not only that, for the first time they'll get you for free. We're giving away that issue. Of course, I'm not counting the books of yours they take from the library. They don't pay for those, either. But still, what a coup for the *Gazette*. Matilda will be ecstatic. Have you told her?"

"No, I haven't seen her recently," I said, amused at her enthusiastic response.

"Well, don't tell her Gwen set it up. I'd like her to think it was my idea. Another feather in my cap. No need to frown. Gwen won't mind a bit. She's a great kid. Actually, I'm a little annoyed I didn't think of it myself. A byline by Jessica Fletcher. That's terrific. I'd better put your story on the front page."

"I think you'd better wait till I've gotten permission to do the story in the first place. That's why I'm here."

"You'll convince them, I'm sure," Evelyn said, reaching into her bag and pulling out a skein of yellow yarn and two knitting needles. One held the beginnings of a project, and she settled in to knit, casting on a series of stitches.

"What are you making?" I asked.

She chuckled. "Someone accused me of 'trafficking in yellow journalism,'" she said, tugging on the wool to loosen a strand. "I figured I'd live up to the insult and make myself a yellow scarf, just to thumb my nose at him. I don't think of the stories in the *Gazette* as being sensational, do you?" She didn't wait for my reply and added, "I try to be 'fair and balanced,' as the fellow says. But you can't please everybody."

The sound of angry voices inside Nudd's drew our attention to the door. I couldn't make out what was being said, but it was obvious from the shouts that some people weren't happy with one of the topics on the agenda. I hoped it wasn't mine.

"I wonder if it was wise to make this request so soon after the article appeared on the troubles Spencer had," I said, half to myself. "I understand the lobstermen were quite upset."

"They'll get over it. Or if they don't, they'll want you to put their side in the paper. Everybody wants 'happy news,' leastwise when it comes to themselves. They don't mind if you trash their neighbor. Makes for good reading, in fact. You wouldn't believe how many letters I get, telling me to check out what so-and-so did. But they don't have the guts to sign their names. Drives me nuts. I won't publish anonymous letters. And I wish I could say I won't follow up on anonymous leads. But it wouldn't be true. It was a tip that put me on to what happened to Spencer's boat. Of course, if you were anywhere near the docks, you wouldn't need anyone pointing it out. That thing did reek."

"For some reason I missed that story," I said. "Did the sheriff look into who dumped the rotten bait on Spencer's deck?"

She shook her head. "Durkee wouldn't file a complaint. I told Mort Metzger what happened and he asked around. I know that for a fact. But no one was talking. He told me to keep him informed if anything like it happened again, but those guys in there"—she cocked her head toward Nudd's—"they'll cover for each other, even if they don't like what happened. Kind of a force unto themselves. Don't let them push you around. They can be very demanding about what appears in print."

"I'm not a journalist," I said, beginning to wonder what I'd gotten myself into. "I hope you don't expect investigative reporting."

"It would be interesting to read your take on the lobstermen's issues—which, by the way, they refuse to discuss with me." The click of the knitting needles accompanied Evelyn's voice. "But this is the festival edition, and Mrs. Watson wants to present a spit-shined Cabot Cove, all cozy and picturesque, the tourists'-eye view of a Maine village."

"It's not as if we're so far from that image," I said, feeling the need to defend my hometown. "I was planning a nice colorful piece on the lobstermen and what they do for a living. People eat lobsters and never think of where they come from. Oh, they know they're from Maine, but they have no idea what hard work goes into putting that elegant meal on their plate."

Evelyn paused in her knitting, tipped her chin down, and peered at me over her half-glasses. "That's exactly what I had in mind," she said.

I smiled at her. "I knew you did," I said. But what I didn't know was that writing a story on the lobstermen would land me in the same place as their prized catch—in hot water.

Chapter Four

The door to Nudd's was flung open, and Levi stepped outside, shutting it firmly behind him. He started when he caught sight of Evelyn, and his face reddened. Quickly he schooled his features into a bland expression, but he had no control over the flush in his cheeks. "Didn't know you were bringing the press," he said to me.

"Well, actually, Levi—" I began.

"Invited myself," Evelyn interrupted. She looked up at Levi, but her fingers continued to work on the stitches. "Mrs. Fletcher didn't know I was coming. She's as much a victim of my stealthy approach as you."

"I hardly consider myself a victim," I said. "Besides"—I turned my gaze on Levi—"the reason I'm asking a favor of the lobstermen is so that I can write an article for Mrs. Phillips and the *Gazette*. I hope the association understands that."

He nodded. "For the festival," he said. "We know."

"Well, then, why not invite me in, too?" Evelyn said.

"This is not a public meeting," he said stiffly.

"I'm aware," she replied. "But if a controversial decision the lobstermen make is going to affect the whole town, we have a right to know what it is, don't we?"

Levi cleared his throat. "I don't know what you mean," he said. "An article in the paper is not a controversial decision." He turned to me. "Jessica, we're ready for you now."

My eyes darted back and forth between Levi and Evelyn, neither of whom was looking at the other. There was an undercurrent here, another message they were exchanging that I didn't understand. "It was nice to meet you," I said as I stood. "I'll be in touch."

"I'll look forward to reading your piece," she said, returning her focus to the knitting needles.

Levi escorted me inside, indicated a seat in the front row, which I took, and positioned himself by the door, leaning back against the wall.

Nudd's Bait & Tackle was a barn of a building, although all the activity took place on one floor. Tim Nudd had used the extra airspace to hang mounted fish, huge ones, from the rafters. He even had a small whale arched over one door and a fierce-looking shark on the opposite wall. By far the oddest hanging on display was an ocean sunfish, a behemoth weighing over a ton, and perhaps eleven feet from fin to fin. It was more round than long; in fact, it looked as if it were missing a body and was merely a giant swimming head. It was a sight the locals had long since grown used to, but awe-inspiring to the tourists, especially those under ten.

I leaned back in my seat and turned my attention to the speaker. Apparently one piece of business wasn't finished, and I was witness to the end of it.

Lincoln Williams was standing at the front of the

room, his arm draped over a stack of lobster pots. He held a gavel in his left hand. His face was set in a stern expression. Another man stood slightly ahead of him and nervously played with his car keys, using his thumb to flip the remote door opener off his hand and then swinging it back up to his palm. The movement was almost hypnotic.

"Now, this is allst I can say. I can't get you a better price unless the market goes that way, but right now, it's still tight." The speaker was a small, wiry man. Although the evening was warm enough for a shirt alone, he wore a leather jacket with the sleeves pushed up, revealing tattoos on both forearms. There was a sharp crease in his trousers and a high shine on his intricately patterned cowboy boots. His carefully coiffed wavy hair was more pepper than salt. And a flat gold disk with markings on it glinted from one earlobe. I gauged him to be mid-forties. Some might have considered him good-looking, but there was something in his expression that stopped short of handsome.

"They got twenty-five cents more a pound today over in Boothbay Harbor, Pettie," said a man in the audience, confirming my suspicion that the guest speaker was Henry Pettie, the broker.

"And Hull's Cove," another voice said.

"Boothbay is quite a hike from here," Pettie said. "And I wouldn't want to have to hustle to Hull's Cove and back either. Much easier to stay close to home after such a long day on the water, don't ya think? See your family, sit down for a nice dinner together, don't have to break your back to put a few extra pennies in your pocket."

"Twenty-five cents a pound would put some few pennies in my pocket, thank you. If the other men're getting more, why aren't we?"

"You know the prices fluctuate, Ike, some days better than others. Plus, Boothbay, for one, has a much bigger market, bigger distribution system. Cabot Cove is small potatoes by comparison. More costly to get the lobsters to market from here. That's reflected in your price. But believe me, I'm always working for you, looking for ways to shave my expenses so I can give you more."

"So you can keep more," muttered someone in back of me, but I doubt anyone else heard.

"We made a deal in March," Pettie continued, "and I'm keeping to my end of it. I been good to you guys for years. Right, Carver? Paynter? Not a man here I haven't helped out. And you owe me. Any man doesn't trust me, thinks he knows my business better than I do, doesn't want to work with me, well, he knows where he can go. He can sell his catch somewhere else. I'll never stop him. But I might not take him back either." Pettie let that threat sink in a moment. Then he pocketed his keys and straightened. "Now, gentlemen, I'll let you get back to the business at hand. You take care of the fishing—we're still a little low for the festival's needs—and I'll take care of the market. That way, we'll both come out on top."

"Any more questions for Henry?" Linc asked. "There being none, we'll move along." He swung his gavel against a woodblock set atop the traps, and it made a satisfying bang.

Henry Pettie nodded at Linc and slipped quietly

toward the door. Levi reached out his hand and opened it, closing it softly behind him.

"That should satisfy," Linc said.

"Only if you swallow that bucket of fish guts." It was the lobsterman who'd argued with Pettie. "You stand to lose money, too, Linc," he said, pointing his finger at Williams. "Why are you defending Pettie?"

"I'm not defending him. I simply said, we signed a deal, we keep it. We're men of our word, aren't we?"

"Even if it keeps food from our tables?"

"Your family's not going to starve, Ike."

"Not everyone lives high like you, Linc."

Linc came away from the pile of traps he was leaning against. "I work hard for that money," he said. "No man better say otherwise."

"Not sayin' you don't. But I work hard, too. Either he pays me the going price or I'll sail up the coast and sell my catch in the next harbor that's not his."

"And the festival?"

"Let the festival buy its lobsters from the market and pay market price like everyone else."

A rumble of voices filled the room, but I couldn't tell if the majority were in agreement or not. I tried not to look too interested in the proceedings, and stole a glance at Levi. His aggravated expression suggested he was uncomfortable that this argument was taking place in front of an outsider—me.

Linc raised the gavel and banged it on the woodblock until the voices died down. "All right. Give us a day or two. I'll talk to Henry again."

"You can talk to him longer than a hard winter and it ain't gonna do any good," Ike said, his voice rising.

"We want action. And if you won't do it, we can do it ourselves. There are plenty of men here ready to make a move. We don't need the association if you're not goin' to stand up for us." He looked around for support, but the room had grown very quiet.

There was venom in Linc's eyes. "This association has represented Cabot Cove lobstermen for generations, Bower," he said. "Don't tell me we don't have the best interests of our men at heart. You want to go off and form your own group, go. Anyone else here want to leave with him?"

Not a soul moved. It was clear no one else would side with Ike Bower against Linc Williams. Bower sat down, breathing heavily and shaking his head. "Can't believe you guys," he muttered.

There was a long pause. Linc's voice broke the silence. "Now let's move on." He tilted his head in my direction. "You all know who Mrs. Fletcher is," he said. "She wants to do an article on us for the *Gazette*. The question on the floor is: Assuming we want an article on the lobstermen to appear in that rag, who's going to be the one to put her right? Carver, you have something to add?"

Levi straightened. "You said it right, Linc," he said.

A man of few words, I thought. I'd hoped Levi would champion my cause. Obviously, I'd been wrong. I raised my hand. "I'd like to add something, if I may," I said.

"That's not necessary," Linc said. "We know what you want."

"Nevertheless," I said, standing and turning to face the audience, hoping I could move them past the grim mood that had taken hold, "I'd like to make a statement." Without waiting for Linc to interrupt me, and without glancing at the scowl I knew was on his face, I went on. "Cabot Cove is my hometown, and I'm very proud of it, as I'm sure you are. We have an opportunity with the upcoming festival to let visitors see what a charming and welcoming village we live in. What's more important is that we'll be helping the Main Street merchants in their quest to draw more customers."

"What's that got to do with us?" a voice said from the back of the room.

"I'm glad you asked," I replied, looking from face to face, trying to see who had asked the question. "The merchants are as much a part of Cabot Cove as you and I are." I ignored the snorts that greeted this remark. "They live here, pay taxes, and contribute to our community's life."

As I spoke, I scanned the faces looking back at me. There were about thirty people in the store. Chairs had been set between rows of display cases, some of which had been haphazardly shoved to the side of the room. A potbelly stove, the only source of heat in three seasons, sat to one side. There was no fire in it, the weather being too warm to justify wasting wood, but a group of older men, their faces weathered from years of challenging the sea for a livelihood, gathered around it in seats they probably claimed all winter long. Spencer was among them.

Most of the lobstermen were family men, like Ike Bower and Levi Carver; a few had children standing between their knees or sitting next to them. There may have been some women who accompanied them to sea, perhaps even one or two who piloted their own boats, but they obviously didn't feel the need to attend the association's meeting. I recognized fathers of students I'd taught years before, and many whose names I didn't know but whose familiar faces I'd seen around town. In the back of the room was a row of young men, who were obviously uninterested in my speech, and who began whispering to each other while I spoke. I recognized Levi's son, Evan, whose photograph I'd seen in his mother's kitchen. And another boy who might be Linc's son, he looked so much like the association president.

"The success of our business district has a direct effect on the prosperity of the town as a whole, on all of our lives," I continued, hoping to recapture their interest. "If the merchants fail, you and I will have to travel out of town to purchase goods and services that are conveniently nearby right now. But if they do well, Cabot Cove as a community will have greater means to help safeguard, perhaps even improve, our quality of life, our schools, parks, libraries, and cultural and recreation services."

I saw I wasn't convincing them. They were getting restless, looking away, tapping their feet impatiently. What would persuade them? I tried another point of view.

"We're so used to seeing lobsters," I said, "we don't think of them as anything exotic. But they're a delicacy the world over. The article I'm hoping to write will show how Cabot Cove's lobstermen work to provide the meal that Maine is famous for. You're the heroes of the coming festivities. It's the lobster festival, after all."

One of the young men, who wore a red plaid shirt under a brown leather vest, gave a loud yawn and stretched his arms over his head. I was grateful to see several of the fathers turn around to glare at his rudeness. Evan, who sat at the end of the row, reached over to poke the heckler on the knee.

"What?" he said, poking back. "I'm tired. I've been up since dawn. And this is a waste of time. I got places to be."

"I won't take up more of your time," I said, "but I imagine your families would be very proud to see your work profiled in the newspaper for everyone to see, neighbors and visitors alike."

"Okay, Mrs. Fletcher, we get the point," Linc said from behind me. "We don't care what's in the paper— well, most of the time—but the real question is, who's willing to take Mrs. Fletcher aboard for a day so she can get the facts straight for her story?"

Silence greeted Linc's question.

I was afraid my petition was going to be tabled. I'd had enough experience in local organizations to know that if that happened, it would mean the request would never get voted on in time to do the *Gazette* and the festival any good. I don't know why the article had become important to me. True, I didn't want to disappoint Gwen—or Evelyn Phillips, for that matter. And it wasn't just a matter of pride in dealing with a less than enthusiastic response to my little speech. But as I'd mustered my arguments, I began to see the validity of them. If the lobstermen declined to participate, even in so small an undertaking as cooperating with the local newspaper, our town would be the less for it. Of course, if they sold their lobsters ahead of the festival and we didn't have enough to feed our visitors, that would be a lot worse.

"We're all in this together," I said. "We're a community, putting on a community event."

I looked at Spencer Durkee. He was bent forward, his elbows on his knees, rolling and unrolling the unknotted twine. I was sure Spencer would agree to host me if I appealed to him. But if I did, the malicious people who'd victimized him already would torture him again. I couldn't take the chance of making his life more difficult than it already was.

I pointed to the rude young man in the back. "Perhaps you'd like to volunteer?" I said. My remark succeeded in evoking a laugh and breaking the tension that pervaded the meeting. Cries of "Yeah, Holland, you do it," echoed in the room.

Holland colored but wasn't cowed. "Me? Not in this life. Anyway, we don't need any more stupid stories in the *Gazette*."

"Pipe down, Holland," Levi said. "This is a senior decision."

"Brady just don't want no one to find out why his other slicker stinks from rotten bait," called out one of Holland's companions. He pushed Holland in the shoulder, then giggled, elbowing another young man in the ribs.

"Shut up, Maynard," Holland said. "Or you'll step in it tomorrow."

Spencer frowned, but said nothing.

"Benjamin Press, what about you?" Levi said to a fisherman sitting next to the ten year old I'd seen outside.

"Nah, Levi. Women's bad luck on board."

"Who're you kidding, Ben?" Levi said. "Didn't your wife use to fish with you?"

"Yeah, and I never had any luck," Press replied, setting off another wave of laughter. The atmosphere in the room was relaxed now, but still, I had no takers.

"Alex Paynter. Can you do it?" Levi asked.

"I would, Levi, but my motor catched up on me. Gotta get me a new part tomorrow."

"Okay, we don't have all night for this," Linc said.

My heart sank. I glanced at Levi, hoping he'd say something. But he was looking at Linc. I saw his shoulders rise and fall.

"Sorry, Levi, you're stuck with her," Linc said, and my heart soared.

A couple of the men snickered. I thought I knew who they were. I gave Levi a grateful smile, but he didn't respond.

"There's not a lot of room on my boat, Linc. Plus I've got Evan as sternman."

"That's my ruling," Linc said. "Your idea, your project." He raised his left hand and rapped his gavel on the woodblock. "Any new business? No? Remember, what's said here stays here. This meeting is over."

I was surprised at the way Linc Williams ran the association. Plainly his word was law, and few would buck him. Ike Bower must have been expecting others to join his mutiny. Perhaps privately they'd rally to the cause. But in public, the support never materialized. Williams was still the king. No votes were taken. No one raised *Robert's Rules of Order*. The association simply ruled.

As the meeting broke up, several people came up

to greet me or to apologize for the rudeness of Holland and his friends, for which I thanked them. When they departed, I looked around for the association president. There was still a crowd of people lingering in Nudd's, but I managed to spot him across the room and headed in his direction. I wanted to express my gratitude for his aid.

Evelyn Phillips had elbowed her way inside the shop and was advancing on Linc as well. She reached him before I did. "Mr. Williams, do you have a statement on the meeting for the *Gazette*?" she asked.

"No comment," Linc said.

"Come on now, Mr. Williams. The village wants to know if the association is still supporting the festival."

"The lobstermen don't break their word. We'll do what has to be done, and that's all I have to say." He pushed his way into the crowd headed for the door.

Evelyn winked at me and looked around for another likely candidate to interview, but when the men spied her, they turned their backs or hurried toward the exit.

Spencer saw her coming and ducked past me to get away. "I talk to her," he murmured to himself, "and it'll get worse."

"Hey, lady, want a comment from me?" Holland said. He stood with a small knot of his friends, who grinned at his cheekiness. I was sorry to see Evan Carver among them.

"I'll give you a comment," Maynard said, rocking his pelvis at her.

"Aren't you a scurvy-looking group?" Evelyn said, her pen poised above her pad. "But I'll bet you know where to find rotten bait, don't you, boys?"

"I smell something rotten in here right now," Holland said, sniffing at her.

"What're you talking about, Brady?" Maynard said. "This lady's a honker. You like 'em big, don't you?" He put his arms out to Evelyn. "Want to go to a party? We could party some with you."

"Knock it off, sonny, or I'll tell your mother," Evelyn shot back. "And don't think I don't know who she is."

"C'mon, Maynard, let's get out of here," Evan said.

"Don't be so spleeny, Carver," Maynard said to him. "She's not gonna hit you."

"Suit yourself," Evan said, and headed for the door. Confident Evelyn could handle herself with the young toughs, I followed Evan and made my way through the crowd of lobstermen outside to the dock. I didn't see where Evan went, but Levi was waiting for me.

"I'm very grateful—" I began.

Tapping the crystal on his watch, he interrupted, "We'll meet here at five A.M. tomorrow. The forecast looks good. Bring lunch for yourself. You have any waterproof gear?"

"I do," I said. "And thank you."

"Don't thank me. It's Mary deserves the thanks."

"I'll remember that."

"I have to find someone inside. I'll see you at first light."

"I'll be here," I said.

"We'll leave if you aren't," he said, and pushed back into Nudd's, past the men exiting the meeting.

Spencer stepped to the side to let Levi pass, just as Brady Holland and his friend Maynard came out the door. Holland put his shoulder into the old man and knocked him to his knees. The contact was a deliberate attempt to humiliate Spencer Durkee. Outraged, I stepped forward, prepared to give Holland a piece of my mind and to assist Spencer to his feet, but a hard look from Benjamin Press stopped me where I was. This was not my business, his eyes said. He looped a hand under Spencer's arm and hauled him to his feet. "You okay, Spencer?" he asked.

"Sure, Ben. Thanks."

"Can't even keep your legs on land. How ya gonna stay upright to fish?" Holland said over his shoulder as he passed the men.

"Clumsy kids," Ben said, steadying Spencer.

"They're more'n that," Spencer said, dusting off his trousers. "Don't think I don't know what you done," he called after them. "You better watch your step. I've got friends, too. I'll get even. You'll find yourselves facedown in a barrel of bait. And I'll be there to whack your bottoms."

Maynard turned and walked backward. "You never shoulda been on that committee," he said. "You fub everything you put a hand to." He turned back to Holland, elbowing his buddy and chuckling as the pair swaggered toward the parking lot. "Told him good, didn't I, Brady?"

Spencer started to go after the young men, but Ben held him back. "Don't bother," he said. "They're lackin' the wits they were born with. Next time they ask one of us for advice, they'll find out what we think of them."

"I didn't screw up," Spencer said. "Pettie, that sanctimonious pen pusher, he tricked me. I'm gonna get even with him, too."

"Yeah, yeah, not here. We'll talk about it later." Ben put his hand on Spencer's shoulder and they walked away.

"What'd I miss?" Evelyn said coming up behind me.

I turned to her. "Holland knocked Spencer over," I said, "and it wasn't accidental."

"Stupid punk!" she said. "You didn't try to help him up, did you?"

"No," I said, "but I wanted to."

"They'd think the cure was worse than the disease," she said. "Never did see such macho types as these lobstermen."

"I'm learning that," I said. "But at least you'll have your story. I got permission to go on a lobster boat tomorrow."

"Good for you," she said. "You must have been very convincing."

"I don't know," I said. "I got the feeling this was merely a formality."

"What do you mean?"

"They'd already decided to accommodate me before I got up to speak. I'm not sure why they put me through the motions, unless it was just for show." And what was it they wanted to show me? I wondered.

"Well, you get to ride on a lobster boat for a day," she said. "That's exciting. I'm jealous. I'd love to do it myself, but they'd never agree to let anyone from away peek into their world. But I know you'll give me a good story."

"I'll do my best," I said. Now that I had permission

to spend the day on a lobster boat, I began to prepare mentally for the task. It would be a long day at sea, hours upon hours in the company of men who were less than enthusiastic about my presence. But it had been a while since I'd sailed out of Cabot Cove's harbor, and I was eager to feel the roll of the waves underfoot and the stroke of salty air on my cheeks.

Chapter Five

"Will your waders do the trick?" Seth asked, stirring some sugar into his tea.

"They're waterproof, cover me up past the waist, and have built-in boots. I think they'll serve the purpose," I said, taking down another cup and saucer. "Thanks for the ride home. Your arrival was very timely."

"No trouble. I'd finished up at the hospital."

"I didn't expect to see you at the dock."

"It's on the way home, for the most part."

"Did you have long to wait?"

"Now don't start giving me the third degree. You weren't swimmin' in offers of a ride, were you? You gave your thanks, and I said you're welcome. Enough said."

I covered up a smile. "Actually you said 'no trouble.' But you're right: I wasn't swimming in offers."

I poured myself a cup of chamomile tea. If I had to be at the docks by five, I didn't want caffeine keeping me awake at night. I opened the freezer and removed a coffee cake, one of three from the last time I'd baked. I sliced off a hunk, put it in the toaster oven to heat, and sat down at my kitchen table with Cabot Cove's favorite physician.

"How's your patient?" I asked.

"Twenty stitches and a sizable bandage, but she'll live. Imagine she'll have quite a shiner to go along with it. Won't keep her out of the garden, however."

"Maybe it'll make her a little more careful where she leaves her tools."

"One would hope so."

"Spencer Durkee is one of your patients, isn't he?" I asked.

"Ayuh."

"How long have you known him?"

"Must be nigh on forty years if it's a day. Why? Was he lookin' peaked?"

"Not at all. He looks quite fit for a man his age."

"Spencer said good-bye to eighty some years back."

"Have you spoken with him recently?"

"Only to say hello. What are you fussing about? Get to the point, Jess."

I smiled at Seth's impatience. He was often brusque and occasionally cranky, but his gruff demeanor hid the kindest of hearts. He was also loyal, thoughtful, caring, and my dearest friend. We'd been through many adventures together. I relied on his discretion, good judgment, and thorough analysis and, he, bless him, put up with my inquisitiveness and tenacity, even when they put me in the way of danger, which, he was quick to point out, was not all that unusual.

"Spencer seems to have disturbed some of his fellow lobstermen," I said, trying to ease into the topic.

"That incident with the bait? Read about that in the *Gazette*. Bunch of hooligans, picking on an old man."

"Yes, and—"

"Mort says he knows who did it, but Spencer won't press charges."

I sat back. "Well, I'm certainly behind in the news," I said.

"Do I smell something burning?"

"Oh, my heavens, the cake!" I jumped up and opened the toaster. A corner of the coffee cake was singed. I grabbed an oven mitt and pulled the tray out. "Oh, I'm so sorry."

Seth peered over my shoulder. "Doesn't look too bad," he said. "You can cut off that corner."

"Are you sure you still want it?"

"It'll be fine," he said, taking his seat again.

I sliced off the burned corner and served the well-done coffee cake, although my recipe didn't benefit from the overheating. What would normally be flaky simply fell apart when speared with a fork. Seth consumed it anyway, scooping up the crumbs with his teaspoon. While he ate, I filled him in on my talk with Mary and on the part of the lobstermen's meeting I'd attended.

"Do you know Henry Pettie?" I asked.

"Heard of 'im. Never met the man."

"What do you hear?"

"Well, he locked up this part of the coast. He handles the harbors to the north and south of Cabot Cove. Makes it tough for a man to sell his catch anywhere else nearby unless he's supplyin' the local residents. The shore restaurants won't deal with an individual lobsterman. If they do, Pettie will lock 'em out when supplies are short. That's how he controls the market."

"Does he control the prices as well?"

"Not entirely. The lobstermen have ways finding out the going price elsewhere in the state. Pettie'd better not stray too far from that number, or he'll lose even more of his credibility and influence with the men. He's not exactly a popular fellow, I hear."

"If they don't trust him, why do they keep selling to him? Seems to me they could find another dealer."

"Might be more trouble than it's worth," Seth said, brushing crumbs from the front of his shirt. "The system works fine as it is."

"Well, couldn't they form a cooperative?" I said. "They do that elsewhere in the state. That way they'd work for themselves. They could do that, couldn't they?"

"Mebbe."

"Sounds logical to me," I said, sipping my tea. "Why do you suppose they haven't done it so far?"

"Inertia, probably," Seth said. "You know the old saying: 'If it ain't broke, don't fix it.'"

"The men don't trust Pettie," I said. "Sounds to me as if it's broke."

"Well, there's broke and there's broke. They'd have to have a powerful motivation to kick the man out after so many years."

"I hope the lobstermen's difficulty with him doesn't have an impact on the upcoming festival."

"Now, Jess, don't go borrowing trouble."

"There's borrowing and there's borrowing," I said. "Mary Carver hinted that the dispute between the men and their broker might mean fewer lobsters available for the festival's shore dinner. And one of the men at the meeting threatened to sell his catch up coast."

"Idle talk," Seth said. "If a man has to sail up the coast to sell his catch, he's adding hours to an already long day. He might be willin' to do it once or twice to make a point, but beyond that, I don't see it happening."

"I agree," I said, feeling comforted that the festival dinner was seemingly secure. "Would you like more tea?"

"Not for me, thanks. And if you've got to meet Levi Carver at the crack of dawn, I'd better let you get some sleep." He rose and pulled his jacket from the back of the chair. "By the way, I've got something here for you."

"What is it?" I asked as I gathered up our cups and saucers and took them to the sink.

"It's here somewhere," he said, reaching into first one and then the other jacket pocket.

I turned on the water, quickly washed up our tea things, and left them in the dish drainer to dry. "Did I tell you that Matilda Watson is helping Gwen out with the beauty pageant?" I said, drying my hands on a towel. "I heard it from Evelyn Phillips tonight."

"You don't say? That's not an easy picture to conjure up."

"I felt the same way myself," I said, hanging up the towel and turning. "Seth, what *are* you looking for?"

"Got 'em!" he said, triumphantly drawing a pair of broad red fabric rings from his trouser pocket. Each one had a white plastic button protruding from it that looked like half a marble.

"What are they?"

He dropped them in my hand. "Acupressure bracelets."

"I've heard of them," I said, pulling on the bands and discovering they were elastic. "What are they for?"

"Seasickness. Put them on. I'll show you how they work."

I slipped them over my hands, and Seth adjusted them so the buttons were positioned between two tendons on the undersides of my wrists. "Where did you find these?" I asked.

"Truman sent them up from Key West. Says his patients down there swear by them. Thought I might like to give them a go up here."

Dr. Truman Buckley was an old schoolmate of Seth's. They'd attended medical school together and had been good friends, even though Truman came from a patrician Boston family and Seth's upbringing was decidedly more modest. Over the years the men had kept in touch, occasionally speaking by telephone and faithfully sending each other holiday greetings and birthday cards. Truman had retired to Key West, and had invited Seth and me to visit him at his home when we and the Metzgers, Mort and his wife, Maureen, were in Florida to attend the funeral of an old friend originally from Cabot Cove. After so many years apart, Seth and Truman had found themselves knocking heads over medical procedures and philosophy, and some fireworks ensued. Eventually they rekindled their friendship, but it was not without accommodations made on both sides. But that's a tale for another time.

"How do they feel?" Seth asked.

"They're a little tight, but generally comfortable," I said, running a hand over the top of the wristband. "But I'm a pretty good sailor, Seth. I don't usually get seasick."

"You've never spent a whole day on a lobster boat, with the smell of the bait rotting in the sun, and the constant rocking."

"Don't make it sound so appealing."

"Just keep these in your pocket. If you don't need 'em, don't use 'em. But if you do, you'll be my test patient on how well they work."

"Fair enough," I said, accompanying him to the door.

"And better take along this as well," he said, pressing a tiny white envelope into my hand.

"What's in it?"

"Seasick pills."

Chapter Six

"Muckle onto that toggle, will you, son?" Levi said, using his gaff, a long pole with an iron hook at the end, to point at the small buoy that marked where he'd set his trap. He passed the gaff to Evan, handle end first.

Evan hooked the Styrofoam toggle and pulled it into the boat, looping the rope that connected it to the trap over a pulley and then between the plates of the hydraulic lift. Moments later, the rope—or warp—was forming wet coils on the deck at his feet, as the pot hauler, as it was sometimes known, pulled the wood and metal lobster trap up from the ocean floor. As the wheel spun, salt water spilled across the boards, along with slimy pieces of seaweed and other debris the rope had snared on its journey upward.

"Better keep your seat," Levi yelled at me over the noise of the trap hauler and the idling engine. "Gonna be real slippery now."

I nodded to indicate I'd heard him, and tightened my grip on the stool he had brought aboard for me and had tied firmly to a cleat fastened to the wheel-house wall.

I'd met the men at Nudd's that morning, arriving at a quarter to five. But they'd been there for some time before me, tying up at the dock, donning their boots and orange rubber bib pants, taking on fuel, and muscling barrels of bagged bait onto the boat in preparation for the day.

Fifteen minutes later, the edge of the sun drawing red lines across the horizon, we roared out of the harbor, angling toward a fishing territory claimed for Cabot Cove's lobstermen and no others. We passed a flotilla of fluorescent-hued buoys bobbing in the water, careful not to come close enough to snag the lines.

"Every man has his personal colors," Levi had yelled over the noise of the engine. "Makes it easy to pick out your own."

The morning air was refreshing, brushing my hair back from my face, blowing steadily on the boat and covering up its smell, which at that early hour was fishy but not yet sour. We whizzed over calm water, attracting an audience of gulls that circled overhead checking for breakfast and, finding none, winged off toward another possible meal. Before the sun was fully up, we'd reached an area dotted with Levi's buoys, which were painted with alternating stripes of shocking pink and lime green.

"Some of the lobsters're still hardenin' up after the molt," Levi had told me. "We'll start layin' the traps farther out today, where we think they're goin' to go. Each day we move 'em ahead a bit more."

"How do you know where the lobsters are going to go?" I'd asked.

He pointed to his head. "Experience. What got passed to me from my father and his father before him. You learn and you keep a weather eye out all the time. You got to balance the time of year, the tide, the wind, the current, the wave height. It all matters. Today, o' course, we got a lot of technology helping out, too. It'll make it too easy for his generation," he said, eyeing Evan.

Levi's technology included a combination compass and depth finder, a global positioning device, and a citizens band radio, explaining the forest of antennae that sprouted from the roof of his wheelhouse. On the outside wall of the cabin was a piece of equipment that looked like a yellow lantern. Levi said it was an emergency transmitter. He also had something he called a "Thistle box."

"We're part of a study lookin' to track where the lobsters are and make sure they stay healthy," he said, patting the top of a computer screen that was covered with numbers and symbols. "Got to take care o' the little ones or else they won't grow up to be keepers."

Everyone in Cabot Cove knew that Maine had come through several years in a row in which each landing, as the lobster harvest was called, exceeded the previous one, although no one seemed to know exactly why we were so lucky. Some said that global warming was making the lobsters grow faster. Others credited overfishing of sea bass and cod, which like to feast on baby lobsters, and whose declining numbers left the ocean bottom safer for crustaceans. While the lobstermen thrived, other fishermen were not so fortunate, struggling with catches insufficient to cover the cost of keeping up equipment, much less feeding and housing a family. One of Mara's cooks had signed on this year after cashing out, selling his boat, and giving up the sea.

Of course, there were no guarantees of bounties for

the lobstermen. This year had started out slow and
stayed that way, with the rain and fog limiting fishing
and the hauls more meager than expected. Mary had
said the prices were rising. It made sense to me. It
was a logical case of supply not being able to keep up
with demand. And lobsters are always in demand.

The festival committee had arranged with Tim
Nudd to store lobsters for the festival. Tim had a small
lobster pound—a series of holding bins with cold
water flowing through them—on his side of the dock.
But Henry Pettie was the broker, and it was he who
determined what was saved and what was sold.

We'd gotten spoiled by the boom years, I saw now.
No one had ever expected that there wouldn't be
enough lobsters in stock by midsummer for the coming festival. I was still confident the star of the meal
would show up on time, and I prayed I was right.
Today was sunny, not rainy. I hoped the change in
weather would bring the lobsters out of their holes,
or wherever they were hiding, and make them hungry
enough to crawl into Levi's traps. And I was about to
see if that happened.

The whine of the pot hauler was a siren song to the
gulls that materialized so quickly, I thought they must
have been waiting nearby.

The top of the trap broke the surface of the water
and, as the boat swayed from side to side in the swell,
Evan lifted the box onto the rail, deftly untying the
string that held the door shut. Through the metal grid,
I could see three, maybe four lobsters. Evan reached
into the trap and pulled one out, keeping his fingers
well away from its crushing claws. He wore heavy
gloves, but even so, if the lobster's claw caught him,

it would be a painful experience till he could release its grip. He measured the lobster, aligning a brass gauge with the carapace, dropped the animal into a bucket, pulled out the next one, measured again, and dropped it back into the sea. "Short," he shouted at me. The third one went into the bucket, but the last lobster had a notched tail—the sign of a breeding hen—and she was gently returned to the ocean as well.

The state of Maine has strict regulations regarding the size of lobsters that can be removed from the water. Take them too small and they haven't had time to breed. Take them too large and you're removing the breeding stock, endangering the future quantity of crustaceans. Woe betide the fishermen caught breaking the rules. Not only do they reap the penalty of the law; they're prey to the wrath of fellow lobstermen, who understand that their livelihood depends on the health and longevity of the existing lobster population.

While Evan cleaned the trap of any unwanted wildlife that had climbed inside, Levi cranked up the engine and started moving on. Evan rebaited the trap, tied it closed, and dropped it over the stern, the warp uncoiling rapidly as the trap sank back to the sandy bottom.

"Had a numbhead helping out as sternman once," Levi shouted. "Got caught in the warp and went overboard with the trap. Had to crank him back up with the trap hauler. Lost half a day's work getting him to the hospital."

"Oh, my," I said. "Was he all right?"

"Red face and broken leg is all. But he had a hard time finding work on a boat after that. No lobsterman

can afford to take on a novice in the busy season."
He nodded at his son, who was binding the claws of
his catch with thick rubber bands. "He's still a bit
slow, but he's able, Evan is. He's careful and sharp, a
good combination. He wanted the summer off to
spend with friends of his, hanging out at the shore,
playing at being lifeguards. I told him, 'There's plenty
of time for pleasurin' when school's back in session.'
This is how we put food on the table, and he'd better
be knowin' it. Can't abide a slacker in the summer."

Evan glanced up at his father, a small smile playing
around his mouth. I had a suspicion that even given
the hard work, he was happier going out lobstering
with Levi than he would have been parading on the
beach in a bathing suit. Lobstering gave him a chance
to impress the old man, and put him squarely in the
ranks of the grown-ups. He mingled with the other
lobstermen gathered at Nudd's each morning, as they
held their cups of steaming coffee with fingerless
gloves and collectively used the daily ritual to swipe
away the sleepy cobwebs of the mind before the day's
run. He eavesdropped on the advice Jim Patton passed
along to his nephew Ralph, and watched as Levi chose
the best bits of bait for his bags. He attended the
lobstermen's meetings, listening to the men's complaints of interlopers setting their traps in Cabot
Cove's "territory," and joining in their laughter with
tales of when Monica Andresen opened her screen
door and yelled for her husband to "come back to the
yard, Mason. That dog of yours took off with my best
housedress. I'll be making dog pie for dinnah if I ever
catch 'im."

Evan would have stories to tell when school started

again—and the confidence of having mastered a tough job. Whether or not he chose to follow his father to the sea, this summer would make him a man in the eyes of the community.

"We don't bind their claws for our safety alone," Levi said. "It's for their safety, too. Keeps 'em from fightin' and eatin' each other. Crowd lobsters together and they become cannibals. No good to themselves and no good to the market. Used to tap wooden pegs in their claws to prevent them from closin', but it's all rubber bands now."

We moved on to the next buoy and the next, hauling Levi's traps and dumping the buckets of lobster into a water-filled hatch below the deck that would keep them alive and safe till they went to market. Occasionally we'd pass other lobster boats, and the men would nod or hail each other on the radio. Other craft were ignored, unless their captains made a point of greeting us. Common courtesy required an acknowledgment.

At ten thirty I spotted two lobster boats ahead. They were moored side by side, and the men were eating an early lunch, keeping each other company. Levi slowed, cut the engine, and let his boat drift into the huddle, careful not to ram a colleague.

"Hard work whips up an appetite," he said, winking at me. "Didja bring yourself something to eat?"

"I did," I said, unzipping my fanny pack and poking around inside. "I've got an apple and some carrots, a container of yogurt, and a bottle of water."

"Yogurt?" Evan laughed.

Levi merely shook his head in disgust. "We've got plenty, and you're welcome to share. Mother always puts in extra sandwiches, just in case. Right, Evan?"

"Right, Pop."

"I guess we got the 'just in case' today."

I tried to object, but Levi insisted, telling me, "I'm the captain heah, and the crew—that's you—has to obey the captain."

"Yes, sir," I said, saluting. And, in fact, my stomach was grumbling, and the idea of one of Mary's sandwiches was very appealing.

Evan pulled out a plastic pail that had been tucked under the washboard against the transom, pried off its lid, and held out two sandwiches to his father. Levi passed one to me.

"Whatcha got there, boy?" a fisherman from one of the boats called. He was tall and ruddy, and stood with one booted foot propped on the washboard. His sandy hair stuck up in spikes from the pomade he'd combed through it with his fingers, a combination of salt water and sea slime. I almost didn't recognize Ike Bower from the meeting the night before.

"Baloney and cheese, turkey and tomato, and ham."

"You had fried chicken last week."

"Not today. My sister finishes everything on her plate."

"Too bad," Bower said. "I'll trade you a tuna fish for the ham."

Evan tossed him a sandwich and caught one in return.

Levi cocked his head toward the fisherman and looked at me. "You know Ike Bower?"

"I've seen him around town," I said, "but I don't believe we've met."

"Ike, this here's Jessica Fletcher."

Ike nodded at me and scratched his head. "You were at the meetin' last night."

"That's right," I said.

"I've heard of you," he said.

"Sure you have, Ike. She's a famous writer."

"Oh, no," I said, shaking my head, embarrassed. "Not really—"

"That ain't it," Ike said. He squinted in my direction. "Wahn't you a friend of Ethan Cragg?"

"Yes," I said, relieved my literary career wasn't under discussion.

"I thought I knew the name. We were schoolmates. Course, that was way before he captained his own boat. His mother's cousin was my grandfather's nephew on his wife's side. Fair fisherman, but of course he didn't go for lobster. Shared some good times, though."

Lobstermen saved their greatest appreciation for other lobstermen, I knew. A "fair" fisherman was the best kind, worthy of admiration, but a lobsterman was a leader among men.

A man in the third boat, who'd been untangling a line with his sternman, stood up to greet Levi. "Hey, Carver, how they crawlin'?"

"Ain't. Mostly shorts and notches," Levi replied.

I was surprised. I'd thought he'd done really well this morning, getting at least two legal-sized lobsters out of most of his traps. But of course, I didn't know how many would make a good catch. I looked over to Evan, who was trying to cover a smile by taking a big bite of his sandwich. He winked at me. *Ah*, I thought. *Levi is not going to let his competitors know how well he's doing.*

"Alex Paynter, this is Jessica Fletcher," Levi said, introducing me. "And that's Maynard," he added pointing to the sternman, whom I recognized as Brady Holland's buddy.

I waved and the men waved back. I'd heard Paynter's name before, but hadn't been able to put a face to it before last night's association meeting.

Paynter and Maynard took out their lunch bags and settled down to eat, one straddling a box, the other perched on the rail next to a boom box. Maynard flipped a switch and the whine of an electric guitar blared out of the giant player.

"Turn that blasted thing off," Paynter yelled.

"I always play music when I have lunch," Maynard said.

"You been playin' that same record all week. I'm sick of it."

"This is my new album. I just bought it. You never heard this one before."

"That rock noise gives me indigestion. Keep it up and you'll be sternman for Brady Holland again. Then you won't be able to afford a new album."

"No wonder you're not catchin' much," Levi said. "You're scarin' the critters away."

The men laughed and Maynard turned off his radio, but he put on a sour face.

"Hey, Alex," Evan called over to Paynter. "Thought you were looking for an engine part today."

Paynter scratched his jaw. "Ayuh. I was, but now that I think on it, it's not comin' in till next week."

I'd been concentrating on my sandwich, but looked up at Paynter. He tipped his cap to me, and I smiled back.

"Too bad," Evan said, laughing. "Your engine sounds like a sick moose."

"We didn't raise a quorum last night," Bower said to Levi.

"Told you we wouldn't."

"Coulda used you to say a word."

Levi darted his eyes in my direction. "Not the time," he said in a low voice.

"She saw it all last night," Bower said. "Won't make no difference now."

"Told you I'll work behind the scenes," Levi said, conceding the argument. "I'm not gonna challenge Linc in front of a crowd."

"Someone has to or that Pettie will rob us blind. He's slick, that one."

"Did you notice how he dangled the lobsters for the festival over our heads?" Maynard said, deciding to join the conversation.

"What's that bilge you're spillin'?" Paynter said.

"He did. He just about said we won't have enough for the town to serve if we don't shut up and keep fishin'."

"Linc's on the take, I'm telling ya," Bower said. "Just bought himself a brand-new truck, put in a fancy kitchen for the wife. They're goin' to Aruba for Christmas."

"Mary got a new kitchen, too," Levi said, "and I ain't receivin' any donations."

"No, but you're likely in debt to Pettie up to your eyeballs."

"That ain't none of your business."

"No use gettin' green-eyed over Linc," Paynter said. "If he's got another source of income, we'd better be able to prove it. Only way we'll ever push 'im out."

Maynard hooted. "That'll be the day. A Williams

has been head of the lobstermen's association for over a hundred years. That's what Brady says."

Paynter eyed Maynard. "Forget what Brady Holland says," he said. "I don't want to find out you carried tales to that punk, you hear me?"

"Linc ain't a real king, and I can think of a dozen men'ud do a better job protectin' our interests," Bower said, stuffing the last of the sandwich into his mouth.

"Mebbe. But the men don't like change," Levi said. "I ain't for bootin' him unless the charge is true."

"Now, how you gonna prove that?" Paynter said, climbing to his feet and nudging Maynard, who balled up the paper that had wrapped his lunch and tossed it in a bucket. "I gotta skite along, earn my keep," Paynter yelled over his shoulder. The loud growl of his engine drowned out further conversation, until his boat pulled away from the little conclave and headed out to sea.

"Whew, amazing that motor still honks along," Evan said, shaking his head.

"Alex is right, Levi. How're we gonna prove it?" Bower said.

"We're gonna keep an eye out is what we're gonna do, and don't be obvious about it or he'll go all nasty-neat on us and that'll be the end of it. If he sees us watchin' and suspects we're onto him, we might as well be shearin' a pig."

Shearing a pig, I thought. *Well, there's an unproductive task.* Between the meeting last night and the conversations I'd heard today, it was becoming clear that the problems of the lobstermen were more and more complicated. They thought their dealer wasn't dealing straight, that he was underpaying them. Even worse, they feared he was paying off their association president, the one man they looked to to safeguard their interests and to act as their spokesman. Pettie was holding the Cabot Cove Lobsterfest over their heads, and Linc Williams had said nothing. If they didn't cooperate, Pettie had a unique way of punishing them. There might not be enough lobsters put away for the big shore dinner that was to be the highlight of the festival. And who would the town blame for the shortage? Not the dealer. That was certain. Henry Pettie wanted the men to buckle down, take what he gave them, and not complain. But the voices were getting louder, not softer. If he wasn't careful, he was going to have a full-fledged mutiny on his hands.

Lunch hour over, we sailed away from Ike Bower and took up the day's tasks again, Evan reining in his father's lobster traps, relieving them of their cargo, rebaiting, and dropping them back in the water in a new location that Levi determined was better than the last. Fully half the creatures captured were illegal for one reason or another, either too small, too large, or a breeding female, and were returned to the ocean to be caught another day. I began to see that lobstering was a hundred percent effort for only fifty percent gain.

"There's some days we're just feedin' 'em," Levi said, as the third trap in a row without a keeper sank back to the bottom. He held up a notch-tail to show me the eggs that were affixed to her belly. "See these berries?" he said. "You let them grow and they put out twice as much as the smaller hens. Sometimes you gotta sacrifice for the future." He leaned over the side, laid the lobster on the surface, and watched as she drifted down out of sight.

Levi tapped information into his Thistle box and checked his depth finder, looking for the signs that indicated a gravel or hard bottom, and signaled Evan when to throw over the trap he'd emptied. The morning's traps had been set in a straight line, but in the afternoon the buoys that showed where Levi's traps were placed were clustered in small groups. "This spot has been good for us before," he explained. "I want to make sure I've got it covered."

"Yeah, and don't give Holland any room to drop his load on top of ours," Evan added.

"What do you mean?" I asked.

"He's been following us all day," Evan said, nodding at a boat about a half mile aft of Levi's.

I followed his glance. "But we've seen lots of other boats today," I said. "How do you know who that is?"

"That's Holland, all right. Does it all the time," Evan said. "Has no idea where to put his traps, so he shadows the good fishermen and copies them."

"I guess that's flattering in a way," I said.

"Mebbe, but if he comes too close he'll foul our lines, or worse, he'll be stealing our catch. I'd'a thought he'd'a learned by now," Levi said, winking at his son.

Evan grinned. "Okay to tell the story?" he asked his father.

"Only if you don't go printin' it," Levi replied, looking at me sternly.

I looked back and forth between father and son, who were clearly sharing a joke. "Scout's honor," I said.

Evan took off his cap and wiped his brow with his bare arm. "Holland made a mess of our lines one time, and Pop wanted to teach him a lesson. He took about fifteen traps and, when he knew Holland was on his tail, put 'em off a ledge near Arrow Point. But there weren't nothin' in them, only bricks. The lobsters were long gone from there. Holland was sure he'd catch what my father was catching, but all he did was waste his time and bait."

"He finally figured it out by pulling one of my traps," Levi added.

"And made a fool of himself at the association by accusing Pop of staking out a prime fishing ground to keep other lobstermen away."

"I asked him how he knew what was in my traps," Levi said, his eyes twinkling.

"The other men gave him what-for," Evan added.

"You don't mess with another man's traps," Levi said, sobering. "That's his livelihood."

"He would've been booted out if Linc wasn't his uncle."

"Linc Williams is Brady Holland's uncle?" I said.

Levi nodded. "His sister's boy. Troublemaker all his life." He looked hard at Evan. "You keep away from Holland and his friends. I don't want to hear bad about you."

"And when did you ever?" Evan said, smirking at his father. "I'm your best son."

"And the only one," Levi said, trying to suppress a smile.

"Yeah, well, Anna would've liked that title."

"She's a tomboy, all right, but she'll come 'round. So was your mother in her younger days."

"Yeah, I know," Evan said, laughing. "But she took one look at you and—"

"Put on a dress," they finished together.

I joined in their laughter at what was a familiar family story. I didn't remember Mary as a tomboy, but I'd heard tales of how she set her eyes on Levi and nothing would do until they were paired off and married. That persistence was still part of her personality, and she was always in demand when any committee was forming for a purpose. I imagined that was how I got to sit on Levi's boat. Mary had "put on a dress" and convinced Levi to take me along.

The sun was high overhead as the men continued working without slowing their pace. They must have been tired. The work was physical, repetitive and grueling. As the afternoon wore on, the seas became rough, making it more difficult to balance the traps on the rail. Evan had to hold them steady with one hand, and empty and rebait them with the other. Added to the challenge of the rolling pitch, the heat took its toll.

I snugged down my fishing hat to shield my face from the sun's rays. Evan's face was bright red under his cap, and his T-shirt was dark with sweat that poured down his back and left two long stains under his arms. The temperature was working on the bait barrels, too, and the seaborne debris that littered the deck. What had been merely a briny smell in the morning was turning sour and pungent, and I began to regret the sandwich I'd so happily consumed earlier.

As the stench of rotting bait sharpened, I began to feel my gorge rise. At first I tried moving to the rail and facing the wind to get away from the smell. But it was only a temporary respite. The rough waters caused the boat to dip and rise as if caught in a wake. Grabbing the low rail and squatting down, I realized I could easily tumble overboard, and while I might welcome the coolness of the water and temporary escape from the reeking fish, my hosts wouldn't thank me for having to interrupt their routine to save their passenger. I'd promised to stay out of their way, not make more work, and I was determined not to show my landlubber weakness by giving up my lunch to the sea. I've always been a good sailor, and the wave of nausea I experienced was as embarrassing as it was stomach-turning.

Breathing through my mouth, I stumbled back to my stool and fumbled in my fanny pack for the acupressure bands Seth had given me the night before. I drew them over my hands, positioning the hard button on the inside of my wrist as he'd shown me.

"Feelin' a mite queasy?" Levi asked.

I nodded, not sure I could get the words out.

"Thought you looked a little funny. Those work for you?" Levi asked.

"I hope so," I managed to say.

"I never tried them."

"You get seasick?"

"Not anymore, but I did when I was his age," he said, cocking his head toward Evan, who wasn't looking all that well himself. "It's one of the hazards of the trade."

"What did you do for it?"

Levi shrugged. "I threw up."

I managed to hold steady for another hour and

heaved a silent sigh of relief when Levi turned his boat around and headed back toward Cabot Cove. By land standards, it was early to end a working day, but we'd been on the water for almost ten hours, and I could barely uncurl my hand from the cleat I'd been gripping to balance myself on the rocking boat. I was surprised to realize that the acupressure bands had calmed my stomach, and was grateful I hadn't had to take the pills Seth had supplied, which I'd brought with me as a precaution.

Evan spent the ride back hosing down the boat and shoveling overboard what remained of the rotten bait, to the delight of the gulls, which had appeared again as soon as Levi gunned the engine and turned toward home. My body was sore and my hair was stiff from the salty spray and flecks of things I didn't want to think about, but when the harbor hove into sight, I felt the relaxation that accompanies a good day's work, and the exhilaration of having landed what appeared to me to be a good-sized catch.

Levi slowed down as we passed the buoys that marked the mouth of the harbor, and navigated around other boats in the shipping lane, angling his boat toward a dock about a quarter mile down the shore from Nudd's. There was a large shack at one end and two gasoline pumps at the other. We were not the first lobster boat in and had to wait as Henry Pettie's assistants weighed several catches ahead of ours.

While Levi tied up the boat and went to check on the day's price, Evan climbed onto the boards and grabbed two of the blue plastic bins that lined the dock. He dropped them onto the deck and jumped down after them, leaning down to pull off the board that served as the hatch cover.

"May I help?" I asked, looking down at the mass of green and orange lobsters that gleamed in the afternoon sun.

"Sure, if you want to."

"What do I have to do?"

"Grab my father's gloves over there, and I'll show you."

Evan used a net ring with short handles on either side to scoop out the lobsters. He balanced the ring on the corner of the blue bin. "You have to be real careful with them," he said. "Rough handling makes 'em drop a claw. The culls are less valuable." Together we transferred the lobsters by hand to the cart, which Evan called a tote, placing them gently inside. Each bin, the sides slotted to let water flow through, held a hundred pounds of lobster, and we'd filled two of them before Levi returned, his eyes stormy.

"Why are you letting her work?" he said. "She's a guest."

"I asked to help," I said quickly, not wanting Evan to get the brunt of Levi's anger.

"That's not the point."

"I've been watching you work all day," I said. "There wasn't anything I could do before but get in your way. Don't be angry at Evan. I just wanted to be able to say I helped, at least in some small measure."

Levi frowned at me and held out one hand. I stripped off the gloves and laid them in his palm. "You're making me feel like a naughty child," I said.

"Not blamin' you."

"I know that, but don't blame Evan either. It was my idea."

"You're a guest."

"And guests should know their place. I'm terribly sorry for overstepping my bounds. I hope you'll forgive me."

He grunted but didn't argue further, taking the scoop and bending over the hatch.

I smiled at Evan and he winked back at me, both of us pleased we'd escaped the tongue-lashing that had surely been awaiting us had I not apologized so quickly.

"What are they goin' for, Pop?"

"Ten cents a pound less than yesterday," Levi ground out, resting the scoop on the edge of the tote. "And he's blamin' the big companies down in Boston this time. When the price goes up, it's all his doing. When he's cheatin' us, it's Boston's fault."

"Why don't we form a co-op?" Evan asked. "They've got them in Stonington and South Bristol and Swan's Island. No reason we couldn't do it, too."

"It's hard for the men to change what they know," Levi said. "But a little more of this may convince them. You keep researchin' it on the computer."

"Is ten cents a pound a big drop?" I asked.

"It's more than forty dollars out of my pocket. You multiply that by all of Cabot Cove's lobstermen, assumin' he's payin' us all the same price, and I'll bet it's almost two thousand bucks a week to him. That's a big incentive to cheat us, don't you think?"

"It's a lot of money, yes. But haven't you been working with Mr. Pettie for a long time? Why would he jeopardize his relationship with you?"

"If he can get away with it, he will. That's human nature. But we have ways of finding out what other dealers are payin'."

"I can find out on the Internet," Evan put in.

"They can't hide it from us anymore," Levi said, ignoring the interruption. "And if we see he's living off what he steals from us, I can make the case to change dealers or start up a co-op."

"It won't be that hard, Pop. I know I can find it on the Internet," Evan said. "I'll get everything we need to start a co-op."

"You're talkin' a lot of work, son. It's not as simple as all of us deciding to sell the bugs on our own. We need a manager, someone with the right connections in the market. Someone with the experience of a dealer, but working for us instead of himself. And somebody who doesn't gain anything unless we all gain."

Levi and Evan dropped the topic while they filled two more bins, four altogether, and part of a fifth— over four hundred pounds of lobster for the day—and took the totes to be weighed. Pettie's assistants gave Levi a chit and dropped the buoyant bins into an area of the water that was cordoned off by floating booms. On shore, three large trucks waited to take their live cargo to market, and a gaggle of tourists surrounded one of the drivers, trying to bargain for some lobsters to take home.

I followed Levi into the shack, where Henry Pettie leaned back in an office chair, resting his cowboy boots on a scarred table, and argued with someone on the other end of the telephone. The room was large and mostly bare. In addition to his office furniture,

Pettie's shack contained three stacks of lobster traps in one corner and boxes of what looked like replacement parts for them. Alex Paynter's sternman, Maynard, was sifting through the boxes, looking for something.

"We'll be there by six. That's what I promised and that's what I'll deliver. They're coming in right now. I can't make the boats go faster. Don't tell me what I've got in the lobster pound. That's not for you anyway. You'll get when I said you'll get and not a minute earlier." He dropped his feet to the floor and raised his index finger at Levi to indicate he knew he was there. "Sam, if I put you at the top of the list, I got to charge you more. My men are suffering down here because no one wants to pay more, you understand. That's what I thought. Don't you worry. I'll take care of you."

He hung up the phone and pulled his checkbook toward him, reaching a hand out to take Levi's receipt. "It's tough this year," he said, selecting a pen from a mug filled with them. "No one wants to pay more than last year even though the hauls are smaller. I know the men are angry. But what can I do?"

He sounded as if he were talking to himself, not us. But Levi was listening and wasn't happy with what he was hearing.

"Last year we were swimming in lobsters," Levi said. "When they're plentiful, I expect I'm not goin' get much per pound, but I'll make it up in volume. But this year they're scarce and you're paying the same price. It don't fly with me. I want to know why."

Pettie tore the check from his checkbook and waved it around as if to dry the ink, although he'd used a ballpoint pen to write it. "You heard what I told Sam. No one wants to pay more than they paid last year. That's the market. When Boston pays less, we all get it in the neck." He opened his desk drawer and took a piece of paper from a pad, scribbled something on it, and gave it to Levi along with his check.

"I don't want you mad at me, Carver," Pettie said. "You're one of my highliners. No better fisherman around, not even down the coast. I rely on you guys, but I can't control the market. You know that. Give that note to Nudd. He'll give you a discount on the bait for tomorrow. It's not much, I know, but it's the best I can do right now. Things'll turn around soon, I'm sure."

Levi glanced at the amount of the check, stuffed the papers in his shirt pocket, turned, and left without saying another word to Pettie.

The broker shrugged at me. "He'll get over it," he said. "I'm the only game in town." He pulled a small black notebook from his hip pocket and made notations in it. Then he picked up the phone and dialed a number.

I followed Levi back to the dock. Evan had moved the boat to where the gasoline pumps were located and was filling the tanks.

"That man's cheating us. I just know it," Levi said.

"He told me you'll get over it," I said, "because he's the only game in town."

"He said that?" Levi looked back toward the shack, his mouth in a tight line. "Not for long, he ain't. Not for long."

Chapter Seven

"How's the coffee, Mrs. F?"

"Just fine, Mort. Do you like the doughnuts?"

"What cop doesn't like doughnuts?"

I had stopped at Charlene Sassi's bakery on the way to see Cabot Cove's sheriff and my friend, Mort Metzger. Charlene had just taken a tray of plain doughnuts out of the oven and iced them with her special recipe for vanilla glaze. I'd bought half a dozen, and while she boxed them up I perused notices taped to her front window. Next to a plea for help finding a missing cat and an announcement of yoga classes forming at the hospital was a photo of Katherine Corr, the young lady Sassi's Bakery was sponsoring in the Lobsterfest pageant.

"Is that Jim Corr's daughter?" I asked. Jim was the high school choirmaster.

"That's her," Charlene said, handing me the box tied up with several strands of string.

"They grow up so fast. I think I had her in one of my classes, years back. Tiny girl with an elfin face. Very bright and very shy."

"She's not so shy anymore. All grown up and gorgeous now. Wait till you get a load of her."

"I'm planning to stop by the pageant rehearsals this

afternoon," I said. "I'll look forward to seeing her again."

Mort had a weakness for Charlene's doughnuts, and I allowed myself one while we shared the latest news over a cup of his jailhouse coffee. Mort had worked in New York City before coming up to Cabot Cove to take over as sheriff after Amos Tucker retired. He was a bit of a coffee snob, claiming our local brew was not up to his standards, and sending to the city for special blends from a secret source he wouldn't reveal. I suspected his secret source had moved closer to home when a Starbucks opened out near the new mall. But Mort wasn't saying and I wasn't pressing. The coffee was good and the company even better.

"Heard you went out with Levi Carver and his son. How did that go?"

"Who told you about that?"

"I met the doc in the emergency room yesterday. Said you were writing a piece for the *Gazette*."

"What were you doing in the ER?"

"We had a fender bender over by the high school."

"Any serious injuries?"

"Nah. One of his patients. She already had a bandage on her head. I figure it may have distracted her while she was driving. The other guy was fine."

"Oh, dear. That must have been the lady who stepped on a hoe."

"That sounds right."

"She's not having a good week. Was she okay?"

"I think so. Maybe a little whiplash, but that's all. So how'd the lobstering go?"

"Pretty well, I thought. We brought in over four hundred pounds," I said. "Will you listen to me? *'We* brought in.' *They* brought in over four hundred pounds. I just watched."

"Did you take notes?"

"No. I'm relying on my memory. There's just no way to write on a rocking boat. I knew if I tried, the salt spray would smear the ink and curl the pages, assuming I could even read my handwriting once I'd gotten home. I typed up a first draft last night, but I was too tired to work on it in earnest."

"Think you'll remember everything you need?"

"Enough to finish the article, I'm sure. And Levi isn't moving away, so if I have any questions, I can call him up and ask."

"Tough business, lobstering," Mort said, reaching into the box for his third doughnut. "Those guys work long hours for not a lot."

"Maureen is not going to be happy with me if you finish that whole box," I said. Maureen, Mort's second wife, was always putting him on a diet. "Why don't you save some for tomorrow?"

"The deputies will finish whatever I don't eat right now. Are you sure you don't want another?"

"I'm fine," I said. "One's my limit."

"I've been thinking about joining a gym or taking an exercise class," Mort said, licking the sugar off his fingers and wiping them on a napkin. He closed the box, carried it across the room, and put it on the top of a file cabinet. "Out of reach, out of mind," he said. "For now anyway."

"Where are your shoes?" I asked, noticing he was in socks.

"Under the desk. They're new. Don't want to scuff them up."

"If you're interested in exercise, they're starting yoga classes at the hospital," I said. "I just saw the flyer hanging up in Sassi's."

"Can you see me standing on one foot and humming?"

"I'm sure there's more to it than that."

"Maybe, but I want something more active, like weight lifting."

"I like to jog myself. I've gotten out of the habit with all the traveling I've done recently. But yesterday convinced me to start again."

"Yesterday? What happened?"

"Nothing, really. I spent the day sitting on a stool and holding on to keep from falling off. But even with a long bath last night, I woke up pretty sore today. It's too easy to get out of shape and hard to get back into it. Those men did all the work, and I got the charley horse."

"Maybe *you* should look into the yoga classes."

"Maybe I should," I said, thinking that wasn't a bad idea. "But tell me, what's new? Any more cases of rotten bait being spilled on a boat?"

"You're talking about the *Done For*. I know who did it, but Durkee won't press charges."

"Brady Holland and his friends, I'm guessing."

"How did you—"

"I was at the lobstermen's association meeting the other night. They're still giving Spencer a hard time."

Mort shook his head. "It took me two days of investigation to track down that information. I should just have waited and asked you."

The phone rang and Mort picked it up. "Sheriff's office. Metzger here." There was a long silence. I started to rise, thinking it was time to get over to the high school gym, where the pageant rehearsals were scheduled to start in another half hour, but Mort waved me back into my seat. "Where are you now?" he said. He picked up a pencil and hunted for a clean sheet of paper on his desk, which was covered with stacks of folders and forms left from the change of shift. He finally settled on writing in the margins of the morning newspaper. "And where is he? Okay, we'll be right over. Stay where you are."

He hung up, pushed his feet into his shoes, and plucked his cap from the coatrack behind his desk. "Coming, Mrs. F?" he said.

"Where are we going?"

"Down to the harbor. There's been another incident."

"What happened?"

"Someone chopped a hole in Ike Bower's boat."

Chapter Eight

Mort paused on his way out of the office to cast a final look at the doughnuts on top of the file cabinet. For a moment I thought he was going to grab one for the road. He exercised admirable restraint and led me out of the building to his patrol car with SHERIFF emblazoned on its sides. We climbed in and headed in the direction of the docks.

"Care to fill me in on who called?" I asked. "Was it Ike?"

"No, Mrs. F. It was Evelyn Phillips from the *Gazette*."

"Oh? She said someone made a hole in Ike's boat?"

" 'Chopped' is the word she used."

"How terrible."

"If it's true. Remains to be seen."

He was right, of course. Our sheriff was not a man who jumped to conclusions. When it came to crime in Cabot Cove, Mort functioned under the old Missouri adage of "Show me!"

The trip to the waterfront usually took only minutes from Mort's office, but a knot of tourists blocked our way at the entrance to the parking area that abutted the docks. The visitors to Cabot Cove were gawking at a sight that was familiar to residents—my friend

Tobé Wilson, who with her husband, Jack, ran the leading veterinarian practice in town, was walking her pet pig, Kiwi. When she wasn't managing their office, Tobé occasionally exercised one or other member of the Wilsons' sizable menagerie with a stroll downtown, to the amusement of onlookers. Tobé is petite, not quite five feet tall, and the pig is enormous. The combination of mistress and swine always attracts attention.

Mort gently tapped his horn, and the crowd parted to allow us to pass. He pulled into an empty space near Nudd's Bait & Tackle, not far from where Ike Bower's lobster boat was tethered to the dock. We exited the car. Ike, who was on board, saw us approach but turned away, tugging down on the bill of his cap to mask his eyes from us.

"I don't see Evelyn," I said.

"Probably around somewhere," Mort said. "We'll catch up with her later."

"Hello, Ike," Mort yelled.

Ike tossed us an indifferent wave and returned to what he was doing.

"Mind if we come aboard?" Mort asked, not waiting for an answer and jumping down onto the deck. He winced, then took my hand and helped me join him. In a shirtwaist, stockings, and pumps, I wasn't exactly attired for boating. Bower, in stained, frayed tan coveralls and rubber boots, was dressed more appropriately for his task. He was in the process of rigging up a small table saw. Other carpentry tools were spread at his feet.

"Heard you had a little problem," Mort said.

"Nope," Ike said, not looking at us. "No problem."

"That's good to hear," Mort said, casually examining the boat's hull from deckside. "Somebody called, said you'd sprung a leak."

"Happens with boats all the time."

"Well, this was maybe not expected?"

"Had a little accident, is all," Ike said as he plugged in the saw to a long orange cord that snaked across the boards from where he'd connected it to a power source on the dock. He switched on the tool and its loud drone filled the relative quiet of the harbor at that hour, the other fishermen long gone.

"What sort of accident?" Mort asked, continuing his perusal of the craft.

"Must have had some driftwood come in overnight on the current," said Ike. "Nothin' major."

Mort and I watched Ike lean over the side of the boat. We flanked him and did the same. A jagged hole the size of a football was slightly above the waterline.

"Must've been one big piece of driftwood," Mort said, "and traveling at quite a clip to pierce the side of the boat."

"Seems strange it made a hole above the waterline," I added.

Mort pulled out his notebook. "Of course, I don't know a lot about boats, but it seems to me that—"

Ike straightened and looked down at Mort, who was a good deal shorter than the strapping lobsterman. "Like you said, Sheriff, you don't know a lot about boats. You can put your pad away."

"Don't you want to file a report?" Mort asked. "For insurance purposes?"

"Insurance don't pay for accidents like this. Now, I've got some work to do to get this here thing fixed before I lose another day's work." He looked at me and said, "Ma'am," in such a way that it was obvious I was being dismissed, along with Mort.

Mort and I climbed back up onto the dock and walked toward the parking lot.

"He's hiding something," Mort said.

"One thing is certain," I said. "That was no accident."

"What's he afraid of? Why won't he file a complaint?"

"Maybe he's worried about reprisals."

"For what?"

I thought back to the meeting of the lobstermen's association at which Ike had spoken openly of not needing the association and Linc Williams if they weren't going to support the lobstermen. Had someone chopped a hole in Ike's boat in retribution for his stand, the way another someone had dumped rotting bait on the deck of Spencer Durkee's boat? Were Ike's fellow lobstermen so vindictive as to resort to such physical threats in order to keep everyone in line? Did the hole in Ike's boat carry with it a message? That was a distinct possibility, although I reminded myself to adhere to Mort's philosophy of not jumping to hasty conclusions.

We stood alongside Mort's marked vehicle and looked back to Ike Bower, who was engrossed in repairing the hole in his hull.

"I wonder," Mort said, squinting against the sun.

"Wonder what?" I asked.

"I wonder why Evelyn Phillips said that somebody chopped a hole in Ike's boat. Maybe she knows something we don't, and that Ike's not willing to admit."

"I suggest we ask her," I offered, pointing to the far end of the parking lot. Evelyn was walking toward us.

"Good morning Jessica, Sheriff," she said.

"Morning, Ms. Phillips," Mort said. He glanced in the direction of Ike's boat before asking the newspaper editor, "So, what's this about somebody chopping a hole in his boat?"

"Why don't you go on and see for yourself?" Evelyn said.

"We just did," I said. "Bower says it was an accident."

"That's not what he told others," she said.

"What others?" Mort asked.

"Other lobstermen. I was down here early, before the sun came up," she said. "I don't sleep well, and I like to come down the docks and watch the fishing boats get ready for the day. I was here when Ike Bower arrived and discovered what had happened to his boat."

"And you heard him say something about it to others?" I asked.

"Yes. He didn't see me. The docks are pretty busy at that time of day, what with the lobstermen and the fishing boats going out, and the party boats getting ready for the tourists." She patted her tote bag. "I had my little stool with me, and I was sitting over there, near Spencer Durkee's boat, over by a pile of lobster traps. I didn't see when he found the hole, but I sure as heck heard him. He was furious, swearing up a storm; I wouldn't dare repeat what he had to say, let alone write it in the paper. But I heard him yell that somebody'd taken an ax to his boat, and he swore he'd get even."

Mort and I looked back to where Ike continued making repairs. What had intervened between the time he expressed his anger at what someone had done to his boat and the time we arrived? Was this another case of lobstermen keeping their troubles to themselves? Or had someone convinced him he'd better accept what had happened, chalk it up to an accident, keep quiet, and not make waves?

"Anything else you remember, Ms. Phillips?" Mort asked.

"I don't think so. After Mr. Bower vented his anger to his colleagues, he went back to his truck and took off. I didn't see him again after that."

"Who were the others he told?" I asked.

"Well, one of them was Linc Williams. And Levi Carver was there. I don't know the names of the others. I think I've seen them around town, though."

"You'd know them if you saw them again?" Mort asked.

"Oh, sure. But there must've been a lot of people who heard him. He was pretty loud." She pulled a slim reporter's pad and a pen from her canvas shoulder bag, opened the pad, and said to Mort, "Any statement, Sheriff?"

"Statement? About what?"

"About what happened here," she replied. "Obviously a crime has been committed. You're here investigating it. Aren't you?"

"I'm here because you called me," said Mort. "According to you, based on what you claim you heard Ike Bower say, somebody cut a hole in his boat. Unless Bower chooses to file a criminal complaint, there's nothing I can do."

"But I heard it," Evelyn said.

"Hearsay," Mort responded. "*You* want to file a complaint?"

"Of course not."

"I'm not sure there's anything to base a story on for the paper," I said to her. "If Ike claims it was an accident, it'll have to stay that way." But I had the feeling she wasn't about to let it go that easily.

She proved me right a moment later. "I write about car accidents all the time," she said. "I can write about boat 'accidents' too." She emphasized the word to make sure we knew she didn't consider it an accident at all. "I'll come back when the lobstermen come in with their catches and see if I can interview the men who talked to Ike Bower this morning. Then, if one of them confirms it, I—"

"Suit yourself, Ms. Phillips," Mort said. "Meantime, I've got to get back to my office."

"How'd your day on the lobster boat go?" she said to me.

"Fine," I said. "I'm hoping to have something to give you tomorrow."

"Can't wait," she said. "I'm sure it'll be terrific."

I looked at my watch and said, "I want to stop in on rehearsals for the beauty pageant. Any chance you can drop me off, Mort?"

"Happy to."

Mort opened the passenger door for me and I got in. He came around to the driver's side and was about to join me when he called after Evelyn, who'd started to walk away.

"Ms. Phillips," he said.

"Yes?" she said, turning.

"How about you making a statement for the record?" he said.

She thought for a moment before saying, "I don't think that would be appropriate, considering I'm a journalist."

"I don't see what that has to do with anything," Mort said. "You claim a crime has been committed. Seems to me being a good citizen is more important than being a journalist."

"I don't think so, Sheriff," she said. "But I'll let you know if I uncover anything else."

"You were a little short with her," I said when he climbed into the car.

"Yeah? Didn't mean to be. Must be feeling a little cranky today."

Mort fell silent as he drove me to the high school, where the pageant rehearsals were taking place. He pulled up in front of the school, reached across, and pushed open my door.

"Thanks for the lift," I said.

"She's right, you know," he said.

"That it wasn't an accident?" I said. "I was thinking the same thing."

"First Spencer's boat, now Ike Bower's. I've got a bad feeling about what's going on with the lobstermen."

"So do I," I said. "Let's hope they can resolve whatever differences they have before the festival."

Mort's laugh was wry. "We can't have a lobster festival without lobsters, now, can we?"

"I'd hate to see us have to serve hot dogs and hamburgers; that's for certain." *But it might come to that,* I thought.

Chapter Nine

The high school gym was set up as if a game were to take place. There were bleachers on either side of the basketball court, with a sprinkling of onlookers lolling on the benches. It was warm inside, even with the ceiling fans on and the doors to the outside propped open. A group of teenage boys sat on the floor near the exit, watching the girls and whispering to each other. I spotted Gwen Anissina sitting in the first row of the bleachers, with an open binder on her lap. Next to her was Matilda Watson, the *Gazette*'s publisher and Evelyn's boss. Wheeled in for the occasion and sitting under one of the baskets was the upright piano the school used for assemblies. I couldn't see over the top, but someone was pounding out a tune while the gym teacher shouted instructions.

"One, two, three, four. Arms up, ladies. Don't look at your feet. Big smile. That's it. Turn, bow." Lynda Peckham clapped her hands. "One more time. Mrs. Fricket, please take it from the top."

The eight young women who were contestants vying for the title of Miss Cabot Cove Lobsterfest arranged themselves in two rows and began their presentation. I recognized Abigail Brown right away from her picture in Charles Department Store. She was a stunning brunette with long straight hair and a twinkle in her green eyes. And I thought I picked out Katherine Corr, too, although she certainly had grown up from her days as one of my students. Charlene was right: She was a curvaceous beauty now.

Lynda Peckham tapped out the rhythm with her toe and put the girls through their paces; the performance was not quite a dance but involved a large number of arm movements and poses. Miss Peckham had a lot of experience choreographing for the cheerleading squad, but perhaps her familiarity with dance was more limited. Or maybe it was the talent of the contestants that required more simplified steps.

"We should have the costumes tomorrow, ladies, so remember to leave enough room between you for them. They tend to be quite full. Arm lengths apart, now. Follow the music."

I waved to Gwen, who motioned me to join her and Matilda.

"Jessica, you're just the one I wanted to see," Matilda said when I sat down. "Would you mind proofreading this for me?" She handed me a piece of paper headlined *Pageant Rules.* "I wrote it out this morning but I never can find mistakes in my own work. I need a fresh eye."

I scanned the sheet, my eyebrows rising as I took in the list of rules, which, along with demands for participation in all the events leading up to and following the coronation, included several paragraphs on morals, as well as a ban on piercing any part of the body other than ears, and instruction on how much jewelry was permissible. "I don't see any errors," I said, handing it back to Matilda. "But it's quite stringent, don't you think?"

Gwen gave me a wan smile, and I wondered if she, too, had just seen this communiqué for the first time.

"You have to police these things," Matilda replied. "Otherwise we could crown someone and discover later she's inappropriate to represent the community. This way we know we won't be embarrassed. I don't want to put some girl's picture on my front page only to find out she has a questionable reputation."

"But these girls have already been accepted as contestants. Is it fair to change the rules on them now?"

"This is standard stuff, Jessica. All the pageants have rules like this. You're just behind the times."

"I may be," I said. "But I thought this kind of thing went out of style long ago. What happens if you lose several of them after issuing this edict?"

"Then they never should have been contestants to begin with," she said, a satisfied grin on her face. "That just proves my point."

Gwen's eyes flew up to the ceiling, but she remained silent.

"Okay, ladies, take five and we'll try it again," Miss Peckham called out. "Do not leave the room. I don't want to have to hunt you down."

Several of the young women needed no encouragement. They flopped down right where they were on the glossy varnished floor, stretching out or sitting cross-legged, while the others wandered over to talk to their mothers or friends waiting in the bleachers or to flirt with the boys near the door.

I heard Elsie Fricket play two final chords and close the piano cover. A former guidance counselor, Elsie had always supplied the music for the school's plays and other theatrical events. She was retired now, but obviously had been called into service for the pageant rehearsals. I looked over as she stood up from the piano, and I did a double take. Elsie was wearing a white plastic neck brace, and there was a large bandage on her forehead, just above a black eye worthy of a pugilist.

Oh, dear, I thought. Elsie must be the lady who stepped on the hoe. Seth hadn't told me his patient's name, but it was clear to me between the bandage and the neck brace that Mrs. Fricket had also been the victim of the fender bender Mort had attended to.

"Elsie, are you all right?" I asked, coming to take her arm and lead her to where Gwen and Matilda sat.

"Oh, Jessica, how nice to see you. I'm fine," she said, looping her arm through mine. "Thank you. It's a bit hard to get around with this neck brace on. I can't look down. Makes it tough on the stairs."

"I can imagine," I said.

"I've been playing the piano by feel—I can't see the keys. Hope I didn't hit too many sour notes."

"You sounded fine to me. You know Matilda. Have you met Gwen?"

"Darling Gwen, of course. You and I are old pals, aren't we?" Elsie said, sinking down on the bench and patting Gwen on the arm. "How are you, Matilda? Still the scourge of downtown?"

"I'm just fine, you old bat. That husband of yours take a Louisville Slugger to you?"

"He probably would if he could see enough to find one." Elsie laughed. "No, stepped on a hoe getting my lettuce and zucchini in."

"Gardening did all that?" Matilda asked. "I thought it was a peaceful pursuit. Journalism is easy in comparison. I'm still in one piece."

"You just have a harder shell," Elsie said. "Surely someone must want to beat you up by now."

"Well, they'd have to catch me first. Who's doctoring you these days?"

"Seth Hazlitt. But the neck brace is courtesy of the hospital. Some guy sideswiped me on my way here the other day."

Mort had presented the picture the other way around, saying that Elsie may have been distracted by her bandage and caused the accident, but I didn't say anything.

Gwen lay her binder on the bench, stood, and looked over to Matilda. "Would you like to address the girls now, Ms. Watson?"

"It's as good a time as any," she replied.

"Beauty tips from the Wicked Witch of the West, huh?" Elsie asked.

"Very funny. I'm giving them the pageant rules and asking them to sign the qualifying statement."

"Oh, that should be fun. You always did like giving orders."

"Some are born to be leaders," Matilda said, and marched off with Gwen.

Elsie hooted. "Give 'er hell, girls," she called out. "Don't let her get away with anything."

Matilda flashed Elsie a dirty look, and I tried hard not to smile. The women had been friendly enemies

all their lives. No one knew when their gleeful banter-
ing had begun, but it was an old habit now, one that
was enjoyed as much by them as by whatever audience
was witness to the exchange.

Lynda Peckham gestured to the contestants to
gather 'round, and Matilda soon had eight pretty girls
sitting at her feet.

"Ladies, you all met Ms. Watson the other day,"
Gwen began. "She has kindly consented to help organize the pageant, and she has something she wants to
talk about with you today."

Gwen stepped back and Matilda walked forward to
distribute her manifesto.

"I've done quite a bit of research," she said, handing out the papers. "Every pageant worth its salt has
guidelines for the contestants and rules for participation. These are ours. Please return the signed statement to me before you leave today."

I watched the faces of the young women as they
read through the rules.

"You're kidding right?" asked one.

"Not at all," Matilda said, stiffening. "All pageants
have rules like this."

" 'I am and have always been a female,' " another girl
said, reading from the paper. "What's up with that?"

" 'I am of good moral character and I am not now,
nor have I ever been, married, pregnant, nor involved
in any act of moral turpitude.' What's 'turpitude'
mean?"

"It's the same as depravity," Matilda said, looking
down into a small sea of blank faces. "I see that the
vocabulary lists in our English classes can stand
updating."

A wave of giggles took hold, and Matilda scowled down at her charges.

"Let me put this simply. You are to do nothing before, during, or after the pageant that would in any way embarrass your parents or this community. No criminal activity, no dishonest, immodest, or immoral behavior of any kind, which means no canoodling with your boyfriends." She put extra emphasis on the last part.

A small gasp escaped from several mouths.

"In other words, you are to be models of chaste, maidenly comportment. Anyone found in breach of these rules will be summarily dismissed from the pageant."

"Does that mean we'd be kicked out?"

"That is precisely what it means. So don't embarrass us or yourselves."

Abigail spoke up. "That's not fair. We were never told this before."

"You can drop out now if you don't think you can live up to our standards," Matilda said icily.

Gwen, who'd been standing nearby with her arms crossed, dropped her head and massaged her eyelids with her fingers.

There was a long—dare I say pregnant—pause. "I have a pen, if anyone needs it," Miss Peckham said. "C'mon, girls. You can do without the boys for a little while. You're strong, independent women. You can weather any storm for good old Cabot Cove."

Her cheer evoked a few smiles, but Matilda had managed to leach out much of the fun of the pageant for its eight contestants. Slowly they got to their feet and shuffled to the benches on the side, where they took turns with Miss Peckham's pen and signed the qualifying statement.

"Oh, boy," Elsie said. "She always was a wet blanket. Gwen may as well cancel the rest of the rehearsal. Those girls don't look like they can muster up any enthusiasm for good old Cabot Cove this afternoon."

"I wonder what set her off?" I said.

"She always has to be in charge. Been like that since she was a tyke. I oughta know. She's been trying to boss me around since primary school."

"Who has?" came a deep voice from her other side. David Ranieri, one of the owners of Charles Department Store, slid in next to Elsie and put his arm around her shoulders. He grinned at me. "No one bosses my aunt around, do they, Elsie?"

"Well, not if I can help it, Davy. How's the family?"

"Everyone's fine. I had a delivery over this way, and thought I'd stop in and see how rehearsals are going. I see Abby's got some competition. They're all pretty girls. It's going to be hard for the judges."

"They can't go wrong with any choice," I said.

"Hi, Mr. Ranieri," Abigail said, coming over to greet him.

"Hello, Abigail. Working hard?"

"We are. We've been rehearsing all morning. Right, Mrs. Fricket?"

"They're drivers, every one of them," Elsie said. "The pageant will be spectacular. Eight beautiful and talented girls. Couldn't want anything better."

Abigail smiled.

"Do I get a chance to see you dance?" David asked.

"I'm not sure if we're rehearsing anymore," she said. "We're supposed to go for a costume fitting next. I might be a little late to work. Is that okay?"

"Not to worry."

"David!" Matilda called from across the gym where she was collecting signed statements.

He stood up. "Uh-oh," he muttered.

Abigail looked from David to Matilda, excused herself, and scooted away to where her friends were gathered.

"You're just the person I wanted to see," Matilda said, hurrying over to catch him. "I didn't get your ad for the next issue."

"I was planning to advertise in the festival edition instead."

"You can do both. Retail businesses rely on display ads. How would people know where to go if they didn't see your ad in the paper?"

"They might be attracted by our windows," David said, inching toward the door. "Which reminds me, I've got to get back. Jim's all by himself today. Two people called in sick."

"Wait, I have an advertising insertion order in my bag," she said, leaning over to pull a black briefcase from under the bench. "Do you have a pen, Elsie? I'll stop by this afternoon, David, and you can tell me which ad you want to run. Or we can make up a whole new one for you. No charge for the mechanical. You won't find a better deal than that."

"Please pardon the rush. 'Bye, ladies. I've got to go," he said, and was out the door before Matilda could twist his arm.

"Well, I think I got all the forms signed by the girls, anyway," she said, waving a sheaf of papers.

"Is that all you do as pageant coordinator, terrorize the contestants?" Elsie said.

"Don't be ridiculous. I'm going with them to the costume fitting right now, and I'll be there later when the photographer takes their pictures for the paper. I don't want any of those standard poses either. We should do something different and imaginative. In fact, I've been meaning to talk to Gwen about that."

"Oh, boy, those poor girls," Elsie muttered as Matilda hustled back to where Gwen was talking with some of the mothers. "I guess they're done with me for the day. Can I give you a ride somewhere, Jessica?"

"That's very kind of you, Elsie, but can you drive with that neck brace?" I asked, apprehensive about trusting my life to her driving skills.

"Don't tell Seth, but I take it off when I get behind the wheel. Couldn't see a thing otherwise."

Elsie and I bade good-bye to Gwen and Matilda, and waved to the girls. On our way out the door, we met Evan Carver coming in.

"Hi, Mrs. Fletcher, Mrs. Fricket. Is Abby . . . uh, the girls . . . I mean, the pageant . . . Are they still rehearsing?" he asked.

"They're just about to leave for a costume fitting," I said, "but I think you can catch them."

"Oh, good."

"What are you doing here?" I asked. "Didn't you go out with your dad today?"

"Sure. But we only put in a half day. Pop wanted

to come back early to help one of the guys with his boat. Ike. You met him yesterday."

"That's right."

"Someone stove in the side of his boat. Oh, darn, I guess I shouldn't say that."

"I didn't hear it from you," I said.

Evan blushed. "Thanks. I-I'd better get inside before I, um, miss them."

"Handsome devil, isn't he?" Elsie said when Evan left. "Levi looked like that when he was young. Mary couldn't take her eyes off him. He and Abigail Brown are an item, Evan, that is. Gonna be hard for them to follow Matilda's rules."

But I barely heard what she was saying. Evan had confirmed Evelyn Phillips's story. Someone had bashed in Ike's boat. Who had done that—and why? I knew it wasn't my business, but that hadn't stopped me before. I wanted to know what was behind the turmoil in the lobstermen's community. After all, it might have an impact on our festival. At least, that was what I told myself. It was as good an excuse as any to do a little investigating.

Chapter Ten

After Elsie dropped me off at the docks, I went into Mara's to get something to eat, and to see if news of Ike's repair work had made its way to the lunch counter. Cabot Cove had three reliable sources of gossip: Charlene Sassi's bakery, Loretta Spiegel's beauty shop, and Mara's luncheonette. Since I was unlikely to encounter any fishermen at the bakery or beauty shop, Mara's was my logical destination in search of scuttlebutt about the lobstermen.

"We've got a soup-and-salad special today," Mara said, bringing me a glass of iced tea, a straw, and a saucer of cut lemon without being asked.

"What's the soup?" I asked.

"Clam chowder or clam chowder."

"I guess I'll have the clam chowder," I said, "and salad dressing on the side, please."

"You're not going to save a lot of calories that way, you know. Dressing on the side—and broken cookies—still have calories."

I laughed. "I know," I said, "but it makes me feel more virtuous, especially since I know you believe in the Julia Child school of cooking, lots of butter and cream in that chowder."

"Have you got spies in my kitchen?"

"If I did, I'd never admit it."

"Must be my new cook. Don't you know you can't trust a fisherman not to exaggerate?"

"Speaking of fishermen, Mara, I was wondering if there's been any talk in here today?"

"There's always talk in here, Jessica. What kind of talk do you mean?"

There was no point in being subtle with Mara, so I came out and asked, "What do you hear about the lobstermen?"

"Quite a bit, actually," she said. "Let me put your order in and I'll be right back."

Mara stopped at three more tables to take care of other patrons before she reached the kitchen to put in my order. By the time she found her way back to me carrying a steaming bowl of chowder, my impatient fingers had folded the paper covering from my straw into a tiny square.

"You heard about Ike Bower's boat, I take it," Mara said, sliding into the booth next to me.

"Yes. I saw the hole myself. He said it was an accident."

She guffawed. "Sure it was an accident—if someone accidentally took a swing at his hull."

I nodded. "Who told you about it?"

"Barnaby Longshoot. You know he can't keep a secret to save his soul. He was hanging around this morning when Bower was griping to some of the other men, swearing revenge, according to Barnaby."

"That doesn't sound good."

She looked around her luncheonette to be sure we weren't being overheard. "And at breakfast time, I saw that Holland kid and his buddy Maynard out front on the dock, giggling and punching each other in the shoulder, giving high fives, like they'd just done a great thing."

"Do you think they were the ones who damaged Ike's boat?"

"I wouldn't swear on it in a court of law, but when Barnaby went out back to get me an extra tray this morning, he saw Holland. He said the guy took one look at him and darted around the corner and down the alley next to my building."

"What he was doing back there, do you know?"

"No. But later Barnaby found a sledgehammer in with the garbage, which he swears wasn't there earlier."

"What did he do with it?"

"Put it in the back shed. It was a perfectly good tool. Nothin' wrong with it."

"When is your garbage picked up?" I asked.

"Around six in the morning. Why?"

"Just curious. Do you mind if I take a look at the hammer?"

"Help yourself. Why do I have the feeling you're onto something sinister, Jess?"

"I can't imagine why you'd think that about me," I said lightly.

"I can't imagine why I *wouldn't* think that about you, Jess." She turned serious. "Do you think I should report that to the sheriff?"

"It couldn't hurt," I said. "Bower said it was an accident, and he refused to file a report, so technically there's no crime for the sheriff to investigate. Still, I think he'd like to know what Barnaby saw and found."

"Mort usually stops by for a snack in the afternoon.

I'll talk to him about it then. Enjoy your soup before
it gets cold."

The soup and salad were delicious—there was good
reason why Mara's had become such a popular place
with both locals and visitors alike—but I finished my
meal quickly, eager to see what was behind the
luncheonette.

Mara's back door was off the same hallway as the
restrooms and the entrance to the kitchen. I pushed
on the door's metal bar and stepped out onto a concrete block, the only bit of paving in sight. The constant rain had left the rear yard a sea of mud, and
even though we'd had a few dry days strung together,
it was not enough to keep my shoes from sinking in
as I tiptoed in the direction of the Dumpster. I looked
down at footprints that had been left in the soil
around the big bin and counted at least four different
sets. I could easily account for three of them—Mara's,
her cook's, and Barnaby's. The fourth looked suspi-
ciously like it had been made by a rubber boot of the
sort favored by commercial fishermen. Barnaby had
seen Holland in the back here, so there was a good
chance those prints were his.

A prefabricated shed sitting on a bed of gravel was
on the other side of the Dumpster. The padlock wasn't
closed, and I slipped it out of the latch and pulled
open the door. Mara had an assortment of boxes on
metal shelves, all labeled with black marker, indicating
which were dishes, glassware, extra cooking utensils,
and trays. A toolbox rested on the wooden floor. In
one corner were three colorful umbrellas, the kind
used with picnic tables, and next to them, standing on

its metal head, was a sledgehammer. I didn't touch it just in case it became a piece of evidence at a later date. But I did examine the top, thinking it might still hold a splinter of wood. If there had ever been wood or paint residue on it, it didn't appear to be there anymore. The hammer had been thrown in a Dumpster and retrieved, and—who knows?—Barnaby might have wiped it off before he left it in the shed.

I closed the door, careful to replace the padlock but leaving it open as I'd found it. I traversed the mud and walked through Mara's back door. Coming down the hall was Barnaby Longshoot.

"Hello, Barnaby, how are you?" I asked.

"Okay. Okay," he said. He seemed uncomfortable at seeing me.

"I wonder if we could sit down for a bit, Barnaby. I understand you were at the docks when Ike Bower was talking about the hole someone made in his boat."

Barnaby raised two fingers to his lips. "Shhh, shhh," he said. "Can't talk about that now."

"If now isn't good, we could meet whenever it's more convenient," I said. "I won't take up too much of your time. I just have a few questions, and since you were on the scene, you're the perfect person to answer them."

"Hey, Barnaby, you're blocking the door to the men's room."

I looked over Barnaby's shoulder and saw Alex Paynter. Evidently some of the lobstermen had put in an abbreviated day.

Barnaby made a face indicating I shouldn't say anything, and stepped aside to move out of Alex's way.

"Oh, hello, Mrs. Fletcher," Paynter said, poised to enter the restroom. "Didn't see you there behind Barnaby."

He went through the door as Mara arrived carrying a large tray laden with dirty dishes. "This hall's not big enough for all of us," she said. Barnaby and I pressed our backs against the wall to allow her to pass.

"So, Barnaby," I said. "It's a little busy here. Why don't we—"

"Not here, not now," he said. "I got work to do."

"Okay. When's a good time?"

"Tonight, after Mara's is closed. I'll meet you out back."

"Out back? Do we really need to be so secretive?" I asked.

"Okay, out front then."

The door to the men's room opened behind me. Barnaby put his fingers to his lips and scuttled back down the hall to the dining room.

"Excuse me, Mrs. Fletcher," Paynter said.

"Of course," I said, moving out of the way.

I shook my head. Was it me, or was there something strange afoot? Barnaby had been visibly spooked when I asked to speak with him. And the sight of Alex Paynter seemed to unnerve him even more. But I'd have to wait to find out what was bothering him.

The way my mind was working at the moment, it was like preparing a plot outline for one of my murder mystery novels, or crime novels as the British prefer to call them. Of course, there hadn't been a murder, or anything close to it. All that had happened was damage to one lobsterman's boat, and the dumping of rotting bait on another, unpleasant incidents to be sure, but amounting to nothing more than unfortunate vandalism.

But my instincts had started shouting at me that what had happened to Ike Bower's and Spencer Durkee's boats had a deeper significance. Maybe it was the concern over the upcoming lobster festival, and whether there would be enough lobsters to feed what we hoped would be a large crowd of visitors, that added gravity to the situation for me.

No matter what the impetus of my growing concern, I'd now allowed myself to become involved, and once that happens . . . well, ask Seth Hazlitt about what happens to me once I reach this stage of curiosity.

Chapter Eleven

The tourist fishing boats had come in, and the docks were teeming with sunburned faces. Most were smiling as families admired the bags of fish, cleaned and filleted by the crew, souvenirs of a successful fishing trip. Others looked a bit green, grateful to be off the boat and back on terra firma, or at least a sturdy dock. The rain on previous days had kept down the number of tourists on the dock, but the welcome sun had brought them back, cheerful and noisy, like gulls that follow fishing boats in search of a tossed handout.

I saw Evelyn Phillips at the end of the dock taking a picture of a father and son holding up their prize catch of the day, which would probably end up in the next edition of the *Gazette*. Photos of visitors to our town with tangible proof of a successful fishing trip were staples in the paper during tourist season, along with kids and dogs enjoying what our lovely town has to offer.

Picture taking completed, Evelyn engaged in an animated conversation with the father and his boy, and I had the feeling she was urging them to return for the upcoming Cabot Cove Lobsterfest. They would be reminded as well, of course, by the colorful banners the committee had strung up along the shore, and

which hung from every light post up and down Main
Street.

Wedged between two of the party boats disgorging
their passengers was Spencer Durkee's lobster boat,
easy to pick out in the harbor thanks to the purple
roof of its wheelhouse. In light of what had happened
to Ike Bower's boat, I wondered if Spencer would
now be more willing to talk about the incident that
had landed him in the *Gazette*. I didn't know whether
Spencer was aboard or not, but I decided to see if he
was. I dove into the crowd, fighting the tide of human-
ity surging toward the parking lot, holding the skirt of
my dress out of the way of the damp bags of fish.

You can always tell the townies from the tourists, I
thought. There I was in a dress, stockings, and shoes,
and all our visitors were attired in T-shirts, shorts, and
sneakers. But, of course, I wasn't coming ashore after
a day's fishing, or hiking, or shopping for bargains and
souvenirs in our shops. I waited while a cluster of
tourists passed me by before scooting across the dock
to where the *Done For* was berthed.

"Spencer," I called out. "Spencer Durkee, are you
there?"

"He's not, ma'am. He went ashore just as we were
comin' in," said a crew member from one of the party
boats who was busy untying the lines that secured his
craft to the dock. The large boats were allowed to tie
up when picking up passengers at the beginning of the
day and when letting them off at the end. The rest of
the time they were moored out in the harbor, leaving
space for vessels that took up less room.

"Did you happen to see which way he went?" I
asked.

"No, ma'am. Sorry."

I walked toward Nudd's Bait & Tackle, thinking Spencer might have gone there for supplies; maybe Tim Nudd would be able to tell me where to find him. Ike Bower's boat was no longer anchored near the store, which didn't matter. I'd decided that Ike was less likely to provide information than the more verbose Spencer. He was like so many older people I've come to know who seem to become more talkative as they age, possibly because they have more to talk about—and perhaps because they realize their time is running out.

Across the harbor I saw the lobster boats starting to line up at Pettie's dock, waiting to unload their precious cargo and take home the day's pay. I felt a pang of envy. Notwithstanding a bit of queasiness, helped immeasurably by the acupressure bracelets Seth had given me, I'd had a wonderful time on the water accompanying the lobstermen and learning about the creatures that were a big part of Maine life and one of the state's major industries. It was fun being part of their special community—even if it had been for only a short period of time.

The entrance to Nudd's was held open by an iron lobster doorstop, one of myriad items Tim stocked to attract tourists during the hours the fishermen were at sea. Many of the passengers who'd just disembarked from the party boats were wandering his aisles, hanging over the counters that held trays of colorful lures, and examining fishing tackle and professional gear. Little ones gawked at the mounted sunfish, a giant specimen, and the whale and shark that hung high up in the rafters, while their parents flipped through the racks of windbreakers, slickers, overalls, and other seaworthy attire. A group of teenage girls clustered around a display of hats and caps, trying them on and admiring themselves in a full-length mirror.

I found Spencer, in green work pants and a tan shirt, sitting near the potbellied stove and fixing a broken lobster trap. I was willing to bet Tim Nudd had encouraged him, maybe even paid him, to do his repair work in the store as a special tourist attraction—an authentic Maine lobsterman.

"Hello, Spencer," I said. "How are you?"

"Nicely, thanks."

"Mind if I join you?"

"Seat's free," he said, concentrating on his work.

I pulled a folding chair near him and sat.

"What are you doing?" I asked.

"Ring's broken. Them bugs'll dance right out of the pot, I don't fix it."

A few children had gathered to watch while Spencer removed the broken ring and threaded a new one into its place.

"You heard about Ike Bower's boat?"

"All over town."

"Do you know who did it?"

"Mebbe."

"Do you think the same boys were responsible?" I didn't have to add "for putting rotten bait on your boat." He knew what I meant.

"Wouldn't be surprised," he said. "Young punks. Like to give 'em what-for."

"Here's your chance, Durkee," said Nudd, who'd been standing nearby, keeping an eye on the customers.

We looked up. Framed in the doorway were Brady Holland and his pal Maynard. They were in their rubber overalls and boots, still damp from a day out on the water.

"Hey, Brady, look who's posin' for pictures." Maynard chortled, pointing at Spencer.

Holland didn't hear him. He was focused on the young women pretending to model hats for each other while they stole glances at the new arrivals. Holland pulled on the peak of his cap and winked when he caught the eye of one of the girls. "Nice to see you, ladies," he said, strolling over to them. "You stayin' in Cabot Cove?"

A peal of laughter rang out, and a chagrined Maynard followed his friend to the hat display.

"What're you boys still in uniform for?" Nudd called, eyeing their boots. "You're gonna traipse fish guts on my newly polished floor."

"They're showin' off for the girlies," Spencer said. "And showin' off their ignorance. No true fisherman goes shoppin' in his gear."

"Well, if it ain't the old man of the sea," Holland said. He looked embarrassed that he'd been caught out. "How's yer boat smellin' these days?" He sidled in our direction.

Spencer squinted at him. "I don't bother with buggers don't know their bulkhead from a barn door. Go 'way, sonny. Come back when you're growed up."

"Why, you old bahstid. You're crazier than a backhouse rat."

"Watch your language, Holland. I've got customers here," Nudd said.

The teenage girls had stopped feigning disinterest and overtly stared.

Maynard pulled on Holland's arm. "Let's get out of here, Brady," he said. "There ain't nothin' I want to buy."

Holland shook off Maynard's hand and squared himself in front of Spencer, smiling. "You want to challenge me, old man? You're just a toothless goner, no good to yourself or anybody else."

Spencer dropped the lobster trap on the floor and stood. "I'll take you on anytime. It's common talk you've a big mouth and a small brain."

"I'll drop you in a second."

Nudd grabbed Spencer's shoulder. "Don't get all humped up. He ain't worth it."

"He come at me, I'm ready."

I knew better than to step in front of Spencer, but I stood, too. "Mr. Holland," I said. "Don't you think it's time you left?" I looked at Maynard. "And you, too. You don't want to make a scene and shame yourselves in front of those nice young women who are watching."

Holland spun around and saw that all eyes were trained on him. "I'm outta here," he yelled, and stomped toward the door.

"Brady, wait for me," Maynard said, hurrying after him.

Spencer sat heavily, his hands making a series of fists. He trembled, and I touched his shoulder. "They're just ignorant boys," I said, "all puffed up and anxious to show how macho they are."

"They've got no respect," Spencer said, "not for

their elders, not for their parents, not for the sea, not for nothin'."

"I know, I know," I said, concerned for his health at that moment. His face was very red, and I feared he might have a heart attack or stroke. "But they aren't worth getting sick over." I sat in the folding chair again and waited for him to calm down. When he had, I said, "Spencer, I want to talk to you about Ike Bower's boat."

"Gangsters is what they are," he said. "Somebody chops a hole in a lobsterman's boat, they chop a hole in his income. It'll take Ike a couple'a days to mend it, and it'll never be good like it was before. Like strikin' a hole in a man's heart."

"I understand," I said. "Ike claimed it was an accident."

"Like I accidentally dumped a boatload of rotten bait on my deck. Some accident. He just don't want trouble, but he got it anyway."

"Why would someone do that to Ike? Does he have any enemies?"

"Nah. He's hotheaded, but he's solid." Spencer picked up his lobster trap from where he'd dropped it when Brady Holland confronted him, and began working on it again.

"But someone is angry with Ike," I said. "Why else would they single him out?"

"Mebbe."

"Did he ever get into an altercation with Brady or Maynard?"

"Don't think he ever paid them no never mind. Not worth thinkin' about them two or their friends."

"Then why would they do something so nasty—if

they were the ones?" I asked. "It's more than just malicious mischief."

Spencer shrugged, but didn't reply.

"Do you think someone put them up to it?"

"Mebbe."

"Has this kind of thing happened before?"

"Mebbe."

"Boats have been damaged before?"

"Boats've been damaged. Bait's been spilled. Lines've been cut. Catch has been stolen."

"Why hasn't the association stepped in to stop it?"

Spencer glanced up at me, and then dropped his eyes back to his work. I was missing something here.

"Holland is Linc Williams's nephew," I mused. "Even if he doesn't want to turn him in, you'd think Linc would have enough influence to put a halt to Brady's crimes, if he knew his nephew was involved with this kind of activity."

"You'd think."

"But he didn't. Why?"

"Have to ask him."

"Linc and Ike argued the other night at the association meeting. Could Brady be getting even for his uncle?"

"Mebbe."

"Linc wouldn't have put them up to it, would he?"

Again Spencer didn't answer, but I took his silence for confirmation.

"Why, Spencer? What reason could Linc have for hurting one of his own lobstermen?"

"He's the king. Likes to keep it that way."

"And Ike said the men could find another leader if Linc didn't stand up for them against Pettie."

"He did."

"So anyone who disagrees with Linc or challenges his administration risks retaliation?"

"I'm not sayin' that."

"But you're not disagreeing with it, either, are you?"

"Not sayin' any more," Spencer said, shaking his head. "As it is, word gets back I was talkin' to you, there's more hell to pay. Probably should stick on my boat tonight, just to be safe. Those hooligans show up again, I'll be ready this time."

"I'm sorry if talking to me causes you any trouble," I said. "If there's anything I can do to help, please let me know."

"I'm an old man. I don't worry what they're gonna do to me anymore. But you take care."

"I'll be careful," I said.

Chapter Twelve

In summer, Mara closes her door and locks up by ten, so I planned to be down at the docks at that time for my meeting with Barnaby Longshoot. When I arrived, the luncheonette was already shuttered and dim, the light from a crescent moon barely visible through the incoming cloud bank, and failing to illuminate the front of the building or reflect off the plate-glass window. It was dark. Light from the street lamps, back in the parking lot, didn't reach the front door.

I took off my sweater and laid it on the glass top of one of the tables Mara leaves outside. I put my handbag beside it. The heat of the day seemed to hover, reluctant to let go its hold on the waterfront, and the air was still; no breeze rattled the lines against the masts or ruffled the fringe on Mara's awning. The only sound was the lapping of the water against the pilings and the irritating warble of a radio on one of the boats across the harbor. Someone was playing loud music, which clashed with the serenity of the waterfront.

I sat at the empty table and waited for Barnaby. What did I hope to learn from him? Spencer had been surprisingly forthcoming, although I'd had to phrase my questions carefully. He'd all but accused Linc of complicity in the two incidents I knew about firsthand—the pile of rotten bait spilled on Spencer's boat, and the smashing-in of Ike's hull—and had hinted at his involvement in others. That power is corrupting is an old maxim, but who would have thought that a pillar of the community like Linc Williams would be so intent on defending his lofty position that he would resort to violence to keep his fiefdom under control? A Williams had headed the Cabot Cove lobstermen's association for a hundred years. Was I naïve to hope that good management, proper care for the people who relied on them, and honest hard work had helped hold on to that tradition? What had happened to this generation? Was the crown more important to the king than his subjects? There had been no bloodshed yet, but it was only a small leap from smashing in the hull of someone's boat to taking out that fury on someone's person. Brady Holland had nearly come to blows with Spencer. He was a volatile young man, and I hated to think of how that contest would have come out had he acted on his intentions.

The song on the radio ended. I sat up straight. What was that noise? It sounded like a moan. *It's your imagination, Jessica,* I told myself. *You think about the possibility of violence and your brain supplies the sound effects.* I strained to hear the noise again, but couldn't make out anything when the music resumed.

Time seemed to move slowly. The clouds obscured what little light might come from the sky. The buzz of a mosquito broke my concentration and had me batting the air. I stood up. Maybe Barnaby wasn't coming. Perhaps he'd had a change of heart. He'd been reluctant to talk to me in the luncheonette. Had someone convinced him not to come, arguing that whatever he told me might wind up in the pages of the *Gazette*? Not true, but how was he to know that?

Wait a minute! Hadn't he said that he'd wanted to meet me behind Mara's? Could he be waiting out back, while I'm sitting out front? He must be wondering what happened to that crazy lady who insisted upon speaking with him and then never showed up.

Certain I'd solved the mystery, I zipped open my bag and took out my flashlight. Enough of this flailing around in the dark. I switched it on, picked up my sweater, shouldered my bag, and walked to the corner of the building. A narrow, pitch-black passage separated it from the neighboring shop. I aimed the beam down the alley, and jumped when the light caught a pair of eyes. A rat? They're a common plague where land and water converge. But the creature turned tail, revealing itself to be a cat, for which I was thankful, and disappeared into the gloom. Tentatively I moved into the tight space. If I reached out my arms to the sides, I could touch the cedar siding of both buildings. The slender ray of the flashlight bounced up and down with each step in the soft, damp earth. It was impossible to see clearly. Fighting an encroaching sensation of claustrophobia, I picked up my pace, feeling the walls lean in on me, the sky disappear overhead; the alley's end seemed to move farther away as I approached it.

Moments later I was in the backyard of Mara's luncheonette and heaved a sigh of relief despite the dank air, redolent with the odor of refuse coming from the overflowing Dumpster. My relief was short-lived. The night, which had been so silent at the tables in front of the building, was abuzz in the back. Flies and mosquitoes and other winged insects drawn by the lure of rotting garbage now discovered other enticements, banging against the flashlight, circling my head, and diving at my face and arms. I swatted at the swarm and quickly put on my sweater, but I knew I couldn't escape them. I flicked the flashlight over the back door and the concrete block at its base. No Barnaby. Should I leave?

I was about to go when a soft groan reached my ears. I hadn't mistaken that. It was not a figment of my imagination. I knew a human sound when I heard it. I trained the flashlight on the ground and swept it back and forth in wide arcs, trying to ignore the cloud of insects reflected in its glow. At the base of the Dumpster were the vermin I'd feared to meet in the alley; two rats fought over scraps of waste that had fallen from the too-full bin. And not ten feet away from their sharp teeth and claws lay a human form, his face bloodied and covered with flies.

"Barnaby!" I raced over to him, my sudden scream and movement startling the rats, which scurried into the shadows under the Dumpster. I whisked the flies away and shook Barnaby's shoulder. "Can you hear me, Barnaby?" I fumbled in my bag for my cell phone and pressed 911.

I knelt by his side, waiting for the emergency crew to arrive, and took a packet of tissues and a bottle of water from my bag to wipe away some of his blood. He'd been beaten severely. His right eye was swollen shut, and his nose was broken. A gash had been opened on his cheek beneath the damaged eye, where a fist had connected, and there was a cut on his lip. I pressed the tissues against it to stanch the bleeding, and waved away the flies that kept landing on his skin.

"Barnaby, it's Jessica Fletcher," I said. "You're safe now. Help will be arriving any moment. Just hold on." I doubted he understood me, but hoped the sound of my voice would give him reassurance, even if he couldn't grasp the words.

The ground was damp and chilly. Barnaby's skin was clammy and pale. I removed my sweater and tucked the folded garment under his head.

With my right hand, I aimed the flashlight on the ground surrounding us to see if a weapon had been discarded, but all I caught in its beam was the red reflection of beady eyes—eyes that were watching me.

Not knowing the extent of Barnaby's injuries, I couldn't take a chance on dragging him away from the Dumpster. We had no choice but to wait. And while we waited the rats crawled out again. Emboldened by my stillness, the pair crept out from under the garbage bin, keeping wary eyes on me as they moved in to graze on the scraps. They were large rodents with greasy brown fur and long, black, scaly tails. A scuffle broke out over a chicken bone. I shouted and waved my arms; the combatants jumped apart, took a few steps back, but then settled down again, no longer afraid of me. One began angling forward, skirting the rubbish on the ground, taking a circuitous path in our direction. I couldn't leave Barnaby alone with them, but was unsure what to do. My experience with rats was limited. Were they rabid? Would they attack? What could I do to protect us?

I reached into my bag and groped around, feeling for anything that might be helpful. My fingers curled around a firm object, and I pulled out the green folding umbrella Seth had given me. I'd forgotten I'd left it in my bag. I slid off the green sleeve, released the tab that held the fabric tight, aimed the point at the rat, and pushed the button. The umbrella snapped open with a whoosh, and the startled rats retreated out of sight. Relieved, I closed the umbrella, keeping it in my hand in case I needed to repeat my defensive tactic.

Trying not to breathe in the fetid odors, I cradled Barnaby's head and listened for the faint wail of a siren in the distance that would mean help was arriving. There it was: first one siren, then two. That would be the ambulance and the police.

"Barnaby," I shouted into his ear. "The ambulance is almost here. Can you hear the siren?"

His response was a weak whimper. He lifted one hand, begrimed with dirt and blood, and dropped it down again.

"Stay awake, Barnaby. Who did this to you? Can you tell me?"

But he sank into unconsciousness again.

The sound of the sirens grew louder. I heard feet running on the boardwalk out front, then down the alley. Two uniformed Cabot Cove officers, led by Sheriff Mort Metzger, burst onto the scene, followed closely by a couple of EMTs from the fire department. To my surprise, Seth Hazlitt was with them. This was his usual night to conduct a medical class for EMTs at the firehouse, and after it to settle in for a friendly game of poker. One of the police officers gently pulled me away from Barnaby, and Seth led me to the side.

"You all right, Jessica?" he asked.

"Yes, I'm fine, Seth. A little shaken, perhaps, but fine."

"Good," he said, leaving me to take a close look at Barnaby, and to assist the EMTs as they placed the battered man on a stretcher and carried him away to the waiting ambulance.

Mort came over to me. "I'll be setting this up as a crime scene," he said. "Then we can talk."

"I'll be here, Mort," I said.

The officers brought in two huge, self-powered floodlights and set them up to illuminate the entire area behind Mara's, their brilliant light flooding the scene. They stretched yellow crime tape from the shed, across the yard, and back to the building, photographed the ground where Barnaby had lain, and combed the area, dropping possible bits of evidence into plastic bags. Seth rejoined me, and we moved out of the way and watched the proceedings. The rats were gone, having fled at the sight of lights and people. Now the back of Mara's looked as it did in daylight—messy and muddy, but not threatening. I shivered, thinking about what had occurred there. Thank goodness the wait was over. Thank goodness help had arrived.

Mort brushed dirt from my sweater as he brought it to me. "This yours, Mrs. F?"

"Yes. Thank you." I examined the sweater in the harsh light of the floods. It was soiled from the muddy ground, but there didn't seem to be any blood on it.

"Will Barnaby be all right?" I asked Seth.

"Not sure yet, Jess. Got himself beat up pretty bad,

but that kind of damage will heal. Can't tell yet if he suffered any internal injuries. I'll head over to the hospital when I leave here."

"How did you happen to find him, Mrs. F?" Mort asked.

"I didn't just happen to find him. Actually, I was looking for him."

"You were?"

"Yes. We were supposed to meet here at Mara's. When he didn't show up, I thought I might have gotten it wrong."

"You don't get things wrong, Mrs. F."

"That's nice of you to say, but hardly true. Anyway, I came back here, looking for him, and found him lying on the ground."

"Sounds like someone didn't want him talking to you."

"I think you're right."

"Any idea who that might be?"

I shook my head. "I don't. But whoever it was is probably left-handed."

"How do you figure that?"

"Barnaby has a bruise on his right cheek, and his right eye is swollen. Assuming his attacker confronted him, the person who took a swing at Barnaby would have to be left-handed to connect with the right side of his face."

Mort drew a narrow leather-covered notebook from his pocket and scribbled on one of the pages. "I'll need to get a full statement, Mrs. F." He looked up at me. "But if you'd rather not talk right now, I can get one of the deputies to take you home and we can get together tomorrow. That'll be okay."

"That could have been you lying there," Seth said to me.

"I'd rather not think about that," I said.

"Listen to Mort. Go home and rest."

"No, no. I don't need to rest," I said. I turned to Mort. "Besides, I'd rather tell you everything I know while it's fresh in my memory."

"That suits me fine," Mort said. "Mind if we go out front where we can sit down? Got a new pair of shoes, and my feet are killing me."

Seth left for the hospital, and Mort and I sat down at the same table where I'd waited for Barnaby. I was grateful to get away from the smell of rotting garbage, and Mort was relieved to slip off his new shoes while I recounted what had happened earlier, and he took notes.

"Rats, huh?" he said, when I'd finished telling him my tale.

"Um-hmm. Big ones."

"Whew! Glad I missed them. When I worked in New York City we would see them all the time, especially down at the waterfront."

"This is the waterfront, too," I said. "I remember when we had a rat problem—what was that, five or six years ago? But the mayor launched a project to get rid of them, and it seemed to work."

"It's the garbage that draws them, not the water," said Mort. "I'd hate to see Mara get a citation, but she needs to close up that Dumpster and call in an exterminator."

"I'm sure Mara wasn't aware of the problem," I said, "but we certainly don't want our visitors seeing rats in Cabot Cove. We'll have a lot of people down here during the festival, and a lot of food, too. I think we'd better let the mayor know what's going on."

"I'll talk to Jimmy first thing in the morning," Mort said.

Harold Jenkins, one of Mort's deputies, stopped by the table. "We're finished back there, Sheriff. Do you want to leave somebody on duty here tonight?"

"Nah. I don't see the sense in it. You can go along back to the office. Make sure you don't leave any of the floods here. Those things cost a fortune. I don't need some kids deciding they'd make good lights for their driveway basketball court."

"Okay. See you later, Sheriff. Night, Mrs. Fletcher."

"Good night, Harold."

"By the way, Sheriff," Harold said, walking backward as he spoke, a smile playing on his lips. "There's someone here to see you."

"Who?" Mort said.

"Oh, I'm so glad you're still here," Evelyn Phillips said, stepping around Harold and hastening to where we sat.

Mort clapped his hands on his head. "How did you know where to find us?" he asked.

"Police scanner," Evelyn said, smiling triumphantly. She turned to me, surprised at my presence. "Were you involved in this?" she asked.

"No, of course not," I said, suppressing a smile.

"So," Evelyn said to Mort, "I heard we had an assault tonight. Any suspects?"

"The case is under investigation."

"No suspects," she said, making a note on her pad.

"I didn't say that," Mort said.

"Saying the case is under investigation is just a

fancy way of avoiding the question," Evelyn said. "Care to change your answer?"

"No! And if I had a suspect, I wouldn't be telling you about it. People are innocent until proved guilty. I don't want you trying anyone in the press."

"Do you think tonight's assault is related to the attack on Ike Bower's boat this morning?"

"We don't have any evidence linking the two incidents," Mort said carefully. "And I'd like to remind you that Mr. Bower claims the damage to his boat was the result of an accident."

Evelyn released a puff of air. "Sure. You can say that, but we both know it was no accident."

"I can only go by what the man says."

"Have you spoken with tonight's victim yet?"

"He was unconscious when Mrs. F found him."

"He was? You found him, Jessica?"

"Think I'm going to follow the doc over to the hospital," Mort said, grimacing as he slid his feet into the new shoes.

"I'll be joining you there shortly," she said. "But I'd like to ask Jessica a few questions, if she's willing."

Mort looked at me and shrugged. "Whatever Mrs. F wants to do or say, it's okay by me. It'll all be in the police report anyway."

"I don't mind," I told Evelyn, "but only for a few minutes. It's getting late and I'm tired."

"Five minutes," she said, "ten at the top."

"You'll be all right, Mrs. F?"

"Of course."

Mort hobbled up the dock toward his cruiser, and Evelyn took his chair.

"What's he worried about?" she asked with a laugh.

"Does he think I'll worm something important out of you?"

I smiled. "I doubt it," I said.

I gave Evelyn an abbreviated version of what I'd told Mort, omitting the swarming insects, the stench of the garbage, and the rats.

"So you didn't hear the assault take place?"

"No. As I said, I was sitting right here. The only sound I heard was a radio on one of the boats." I looked out over the harbor. The radio had been turned off. A slight breeze blew the day's heat away, and the clouds had parted. The sliver of moon cast murky shadows on the boats at their slips. Was that Spencer tottering down his dock? He seemed to be bent under a heavy burden. *What's he doing up so late?* I wondered. *And what on earth is he carrying? It's a crazy time of night to bring supplies to the boat. He really needs to take better care. One of these days he'll fall off the dock into the water when no one's around.*

Evelyn interrupted my reverie. "Any ideas who'd want to beat up Barnaby Longshoot?"

"No idea at all," I replied.

A short series of beeps sounded from her pocket. She pulled out a pager and looked at the message. "I've got to run," she said. "I asked a nurse at the hospital to alert me when Barnaby regains consciousness. Want to come along? Course, it could be a couple of hours till they let us see him."

"No, thanks," I said. "I'll visit him tomorrow."

"Well, appreciate the interview. I'm really glad we're having the opportunity to work together."

She stuffed her notepad in her pocket, shook my hand, and strode toward the parking lot.

I waited till I heard her start her car and drive away. Luckily she didn't know I don't drive, or she'd have been suspicious of why I wanted to stay at the harbor instead of hitching a ride with her.

I picked up my sweater. There wasn't room to stuff it in my bag, so I put it over my shoulders, tying the sleeves in front. It would need a good washing when I got home. I walked up Mara's dock, across the boardwalk, and down to the second of the piers that thrust out into the water, where Spencer's boat was tied.

I'd been tired when the ambulance arrived. The tension of worrying about Barnaby's injuries and keeping the rats at a distance had taken its toll. But now I had a second wind and felt alert and energized. The heels of my shoes made sharp clicks as I walked along the wooden planks. *I'm certainly not sneaking up on anyone,* I thought.

I saw Spencer moving around on the *Done For*.

"Good evening, Spencer," I called. "You're up late this evening."

I couldn't see his face, but he nodded at me and turned away.

"Since you're up, I wonder if you wouldn't mind talking with me for a few minutes," I said. "I've never been on your boat before. May I come aboard?"

He didn't answer, and I took that as an invitation; he hadn't said no.

"It's so dark tonight," I said. "It's hard to see where you're going."

It would have been polite if he'd helped me down, as Mort had done on Ike's boat that morning. But he was obviously not feeling social, and since I was invading his privacy I didn't begrudge him the lack of courtesy. I turned around, put my bag on the dock, and knelt down, holding on to a cleat. I reached down with one foot until connecting with the deck, and jumped the rest of the way. Brushing off the front of my dress, I turned toward the wheelhouse. Spencer had disappeared.

"Spencer? I know you may not be in the mood to talk, but something happened tonight I think you should know about. Spencer?"

There was no answer from inside the cabin.

"Please come out," I said. "We have to talk. Barnaby Longshoot was assaulted this evening. He was beaten up and left for dead behind Mara's. I shudder to think what might have happened to him if I hadn't come along."

I walked to the wheelhouse and leaned down toward the opening. Recessed steps led to the cabin door, which was ajar. "Spencer? This is serious. If Linc Williams is behind this, too, we need to do something—and fast. Are you listening? The lobstermen can't remain silent forever. Someone has to be brave enough to stand up to Linc and demand that this madness be stopped before someone gets killed."

No answer.

"Really, Spencer. I shouldn't have to come in after you." I stepped into the stairwell and pressed the door open. Spencer was lying across the bunk. He wasn't moving. But it was so dark in the cabin, I couldn't see very clearly. He couldn't have fallen asleep so quickly—

unless he was drunk. But he hadn't seemed inebriated. There wasn't any smell of alcohol in the air.

"Spencer?"

Suddenly the hairs on my arms stood up. Spencer and I were not the only ones on the boat. Someone was behind me. I put my hands on either side of the door to brace myself, but I knew I'd walked into the lion's den. I felt the heavy blow, felt my legs crumple beneath me, felt my body being lifted and flung to the side. I'm not sure if I heard the engine start, but I felt its vibrations as the boat backed out of its slip and made for open water. After that, the clouds covered the moon again. And a deeper darkness descended.

Chapter Thirteen

I think it was the smell that woke me.

I'd been dreaming about a lobster boat on the water. I shut my eyes again and tried to recapture the vision. It had to do with the lobster festival. And Spencer Durkee was there. Why? We were on a boat, weren't we? I struggled to remember, but the details kept fading away. Even so, I could still hear the quiet lapping of the sea on the hull, feel the gentle rocking of the boat, and smell the sour tang so reminiscent of a fishing boat.

What a vivid dream, I thought.

A breeze was fluttering fabric against my legs. I felt it move across my body. I tried to turn over to escape the blinding light of the sun, but my bed was all lumpy and hard.

This isn't my bed!

The shock of recognition made me bolt up quickly. I cringed at the pain and reached out to steady myself, my hand pressing against a hard surface. My heart was sounding a tattoo in my chest. I tried, but couldn't take a deep breath, settling instead for shallow panting. Dizzy. Why was I so dizzy?

I looked up. Above me dangled the pulley of the hydraulic pot hauler used to pull lobster traps up to the surface of the water. It was attached to the purple roof of the wheelhouse, a Spencer Durkee trademark.

I'm on Spencer's boat, the Done For. *How did I get here?*

While my brain struggled with the past, I took inventory of the present. I was alone on the ocean. No land in sight, only a straight line of water stretching away to where it met the sky. I was without food, without drinking water, without any way to communicate, without even knowing in which direction to go. All around me the seascape was the same. Water. No land. And a bank of dark clouds heading my way.

Gingerly I probed the left side of my head, discovering a good-sized egg that was tender to the touch. I knew that a bump on the head could cause amnesia. Was I one of its victims? I knew who I was. But I had no recollection of how I'd gotten here.

I stood on the wet floor in the cramped cabin of the *Done For,* staring at the body of a dead man, and little by little the events leading up to my being there returned.

I'd been talking to Spencer. Or was it Spencer? There'd been a man on the *Done For*—at least, I thought it was a man. I'd assumed it was Spencer, but I'd never actually seen his face or heard his voice. It had been so dark, and clouds had covered the moon. Even when there was a break in the clouds, the weak light of the crescent barely reached into the heavy shadows, making it difficult to see anything clearly.

There had been a pressing reason why I wanted to talk to Spencer. What was it? *Oh, yes. Barnaby.* Barnaby had been beaten. *Oh, dear.* I hoped he was all right. Mort had been there, and Seth. Not on the *Done For*. Where? At Mara's. That was right. I was to meet Barnaby at Mara's. They came to help after I'd called 911. I shivered at the memory and looked down at the dirt on the front of my sweater. I'd put it beneath Barnaby's head to shield him from the damp and chilly earth. Evelyn Phillips was there, too. I still needed to finish that article on the lobstermen for the festival edition of the paper. It was all coming back to me now.

The body lay on an angle across the bunk. Booted feet hung off the end. It was those boots that had blocked my entrance; I'd had to push hard to force the door open. They were not fishing boots, but leather, highly polished and intricately stamped. I moved to the side to get a better look at the corpse, but I already knew who it was. The dead man was the lobstermen's broker, Henry Pettie.

Had Spencer killed Henry?

Pettie had been the source of the old fisherman's humiliation. Spencer had signed the contract that had bound his fellow fishermen to whatever price the broker wanted to pay for lobsters for the festival. He had been reviled by his peers and punished in a most public and degrading manner. He'd sworn to get even with the broker. Had he been plotting revenge all this time?

I lifted Pettie's right hand, pushed back the sleeve of his leather jacket, and felt for a pulse in his wrist, but I knew I wouldn't find one. I leaned across his body and turned his head. His earring was missing, and there was little blood on the berth beneath him. I couldn't see a wound without turning over the body, but I knew he hadn't been killed on board. It must have been his corpse I'd seen Spencer struggling to carry down the dock—if indeed that had been Spencer. Had Pettie been bludgeoned, like me, only harder? Was that why I was here? I'd stumbled upon the murderer who was in the process of disposing of his victim. Whoever that was had decided to get rid of the witness—me—at the same time.

Don't disturb the crime scene, I told myself. But I realized that if someone didn't find me soon, it might well be a crime scene that only I would ever see. I remembered seeing Pettie writing in that infamous black book in which he kept a record of everybody's debts to him. I patted his pockets in search of it, but they were empty. No black book. No wallet either.

As my mind cleared and my senses sharpened, I had a sudden urge to flee the cramped, stuffy cabin and Henry Pettie's lifeless body. I made my way out to the deck and surveyed the horizon in search of another boat. Nothing, just the relentless expanse of ocean. I climbed up on the rail for a better view, now confident of my balance after having gained my sea legs. There was no mast in sight, no boat-shaped vision, no faint sound from a faraway engine. I don't know why, but somehow the discovery of a murder seemed to compound my predicament, making the need for rescue even more urgent. I needed something I could use as a signal should another boat come into view, a flare, an air horn, even a flashlight. I had forgotten my hunger and thirst, but knew I had to keep my strength up. Spencer might have emergency supplies—assuming he'd left them, assuming they hadn't been removed.

Reluctantly I went back into the cabin. But my attention was drawn down to its floor. It had been wet before, but now the water came up to my ankles. The *Done For* was taking on water.

I tried to conjure a rational reason for that to be happening. Spencer's boat was, as far as I knew, seaworthy. Had something in the water damaged it, as Ike Bower claimed had happened with his craft?

"Oh, no," I said aloud, and my stomach tightened. The incident with Ike's boat hadn't been an accident. Someone had deliberately opened its hull. The same malicious intent must have been applied to the *Done For*. At least the hole in Ike's vessel had been slightly above the waterline. Whoever made it had wanted Ike Bower to know he could have sunk his lobster boat, but chose not to. That obviously wasn't the case here.

It was evident that we were sinking. I forced my eyes open and closed a few times, as though that would help me think more clearly, the way people in cars looking for a house number invariably turn down their radios for the same misplaced reasoning. Whoever struck at the boat had to have done it after we'd reached open water, and with the intention of seeing it sink, taking Henry Pettie's body to the ocean depths, and me along with him.

Who was that person? More important, at least at that moment, was the question of where he or she had gone after doing the deed. My initial thought was that a lifeboat of some sort might have been the vehicle for escape. But I discarded that possibility as quickly as it had occurred. As far as I knew, lobster boats didn't carry such craft. Besides, we were far out to sea. It would have been a frightfully long row back to shore.

No, someone else must have been involved, probably having trailed the *Done For* and taking whoever scuttled it back to Cabot Cove, or to a neighboring seaside community. Having come to that logical conclusion, I forced myself to think more keenly back to the moment I'd stepped aboard and been struck from behind. What had subsequently transpired? There was little to remember, of course, because I'd been knocked out by the blow. But I'd drifted in and out of consciousness, hearing a sound for a brief second, or detecting an odor that came and went. I recalled a banging noise, like someone hammering away at a wall. Of course. That must have been when my assailant—and presumably Henry Pettie's murderer—had put a hole in Spencer's boat.

What else could I remember? Not much. Oh, yes, there was that period of time, no longer than a few minutes, when the steady drone of a motor had ceased, followed by relative quiet. But then there was another mechanized sound, a deeper, throatier sound I'd heard before. Was that another motor? It was different from the previous one. That might have been the boat used to rescue my attacker from the *Done For*.

I looked down again. The water was rising; it was halfway up my shins. I realized that the boat was now listing to its port side. Quickly I looked around the cabin for storage bays. There were cubbies to my right, above the bunk. I reached inside, desperately groping for supplies or anything that could be used in an emergency. I found a flashlight, an open box of saltines, and a six-pack of tomato juice with two of the small cans missing from the plastic rings. I tossed the provisions through the open door onto the deck, which was two steps up and dry—at least temporarily. The juice and crackers would be breakfast if I ever found the time to eat.

I clambered back on deck and collected my rations, wrapping them in Spencer's slicker, which I'd removed from a peg on the wheelhouse wall. It had been his foul-weather gear that had concealed the door when I'd first looked for access to the cabin. I put the folded slicker on top of the bulkhead. The deck would be wet soon enough.

"We're going under!" I announced to no one, the breeze carrying away my words.

Stay calm, I reminded myself. *Think!*

My eyes searched the horizon. *Could it be? Is that a boat I'm seeing? Yes, it is, a large one, maybe a freighter of some sort, or a tanker.* But it was so far away, a shimmering image that came and went. I started to wave my arms but realized it was a wasted exercise. No one would see me from that distance. But it raised hope. There might be other boats and ships. I knew I couldn't wait for that remote possibility. I had to take action, and do it fast.

I pulled the old-fashioned life preserver from where it hung. It was a hard flotation device, rigid and solid. Would it enable me to survive an extended stretch in the water? The thought of drifting aimlessly in the vast ocean was painful to contemplate. But I didn't have a choice.

There was another problem, however: the very dead

Henry Pettie. Could I simply cast myself overboard and allow him to sink to an icy, watery grave? I would if I had to, I decided, but resolved, at least for now, to attempt to remove him from the boat before it went under.

I entered the cabin, where Pettie lay dead. The notion of having to pull him out on to the deck wasn't pleasant, but it had to be done. Fortunately he wasn't a big man. I knew I'd never be able to accomplish it with a heavier and bulkier person. Gripping the heels of his cowboy boots and using all my strength, I began to yank him off the berth. The thick blue vinyl cushion that served as a mattress came away from the wall along with the body. I stopped. There was something stenciled on its side. I squinted at the lettering. APPROVED FLOATATION DEVICE. *Thank goodness!* There was a real possibility now that I could save Pettie's body for the authorities. I dragged him the rest of the way off the berth and he landed on the floor with a splash, his now-waterlogged clothing adding to his weight. Even so, I was able to maneuver him through the narrow cabin opening, up the steps, and onto the deck. Leaving him there, I went back into the cabin, wading through the knee-high water to retrieve the cushion. I laid it next to Pettie, trying not to look at his face, contorted in death.

Using the coil of rope that had been my lumpy bed, I tied Pettie's body to the blue mattress. As an afterthought, I left a length of the line dangling free and looped it around the hard life preserver I intended to use for myself. As macabre as the thought might be, having him tethered to me in the water would provide a modicum of comfort. A dead, shipwrecked compan-

ion was better than no company. Besides, if Pettie, an
apparent murder victim, went down with the boat, the
chances of ever recovering his body were nil. All the
authorities would have was my word—provided I sur-
vived to even tell the tale.

I looked around the deck. What else could I sal-
vage? The box leaning against the bulkhead that Spencer used as a seat held supplies, too. I unlatched the
top, lifted it up, and rummaged inside, claiming a box
of zip-top plastic bags, a coffee cup, a pad and pencil,
a loop of wire, a nail clipper, and a box of matches,
which I put in my pocket. I used the nail clipper to cut
the wire, and tied off Spencer's yellow rubber pants at
the cuffs and waist in the hope they would hold some
air and provide additional flotation. And I unwrapped
the slicker I'd left on the bulkhead and packed the
crackers into one plastic bag, the juice in another, and
the remaining items in a third, folded up the slicker
again, and laid it atop Pettie's body.

Anything else?

The box! The box was wood. Maybe it would float.
With a strength I didn't know I had, I tipped over the
seat and pawed out its contents, moving quickly but
wary of sharp items that could cut me. I didn't want
the smell of my blood to lure any hungry sea creatures
once I was in the drink. *Don't think about that, Jessica.*

The port side of the boat was slipping under. Water
poured through the drainage holes and flooded the
deck. Pettie's body on the blue cushion began to float
toward the rail, taking my life preserver with it. I
closed the lid, latched it, pushed the box to the port
side, and lifted it up and over into the water. It
bobbed on the surface, then was upended, the weight

of the top pulling it over. But it didn't sink. I should have put the plastic bags inside, I thought, but there was no time to pull the box back on board.

I drew deep breaths in an attempt to ready myself for the plunge. My plan was to hold on to the life preserver ring, push Pettie over the side, and follow him, pulling Spencer's rubber bib pants behind me. I didn't know if it would work, but it was the best scheme I could come up with. But then I decided to take another step. I would set the bow of the boat afire in the hope that it would serve as a signal to someone, anyone in a position to see it. I carried the red metal container I'd found under the transom at the back of the boat and made my way to the roof of the cabin in the bow, where I sprinkled the container's meager contents on the boards. The empty can might also help me stay afloat, and I tossed it into the water in the direction of the wooden box before pulling the matches from my pocket. Hopefully they weren't too damp to strike.

Kneeling down, careful to keep the skirt of my dress well away from the gasoline, I pulled out two matches and struck them on the side of the box. They flamed immediately and extinguished just as quickly. A hum began in my ears as I tried another match, moving my body to shield the small flame from the wind, to no avail. The hum got louder, and I shook my head, thinking that this was no time to allow a buzzing insect to distract me. I waved my arm over my head and concentrated on my task. The hum persisted. I looked up to see the source of the annoyance. A small, single-engine plane was flying low across the horizon. *Help!* I jumped up and waved my arms frantically, bouncing up and down on the slippery platform. *Help! I'm over here. The boat is over here. You're going in the wrong direction. Turn, turn and you'll see me.*

I realized the smoke from a fire would be far more visible than my ineffective frenzy. I fell to my knees and emptied the box of matches, striking and dropping each one till a flame finally caught on the deck and spread. I stood up on shaky legs and scanned the sky for the buzz I'd so doggedly ignored. Why hadn't I paid attention? Where were my vaunted powers of observation when I needed them? Gone, along with the plane. I could barely see it. It was getting smaller and smaller, only a tiny speck against the dark clouds, looking for all the world like the insect I'd initially thought it was.

The flames on the bow began to crackle, the smoke choking me, and I hurried aft to push Henry Pettie, tied to his blue vinyl mattress, into the sea. I lifted the life preserver over my head and squeezed my shoulders through the round hole, grabbed Spencer's overalls, and stepped off the rail, following Pettie on his floating bier.

The ocean was icy. I don't know why I had expected it to be otherwise. The life ring kept my head and shoulders dry, but the rest of my body was stung by the frigid water. For a minute I thought I might not be able to move. Then practical considerations goaded me into action. Pushing Henry ahead of me, holding on to the rope around his body, I kicked my legs to get away from the burning boat and the cloud of smoke it created. When it sank, the *Done For* might create a whirlpool, the suction taking anything in its vicinity to the bottom, along with the ship. I swam a safe distance away and turned to watch. The blaze I'd hoped would be a distress signal was going out. There hadn't been enough gasoline to ignite a conflagration. The flames had managed to consume the "volatile accelerant," as arson investigators would call it, and perhaps a bit of the paint and varnish had burned, but the boards never caught; the fire was dying. It didn't matter anymore. The *Done For* was listing seriously, the port side completely under. The seawater would soon douse the rest of the flames.

I almost didn't notice when it disappeared from view. It was surprisingly quiet, the death of the *Done For*. There was a soft gurgling noise and the sound of bubbles as the remaining pockets of space were submerged. The boat tilted till its starboard side was the only part visible, like a breaching whale exposing its flank to the sky. Then it slid slowly downward and was gone.

With the last sigh of the lobster boat lingering in the air, the enormity of my dilemma came pounding home. All alone, except for my dead companion. How many days could I survive in the water? For that matter, how many hours? The sun was warm overhead, but I had no illusions it would remain that way. Unlike the seaplane, the bank of clouds I'd seen when I awakened that morning was moving toward me, not away. What would I do if it rained? If the seas became rougher and I couldn't even see above the swells?

I treaded water, more to get my circulation flowing to warm my feet and legs than to keep myself afloat. The life preserver would do that. But the cold penetrated through to the bone. My legs felt heavy and slow, my movements clumsy. I considered trying to wrap myself in Spencer's slicker, but I was fearful of losing my grip and having it go under or float away. I needed it, not to keep the crackers and juice dry, but to use it as a banner. Its bright yellow color spread out on the surface would help attract attention should the plane come back. *Please let the plane come back.*

I felt something slither past my legs and leaned over the side of the life preserver to peer down into the water. A school of little silver fish flitted by. There must have been hundreds—no, thousands of them. They moved in unison, yet so quickly I was surprised they didn't bump into each other. How did they know how far to go, which way to turn? How did they communicate instructions for their synchronized movement? Perhaps the currents influenced them, or the temperature of the water. Or maybe they were being chased by larger fish, ready to scoop them up should they move in the wrong direction.

A chill crept up my spine. The little fish knew how to escape. But I did not. One moment they were sparkling below the surface, and in the next they'd vanished. They were gone. But something else was there. I looked over my shoulder and froze. Not twenty feet away was a sharp gray fin poking out of the water. Behind it another one pushed up out of the water, and behind that, a third. And all three were steaming toward me.

Up until that moment I'd been fairly successful in keeping my wits about me. I'd managed not only to arrange for me to stay afloat; I'd brought Henry Pettie's body with me. But the sight of those dorsal fins heading in my direction wiped away any semblance of rational thought.

Those fins represented every swimmer's worst fear—sharks!

I forced my mind into gear, and tried to remember what I'd seen about sharks on TV, on National Geographic and Learning Channel specials, and what I'd read about these fierce predators in books and magazines. I came up blank. What do you do when confronted by a shark? Do you splash the water to scare them away, or do you remain still in the water, pretending to be an inanimate object? Sharks were drawn to blood, I knew. I didn't enter the water with any cuts that would produce blood, but there was Pettie. He had blood on his cheek, and perhaps a wound had produced blood on his scalp. I hadn't bothered to check that, although it really didn't make any difference at that juncture. It was too late to do anything about it.

I decided that holding perfectly still and making myself as small as possible made the most sense. I tried pulling my knees up toward the surface, but the cold had made my legs so numb they wouldn't bend. So I hung from the life preserver, immobile. For a second I thought my actions had been effective. The three fins swerved away from me and began to circle, rather than continue on their course toward me. But after completing a few circles, one of them broke away from the others and bore down on me.

I couldn't help myself; I started kicking, and added my voice to what I hoped would be a deterrent, yelling, "Get away! Get away!"

My attacker reached me, the fin only eight or ten feet away; then the head bumped into my thigh. I closed my eyes against what I was certain would come next, the clamping down on my leg of a large mouth full of sharp teeth. It was over! My life was over!

Except that after bumping me, the huge fish's body slid along my leg. It felt like sandpaper, and the contact was much shorter than I would have thought a good-sized shark would feel like, given the size of that fin. I opened my eyes and dared to look at my "attacker." The fin was enormous and was attached to an even larger head, but there was barely any body to speak of.

The creature swam away, joining the others a dozen yards in the distance. It hadn't attacked me, hadn't bitten down. It swam closer again, but I didn't panic this time. As it neared, it angled its body up toward the surface, looking like a huge oval platter floating in the water. A dark eye stared into mine. I stared back, mesmerized, my heart pounding in my chest. For a moment I felt a connection with this odd denizen of the sea. I was the intruder here, the one in the wrong place, the fish out of water, I thought ironically. The creature rolled over and slowly swam back to its companions. The three fins made another circle of me and Henry Pettie, then left.

I let out a whoosh of relief and watched the fins grow smaller before disappearing. They hadn't been sharks. A vision of the gigantic ocean sunfish mounted on the wall at Nudd's Bait & Tackle came into my consciousness. That was what they must have been, Ocean sunfish, whose fins are virtually indistinguishable from those of a shark.

I took deep breaths in an attempt to slow my racing heart, and force me to think clearly once again. Once I'd succeeded, I took renewed stock of my situation.

That the fins turned out not to be attached to a killer shark didn't mean sharks weren't in the area. That realization, coupled with my obvious helplessness to do anything, struck a stake of abject dejection into me, and I thought I might begin to cry. It was at that low moment that a sound reached my ears; the drone of an engine, an airplane engine.

I'd come to recognize the sound of a plane's engine when I'd taken flying lessons from Jed Richardson. He was a former airline pilot who'd settled in Cabot Cove and operated Jed's Flying Service, giving lessons and ferrying people to larger airports. That I'd earned a private pilot's license but didn't possess a driver's license struck many as strange, even amusing. But I'd loved the experience of piloting an aircraft, and those comments meant nothing to me.

I swiveled my head in search of the sound's origin. There it was, off to my right, and heading in my direction. But it was high in the sky. Would he see me? *Now's the time,* I told myself. I spread out Spencer's slicker on the surface of the water on one side of me. I hoped it would serve as a yellow bull's-eye to draw the pilot's attention. I put the bib overalls I'd made into a float on my other side, hoping to widen the visual target. Henry Pettie, tied to the dark blue cushion, would be less easy to spot from the air. Nevertheless, together with the white wooden box and the red gas can, which were floating about ten yards away, they added to the flotsam in the water. Who knew what might catch the eye of the pilot first?

As the plane got closer, I saw that it was an amphibious floatplane—Jed Richardson's red-and-white, high-wing floatplane. He'd recently added it to his fleet of small planes. Unlike a basic floatplane that can land only on water, Jed's amphibious model had, besides floats, retractable wheels, which allowed him to operate from land or water.

I reached as high as I could and waved and yelled, even though I knew the pilot would never hear me above the growl of the engine. I kept my arms moving as the plane flew over me and continued on, the echo of the motor fading in the distance. *Oh, no. He didn't see me.*

I don't think I've ever been more despondent in my life as I was at that moment. I crossed my arms on the life preserver and bowed my head, praying for strength. I always knew I would die; I never expected it to be this way, cold, alone, without the comforting touch of those who care for me. But just as I was at my lowest, the motor grew louder again. I looked up. Jed was flying lower this time, and coming straight toward me.

The plane flew overhead—Jed wagging his wings from side to side to indicate he'd spotted me—and made a tight turn. I knew what he was doing. He had to make two decisions: One involved the direction of the wind. He would want to land into it, not have it at his tail. The second had to do with the condition of the sea. Landing on a choppy surface was dangerous, perhaps too dangerous for him to attempt it. That possibility didn't dampen my spirits. If he couldn't land, he would radio his position to the coast guard, and they would dispatch a boat to save me. It would take a little longer, but I didn't care.

I felt the breeze against the left side of my face, and watched Jed line up to come in from the opposite direction. There was a distinct chop to the water, and I hoped he wouldn't take an unnecessary risk on my behalf. I doubted he would. Jed was too professional a pilot, with thousands of airline hours behind him, to make an imprudent decision.

He brought his plane down to only a few feet above the water, the nose slightly elevated, and touched down, the rear portion of his floats making contact first, the forward portion immediately following. The plane bobbed up and down in the water as he taxied to within a few feet of me.

"Jessica," he called out through his open window.

I waved, a broad smile on my face.

"Are you all right?"

"Yes, yes, Jed, I'm fine now."

He slowly, carefully maneuvered the aircraft until one of the floats was within reaching distance of me. I extended my hand and grabbed hold of it, just as the first drops of rain began hitting the water.

"Who's that?" Jed yelled, referring to Henry Pettie.

"He's . . . It doesn't matter," I said. "He's dead."

"*Gorry!*" he said, using a popular Maine expression of surprise and shock. "Here's what we do," he said, and proceeded to instruct me on how he would get me out of my predicament.

It took Jed a half hour to securely tie Pettie to the top of one of the floats, and for me to haul myself up onto the other, with Jed's strong hands helping me. He pulled me into the cockpit, where I slumped into the right-hand seat. We were both soaked to the skin, me from my sojourn in the sea, he from the pelting rain.

Until that moment I'd concentrated all my efforts

on following Jed's instructions, and was surprised at the strength I was able to muster. But once I was safely inside the cockpit, that strength and energy drained from me as though someone had opened a valve.

"You okay?" he asked, as he wrapped a silver rescue blanket around me. The space-age material, developed for NASA, would keep my body heat inside and help to warm me faster.

"Yes," I managed. "I think so."

I looked down through my window at Pettie's body strapped to the float.

"Do you think that'll work?" I asked.

"Ayuh," Jed said. "Should work fine. It'll put some weight on that side, but nothing I can't manage. Buckle up, Jessica. You'll be back on solid ground before you know it."

Chapter Fourteen

Jed landed the seaplane in Cabot Cove Harbor and taxied toward shore. The sun was out; the storm hadn't reached the coast. I looked out the window and was shocked by the view. The marina was empty. Not a single vessel was anchored in the water; nor were any tied up at the piers.

"Where are all the boats?" I asked. "What's happened?"

"They're all out looking for you," Jed said, laughing. "The lobstermen's association organized the search. But I got the prize. And there's your reception committee."

While the water was deserted, the dock was not. There were a hundred people or more, all standing and waving to the plane as Jed maneuvered closer to the pier. It looked a little like the crowd we get on Main Street for the Fourth of July parade, but instead of applauding the colorful red-white-and-blue floats, here they were saluting our arrival, cheering and clapping. Practically every emergency vehicle owned by the town was in the parking lot. I could see Mort's squad cars, their red lights circling, an ambulance, a fire engine, a hook and ladder, the EMT truck, and a couple of motorcycles. The only piece missing was the paddy wagon.

"Good heavens, how did they know we'd be coming in?"

"I radioed the coast guard when I spotted you. Word must've gotten passed along."

"How did you even know I was missing?"

"You may not be aware of it, Jessica, but there's lot of people in this town looking out for your best interests. Let's get you ashore. The sheriff can answer your questions."

Jed cut the power and allowed the plane to approach the dock under its own momentum, a tricky maneuver. Cut power too soon and you don't reach the dock. Cut it too late and you risk ending up with twisted metal and splintered wood. But Jed's timing was perfect, and we gently nudged up against the dock, where men tossed out two lines with which to tie the plane securely. Jed opened my door and helped me out into the waiting arms of Seth and Mort. A cheer went up from the crowd.

"You all right, Mrs. F?" Mort asked.

"No sense askin' her if she's all right," Seth said. "She's probably suffering from hypothermia. Won't know her right hand from her left till we get her warmed up."

"I'm fine; really I am," I said.

"She looks pretty good to me," Mort said.

"What do you know? You're a policeman, not a doctor. I want her in the hospital pronto."

Seth had had a wheelchair brought to the dock and insisted I sit in it. I was too tired to argue.

"What's that?" Mort asked, pointing to Henry Pettie's body tied to the float. In the commotion surrounding my arrival, the bundle strapped to the pontoon had gone unnoticed. Jed had covered the body with a tarp; what was beneath it could have been anything.

"Another passenger," I said. "Jed can tell you about him."

"I'll take care of it, Mrs. F. And I'll come see you as soon as we clear out this crowd. We're all happy you're back."

"So am I. Thank you so much."

As Seth pushed the wheelchair up the dock, well-wishers pressed in to greet me.

Matilda Watson patted my shoulder. "Oh, Jessica, thank goodness we found you." There were tears in her eyes. She surveyed the gathered crowd. "Where is Evelyn with the camera?"

I looked around. It seemed everyone I knew in town had heard I'd been found and came out to greet me. Familiar faces surrounded me. Mara was there, and Charlene Sassi from the bakery. Loretta Spiegel and Mort's wife, Maureen. All the Friends of the Library, and David and Jim from Charles Department Store. Elsie Fricket in her plastic collar. And Gwen Anissina with the young ladies in the pageant, among many others.

"Nice to have you back, Jessica."

"Oh, Mrs. Fletcher, thank God you're all right."

"Three cheers for Jessica Fletcher. Hip, hip, hooray. Hip, hip, hooray."

"All right, folks, let's break it up," Seth called out. "She's safe. Make room, please. We need room to get this chair through."

Mort's deputy Harold stationed himself in front of the wheelchair and waved his arms to encourage people to move aside. Our progress was protracted, but eventually we reached the parking lot, where Seth assisted me into the ambulance.

"You know, this really isn't necessary," I said.

"Now don't be your usual stubborn, hardheaded self. Humor me, Jess. I'll feel a lot better once you're in the emergency room and the staff can examine you. You've been through an ordeal, whether you acknowledge it or not. I want them to give you a clean bill of health before we let you go."

"All right, but I'm telling you, the best place for me right now is in my own house, in my own bed."

"Later, if everything checks out, I'll drive you home personally."

"I'll hold you to it."

After examinations, blood work, X-rays, and a CAT scan of my head that revealed only a minor concussion, I was discharged. The hours lying on an uncomfortable hospital bed did more to discomfort me than the time I'd spent dangling in the icy water, fending off giant fish and the danger of despair. After being given painkillers to take with me in the event I needed them at home that night, Seth pushed me in my wheelchair to the main lobby. "You sit tight," he said, "while I get the car."

He'd no sooner exited the hospital when Mort Metzger came through another set of doors, accompanied by two men in suits. "Mrs. F," Mort said. "Glad we caught you before you left."

"Seth's gone to get the car," I said.

"Mrs. F," Mort said, "this is Special Agent Frank

Lazzara, FBI, and Bob Dailey, Maine Special Investigation Unit."

"Hello," I said.

"We've got some questions for you, Mrs. Fletcher,"
Agent Lazzara said.

"Questions? About what happened?"

"Yes, ma'am."

"Now?" I asked.

"Best to get it over with," said Mort. "Recollections
are better the closer to the event."

Seth came through the door; I could see his car
running outside. "What's going on?" he asked Mort.

Mort introduced Seth to the men, and said they
were there to take a statement from me.

"Can't it wait?" Seth asked. "You can see that Mrs.
Fletcher has been through a terrible ordeal."

"Yes, sir, we realize that," said Investigator Dailey,
"but two serious crimes have been committed; a murder, and the deliberate sinking of a boat to cover up
the murder."

"I'm sorry," Seth said, "but as Mrs. Fletcher's physician, I'm afraid I have to insist that any questioning
of her wait until she's had sufficient time to recover."

"I really don't mind," I said.

"Excuse us, gentlemen," Seth said, grabbing the
handles of the wheelchair and turning me in the direction of the doors.

"Tomorrow?" Lazzara asked.

"That will be fine," I said. "I'm sure I'll be feeling
up to it by then."

"How about at my office?" Mort said. "Say, ten
o'clock?"

I agreed, and Seth took me to the car.

Although I'd said I wouldn't mind being questioned, I was glad Seth had insisted on delaying the interview. I was feeling exhausted, and crankier than Seth had ever been, which was saying a lot. But once I was sitting in my favorite armchair in the familiar and dear confines of my own living room, with a cozy fire in the hearth even though it was August, I began to feel myself again. Seth refused to leave, trotting back and forth to the kitchen, making tea and attempting to cook dinner, although all he had to do was heat up the casserole my neighbor, Tina Treyz, had left on the doorstep. A succession of dishes had arrived, and my refrigerator and freezer were full to bursting. I wouldn't have to cook for a month, maybe more.

We'd just finished the lobster pie left by Tina when Mort arrived bearing Maureen's specialty, blueberry apple pie. He happily accepted a slice, and the three of us sat down at the kitchen table. My two friends looked at me, heads cocked, eyebrows raised in question marks. I hadn't offered anything about my tribulations, how I'd ended up on Spencer Durkee's boat, the blow to the head, discovering Henry Pettie's body, the sinking of the boat, and my Rube Goldberg attempt to stay afloat until help arrived. The doctors at the hospital had asked how I'd injured my head, but I said only that someone had hit me, and offered no further details, explaining that it really was a police matter.

Now, in the security of my kitchen, hunger satisfied, my body again warm, I knew it was time to lay it all out, which I did in as much detail as I could muster. It took me twenty minutes to unfold the entire tale. Mort's and Seth's interruptions were few. Mort took notes; Seth was content to nod, grunt, and utter expressions of dismay or shock at appropriate times.

"Well, that's about it," I said. "That's the whole story as best I can remember it."

"Horrific," Seth said.

"You're one lucky lady to be alive," said Mort.

"I'm well aware of that," I said. "I'm curious. How did you learn I was missing?"

"Evelyn Phillips turned up at the hospital last night, around one in the morning, said she knew Barnaby Longshoot had regained consciousness," Mort said.

"I'd like to find out who in the hospital tipped her off," Seth said. "They're supposed to protect patient confidentiality, not call the press."

"Anyway, I wouldn't let her talk to him," Mort said.

"How *is* Barnaby?" I asked. "Is he all right?"

"Ayuh. He's a tough bird," Seth said. "No internal injuries, luckily, but he's pretty bruised up. The hospital discharged him today. He'll be in fine fettle soon enough."

"Thank goodness for that."

Mort cleared his throat.

"Oh, I'm sorry, Mort," I said. "I interrupted your story. You were talking about Evelyn Phillips."

"So she asked to interview Barnaby, and I said no. And then I asked her where *you* were, and she said she didn't know. 'How can you not know?' I said. 'You were together when I left.' And she said she'd left you at Mara's and assumed you were going home. And the doc, here, said—"

"I can tell this part," Seth put in. "I asked her, Didn't she know you don't drive? And she said, How was she supposed to know that? And I said, 'Everyone knows that.' And she said she didn't, and didn't I know she was new to Cabot Cove?"

"So Doc and I hopped in the patrol car and raced around town—"

"With the siren on and the light goin' 'round. Must've woken up half of Cabot Cove."

"Anyway, we came here first, expecting you might have walked home. But we didn't catch sight of you along the way."

"And you didn't answer your door."

"And I said you were probably waiting for someone to come to their senses and realize you'd been stranded down at the harbor without a ride," Mort said. "So we drove over there and looked for you around Mara's and went up and down the dock till we found your purse."

"Very clever of you to leave it there for us to find," Seth said, "or we'd've had no idea where to begin to look for you."

"We figured you'd left us a clue," Mort added. "And when we saw that the *Done For* was gone, that was another clue."

"I wish I could take credit for anticipating that I would be assaulted and kidnapped," I said, "but the truth of it is that I needed both hands to climb down onto the *Done For*'s deck. I simply put my shoulder bag down on the dock so it wouldn't get in the way."

"Whatever," Mort said. "That's what launched the search."

"And not a moment too soon," Seth said. "According to Jed, when he found you you were near to driftin' out to sea. The current where you were flows due east."

"I forgot to ask Jed how he found me," I said. "When I first saw his plane on the horizon, he wasn't close enough to signal."

"He told me he was about to fly back to the harbor when he took one more look around and noticed smoke in the air," Mort said, "and thought he'd better check it out."

"He's thorough, Jed is," Seth added.

"Lucky for me he is," I said. "The fire didn't last long."

I shivered, thinking how close I'd come to losing my life, how, if Jed Richardson weren't thorough—how, if he hadn't looked around one last time—I might still be suspended from a life ring in the bitterly cold water holding on to a dead man tied to a cushion.

"What's happened to Henry Pettie's body?" I asked.

"Down at the medical examiner's office," Mort replied. "We should have a preliminary report on the cause of death by tomorrow."

"I didn't examine him carefully, but I thought he might have taken a hit on the head, just like me," I said.

"So you're assuming the same person who hit you killed Pettie."

"Makes sense," Seth said.

"It's possible," I said, "but I have no proof."

"Then you didn't see who hit you, Mrs. F?"

"There was someone on the deck, but I never saw his face. My back was to him when I climbed down onto the boat, and when I looked around he'd disappeared."

"But you thought it was Spencer?"

"I did, but only because it was his boat. When I peered into the cabin, I saw someone lying on the berth. At the time I'd assumed it was Spencer. It was only when I woke up out on the ocean that I discovered it was Henry Pettie."

"Hmm," Mort said, closing his notepad. "I'd say Mr. Spencer Durkee has got some serious explaining to do."

"That was my first reaction, too," I said, "but on reflection, I can't imagine he had anything to do with it."

"The way I see it, Mrs. F, old Spencer might have made his mind up that Mr. Henry Pettie was responsible for what's been happening recently, decided to get rid of him, and drove his boat out into the ocean to dump the body. You were a witness, so you had to go, too."

"Doesn't hold up for me, Mort," Seth said. "Spencer would never sink his own boat. The *Done For*'s been his livelihood all his life."

"Not much of a living for him lately," Mort offered. "He's getting old. From what I hear, he's not catching much these days, could barely afford to replace the traps those delinquents cut free."

I chimed in. "Let's say you're right, Mort. Let's say it was Spencer who killed Henry and decided to send him down with the boat. There had to be someone else involved, an accomplice who followed him out and took him back to shore."

"I know that, Mrs. F," Mort said, "and I'm hoping Spencer will tell us who that was."

"Have you spoken with him?" I asked.

"I have. Got him under protective custody, but he's not talking."

"You arrested him?" Seth asked.

"Not the same thing, but I've got him. Came busting into my office this morning claiming somebody stole his boat. Acted like a crazy man, ranting and raving that he'd get even with whoever did it. I won't repeat some of the words he used, not in front of you, Mrs. F. I told him you were missing along with the boat, and that if he had an alibi, he'd better come out with it right away. Said he was drinking down at the beach, and he didn't see anyone and no one saw him. I told him that wasn't good enough."

"So you locked him up," I said.

"Yep. And this afternoon, when I told him we'd found you and Pettie and that he'd better say who he was in cahoots with, he wouldn't talk. Clammed up right away."

"So he knows Pettie is dead?" I asked.

"He does." Mort stood and stretched. "I'd best be going. Afraid you're going to have to repeat your story tomorrow morning for the others. Coast guard will have an investigator present, too."

"I'll be happy to help in any way I can," I said.

Seth was reluctant to leave—"You gonna be all right by yourself tonight?"—but I shooed him out the door, promising to call if I needed a comforting voice in the wee hours, if I suffered from nightmares or an attack of nerves should what I'd just been through revisit me in the middle of the night. They left together, but not until Seth gave me final instructions: "You get yourself to bed right away, Jessica."

He didn't have to tell me that. Within minutes of their departure, I was in pajamas, under the covers, and out like a light.

Chapter Fifteen

It was wonderful to wake up in my own bed, in my own room, in my own house.

I'd slept soundly, although I was vaguely aware of distressing dreams that floated just below the surface of my slumber. Too soon, I awakened as the sun's rays squeezed through the slim gap between my shades and the window's frame, painting two broken stripes of light on my bedroom wall. I stretched, appreciating the smooth mattress and sheets, and fresh-smelling air. My excursion on the *Done For* had tapped muscles long unused, but even my sore shoulders, back, and legs were a reason to celebrate. All the aches and pains simply confirmed the joyous fact that I was alive.

There's nothing like a brush with death to bring your everyday blessings into sharp relief. I savored each morning task as I went about my household chores, took pleasure in the flavors of my breakfast, and breathed in deeply when I opened the front door to retrieve the morning paper. I left the paper unread as I took a leisurely hot shower, reveling in the soothing effect of the hot water. I wrapped myself in a terry-cloth robe and went into my study, where a flashing red light on the answering machine indicated that I'd received seven calls while showering. The recorded messages from friends prompted me to go where I'd dropped the paper on the kitchen counter. There it was, a banner headline in huge letters that Evelyn Phillips had put across the top of the front page: MURDER IN CABOT COVE, and beneath it, LOBSTERMAN HELD FOR QUESTIONING. Next to the story was a photo of the deceased that must have been taken years ago, when there was no gray in his hair and no meanness in his eyes. At the bottom of the page in smaller type was: MYSTERY WRITER FOUND, accompanied by a photograph of me being assisted into the ambulance. I could make out in the background the empty harbor and the crowd of people on the dock. Evelyn had chosen her position well from which to take the shot to illustrate the story.

I had just sat down with the paper and my second cup of tea when the phone rang. It was the editor herself.

"I'm calling to apologize," she said. "I feel terribly guilty."

"Why's that?" I asked.

"I've been hearing from some of your friends that they consider me responsible for your having been kidnapped and nearly killed because . . . I 'deserted you,' is how they put it, at Mara's the night you were kidnapped."

"I certainly don't feel that way, and no apologies are necessary," I said. "You couldn't have known that I don't drive. Besides, I deliberately didn't ask you for a ride home because I wanted to investigate something I'd seen on the dock. You assumed I had a car there. So you see, Evelyn, you're not in any way responsible. You can stop feeling guilty."

"Thank you," she said with an exaggerated sigh. "I just wish those sending me vituperative e-mails and leaving nasty messages on my answering machine would see things the same way."

"If it helps, I'll write a letter to the editor exonerating you."

"You wouldn't mind doing that?"

"I made the offer. You didn't even ask. I don't mind at all. It will give me an opportunity to thank all the people who helped look for me. I'll drop it off later today, along with my article for the festival edition."

"It's nice not to have to feel guilty. But I do feel like a fool for not having picked up a fact that everyone in Cabot Cove but me seems to know—that you don't drive."

"Considering your short tenure as editor," I said, "I think you've learned a remarkable amount about our town. It takes years and years to get into the heart and soul of a community, and some never do. I think you're doing a fine job."

"Thank you, Jessica Fletcher. You're a very kind lady. I owe you. And I always honor my obligations."

"Don't thank me yet. I was planning to pick your brain to find out what you know about Henry Pettie, and the people who didn't hold him in especially high regard."

"You can probably include the names of every member of the lobstermen's association, with the possible exception of Linc Williams, and maybe him, too. The men hated him. But am I reading you correctly that you don't think Spencer killed Pettie? I spoke with Sheriff Metzger earlier this morning. He seems pretty confident he's got the right man."

"He may have," I said. I realized I was talking to the press, and didn't want Evelyn to write in the paper that Jessica Fletcher was questioning the competence of our sheriff, and my dear friend. "I'm not giving an interview here," I said. "I don't want to see myself quoted in the paper."

"In other words, this is off the record. I understand. I'll make a deal with you."

"What's that?"

"I'll tell you everything I know and everything I find out, if you'll write up your experience on the *Done For* and let me publish it in the *Gazette*."

I had no intention of satisfying her readers' morbid curiosity by reliving that harrowing experience in print, but I didn't say that. As it was, people would be pressing me for the details. I knew that. But I'd already given the details to the two people who needed to know, Seth and Mort, and who were genuinely concerned for my welfare, not merely eager to hear the lurid story. Perhaps there would come a time when I'd want to write about it, when it might form the centerpiece of one of my stories, altered, of course, with events purposely made more dramatic for a fictitious heroine. But that was for another time. I wasn't about to make a spectacle of myself in the newspaper. Furthermore, I had more important things to do.

"No deal," I said.

"Too upsetting, huh? I'm sorry I asked. I'll tell you what you want to know anyway."

"You could put something in the paper for me."

"What's that?"

"According to Mort Metzger, Spencer claims he spent the night down at the beach. It's August and it wasn't raining. There's a good chance there may have been other people there, someone who might have seen him and can come forward to verify his alibi."

"That's a good point, Jessica. I'll write something up right away. Maybe Matilda Watkins would be willing to post a reward for information. She likes the idea of investigative reporting, except, of course, when it comes to her. Oh, the stories I could tell you."

"Another time," I said. "But you might want to check with Mort before posting any rewards. He might not be pleased with any interference on the paper's part. You don't want to get in the way of his investigation."

"I'll call him right away. When do you want to talk about Pettie?"

"Why don't I stop by your office later today, say around three?"

"I'll be here. See you then." Just before I hung up she added, "And Jessica, I am so relieved you're home safe. It must have been a nightmare."

Chapter Sixteen

The hot shower had felt wonderful on my aching body, but after I'd been talking with Evelyn, my muscles began to stiffen up again, and my joyous mood began to fade. Nevertheless, I wrote the letter to the editor I'd promised, and put the final touches on my article on the lobstermen for the festival edition of the *Gazette,* finishing just in time to head downtown for my meeting with the authorities.

I took a taxi to the small, white building on the village green in which Mort Metzger's sheriff's office and the town jail were situated. It was a relatively new facility, erected six years ago to replace what had become a decrepit, and even unsafe structure. A bond issue was floated, and the new building took its proud place alongside other town government buildings.

Although I'd never conducted a poll, I could only assume that those unfortunate enough to have to spend time in a cell there were pleased that their accommodations were fresh and clean. Actually, for the most part, we have relatively little crime in Cabot Cove—traffic infractions, an occasional domestic dispute, and a citizen who now and then imbibes too much alcohol and becomes Mort's guest to sleep it off. When murder does occur, however, like the one that took place on Spencer Durkee's lobster boat, you can imagine the furor it creates in town.

FBI special agent Lazzara, Maine investigator Dailey, and a uniformed officer from the coast guard, whose name was Grissom, were in Mort's office when I arrived. They apologized for putting me through a round of questioning, but I assured them I understood the necessity for it, and suggested they get started. They were terribly polite and solicitous, and took notes as they encouraged me to tell what had happened in my own words and at my own pace, with few interruptions for clarifications. The session lasted a half hour. When it was over, they thanked me for my cooperation, suggested they might contact me again, to which I readily agreed, and left.

"Nice men," I said to Mort.

"Suppose they are, only it looks like we're about to get into a turf war." His expression was pained.

Jurisdictional disputes between law-enforcement agencies weren't alien to me—I'd been in the middle of them on more than one occasion. While I knew that Mort would have preferred to handle the case alone without interference from other agencies—he'd successfully investigated murders before—I also knew he was a rational enough lawman to accept help when it was offered. He simply didn't have the manpower to launch a thorough investigation while he was also preoccupied with arranging security and traffic control for the upcoming festival.

"Well, Mrs. F.," he said, taking the seat behind his desk and heaving a relieved sigh, "it was good of you to come in this morning. How are you today—you all right?"

"Aside from feeling as though I've been run over

by an eighteen-wheeler, I'm fine. But tell me more about Barnaby Longshoot. How is he doing?"

"He looks like he went twelve rounds with George Foreman, but other than that, he's okay."

"I'm so glad he wasn't seriously injured. You questioned him, I'm sure. What did he say?"

"Couldn't tell me much. Says he was hanging around outside Mara's and he heard a man calling his name. He followed the voice down the alley to the back, and pow!—someone got him with a couple of roundhouse punches. Too dark to see who it was."

"So his assailant lured him to the back of Mara's, where the attack wouldn't be seen?"

"Sounds that way."

"Did he recognize the voice?"

"Says he didn't."

"Whoever it was wanted him off the dock. But did that person know he was there to meet me, or not?"

"It's a good question. You're lucky you didn't end up like him."

"I might have been better off. At least he stayed on land."

"Sorry, Mrs. F. Forgot for a second what happened to you. You look fine, though, apart from a little sunburn."

"The injuries are all in here," I said, pointing to my head. "It's an experience I'm not likely to forget for some time." I gave an involuntary shiver. "Mort, as long as I'm here, I'd like to talk to Spencer."

"Are you sure, Mrs. F? You've been through a lot. We've already got a good handle on the case."

"I'd like to hear what he has to say about what happened the night before last," I replied.

"I can tell you that," Mort said. "He claims he was down at the beach sucking on a bottle of liquor when somebody stole his boat. That part rings true to me. I've had a drunken Spencer Durkee as an overnight guest in our jail on more than one occasion. But I don't believe he stayed down at the beach and slept there. From what I see and hear so far, I think he got himself boozed up, had a confrontation with Henry Pettie, killed him, and decided to get rid of the body at sea."

"I just don't think he'd sink his own boat," I said, "not even if he was in a drunken stupor."

"I've considered what you and the doc said last night. But anything's possible when you're under the influence and not thinking clearly, Mrs. F. All I know is a murder took place on his boat, and I don't need to remind you, there was an attempted murder as well. Until I receive information to the contrary, I'm holding Spencer."

"And maybe it's just as well that you do," I said. "But surely you haven't closed your mind to other possibilities, such as someone else killing Henry and then stealing Spencer's boat."

"Got anything to offer on that score, Mrs. F? Any ideas who that other person might be?"

"Not at the moment. Frankly, Mort, I'm surprised that you're holding Spencer on so little evidence."

"Maybe you don't know how much evidence I have," he said.

"I'm sure I don't," I replied. "Care to share it with me?"

"I don't mind," he said, leaning his elbows on the desk and lowering his voice. "I've got an unimpeachable witness who put Spencer with Henry Pettie the night you disappeared. Of course, Spencer denies it, claims he never saw Pettie that night nor had any intention of meeting with him."

"Who is this unimpeachable witness?"

"Linc Williams, the president of the lobstermen's association. Got to him first thing this morning, before he cast off. He says Pettie told him that he was on his way to meet with Spencer."

"You got an early start," I said, smiling.

"Looking to catch the worm," he said, sitting back, a satisfied expression on his face. "Not only that, the deputies and I combed the beach and never found that bottle where Spencer said he was drinking. So you see, Mrs. F, I've got pretty good reason to view Spencer as the primary suspect—at least till I hear something to change my mind."

"I appreciate your sharing that information, Mort. I don't mean to question your investigation. You haven't wasted any time in interviewing people who might know something. And I know it certainly looks damning. But there's something that bothers me. I can't quite put a finger on it yet, but perhaps if I speak with Spencer, it'll become clearer. May I speak with him? I won't take long. I can't see what harm it could do. Please. Just to satisfy my curiosity."

Mort squinted as though it would help him make a prudent decision. "Sure, Mrs. F," he said. "Maybe you can squeeze out of him who his accomplice was. But I gotta ask you to make it short."

"I'll be as quick as I can, and I appreciate your accommodating me."

"It's nothing. By the way, that new editor of the

Gazette, Mrs. Phillips, called here this morning. Wants to run an item in the paper asking whether anybody was down to the beach and maybe saw Spencer there. She said you suggested it."

"Yes, I did. But she also mentioned the idea of posting a reward for information. I told her to check with you first. I'm glad to see that she did."

"She never mentioned any reward. I guess her boss, Mrs. Watson, wasn't so keen on that idea. I told her it was okay by me to ask for information. Won't amount to anything, and I don't want to be somebody who's accused of being against free speech and the First Amendment." He got up and came around from behind the desk. I noticed he was in his stocking feet.

"New shoes still bothering you?" I asked.

He looked down and wiggled his toes. "You'd think if a shoe is a size eleven, it'll fit a size-eleven foot. Ordered those on the Internet," he said, pointing to the offending pair of shoes. "Don't think I'll do that again."

"Why don't you just send them back?" I said.

"Threw out the box and now I can't remember which Web site it was where I bought them." He scratched his head, looking embarrassed. "Come on," he said. "I'll have one of the deputies stay with you in case old Spencer gets rowdy."

"I'm sure that won't be necessary, Mort," I said as I followed him down a hallway to the rear of the building, where a half dozen cells were located. Spencer was in one at the far end. The other five cells were vacant.

"Your occupancy rate is down," I commented.

"Just the way I like it, Mrs. F. Just the way I like it."

Spencer was sleeping. Mort rattled a set of keys against the bars, causing the crusty old lobsterman to bolt upright.

"Hello, Spencer," I said. "Remember me? Jessica Fletcher?"

"Course I do," he said in a strong, deep baritone. Aside from looking disheveled from having spent the night on a cot in his cell, he was clear-eyed and obviously sober. "This is no place for a lady like you," he said.

I laughed. "I've been in worse places," I said. "Sheriff Metzger is being good enough to let me sit with you for a few minutes and ask some questions."

"Questions? Why would *you* want to ask *me* questions?"

"A writer's habit, I suppose," I responded. "Mind if I join you in there?"

Spencer looked at Mort, who nodded as he unlocked the cell door and opened it for me. I stepped inside. As I did, I heard the door close behind me, and the key locking it again. "I'll send a deputy back here."

"Please don't," I said. "I'll be fine."

Mort said to Spencer, "Don't you go acting up, Spencer. You're in enough trouble as it is."

"I didn't do nothin'," Spencer said to Mort's back as the sheriff walked away. My host, if that was what he might be called at the moment, got off the cot on unsteady legs, went to a small table against the wall, and held its chair out for me.

"Thank you," I said, sitting.

He resumed his place on the cot. "Sorry I can't be offerin' you somethin' to eat or drink. Don't even have coffee in here."

"That's quite all right, Spencer. The sheriff has granted me only a few minutes. You know, of course, that Mr. Pettie was killed aboard the *Done For,* and that your boat was deliberately sabotaged and sunk."

I wasn't certain, but I thought I saw his eyes mist up. "Yup, I heard," he said in a low voice. "Had that boat for more than forty years. Like losin' a wife or something."

"I can imagine. And you know that whoever killed Mr. Pettie and sank your boat also tried to kill me."

He stiffened, his eyes open wide. "You? Somebody tried to kill you on my boat?"

"You didn't know?" I said. "Well, it's true. That's why I'm here, Spencer. I want to know who's responsible for this."

"The sheriff says I am."

"Are you?"

He slowly shook his head and looked me in the eye. "No, ma'am," he said, "I most 'suredly are not."

"And I believe you," I said. "Look, Spencer, I'm told that Linc Williams maintains Pettie told him he was meeting you that night. Is that right?"

"No, ma'am, it's not. Can't imagine why he'd say such a thing about me. I never saw that twerp Pettie, and I'll swear to it on a stack of Bibles—take one of those lie-detectin' tests, too."

"Perhaps Pettie intended to look for you and didn't find you."

"Mebbe so. I warn't there."

"So I've heard," I said. "That's your alibi. You say you were down on the beach with a . . ."

He grinned, exposing a jagged set of yellowed teeth. "It's all right, ma'am, you can say it. Yup, I spent the night down to the beach with a bottle. Drank just about all of it and fell asleep. That's where I was all night."

"Why did you go to the beach to drink?" I asked.

"Not unusual for me," he said, rubbing gray stubble on his chin and running gnarled fingers through his wiry gray hair. "I like it down on the beach at night. Real peaceful there with the stars and the breeze off the water. Didn't plan on it night before last, but—"

"But what?"

"Well, I went down to the boat to do some fix-up early that evening. Might have stayed and done it, 'cept there was a brand-spankin'-new bottle of wine sitting there. Just what I like, too. I decided the fixing up could wait, and took the bottle down to the beach."

"It wasn't your bottle?" I asked.

"Nope. I figured some good soul dropped me off a present."

"Has that ever happened before?"

He rubbed his chin again and frowned. "No, now that you mention it, can't say that it ever did. Must have cost whoever bought it a pretty penny. Expensive stuff. At least, it looked that way. Real fancy label. Liked the bottle too, funny shape. But it's all in the tastin', and this tasted real fine, real fine wine."

"And you don't know who bought it for you?"

"No idea."

I heard footsteps approaching in the hallway.

•

"Spencer," I said, "it sounds like I'm going to have to leave in a minute. Do you have a lawyer?"

He shook his head.

"I'm sure one will be provided to you. In the meantime, can you think of someone—anyone—who might have seen you down on the beach last night? Was anyone else there?"

"Mighta heard some kids messin' around. Can't be sure. But I didn't see a soul. Then again, I warn't looking past the bottle."

"What did you do with the bottle?"

"Haven't the foggiest. Probably threw it away. I allus do. I got a question for *you* now."

"Yes?"

"If somebody killed Pettie and sunk my boat out in the ocean, how'd he get back to shore?"

"How do you think?"

"Well, somebody must've had to come out and collect 'im."

"That's right."

"Means two of 'em were involved in killing Pettie and tryin' to kill you."

"Right again."

He grunted.

Mort appeared, unlocked the cell, and motioned with his head that I should leave. I stepped into the hallway and looked back at Spencer, who sat on the cot, his head in his hands.

"I sure loved that boat," he said to himself. "She were a beauty."

"Drop you someplace?" Mort asked when we'd returned to his office. "On my way out anyway."

"Thank you, no, Mort. I have some stops to make,

including a Friends of the Library meeting I almost forgot."

The phone rang and Mort picked it up. "Yeah? No, I didn't see them." He hung up. "Afraid you got some press camped out out front. You want to sneak out the back door?"

I sighed. "No," I said. "They'll just find me somewhere else. Let's get it over with."

He walked me outside. As we came through the door, a half dozen people, including a two-person TV news crew from a Bangor station, who'd been corralled by one of Mort's officers, started yelling questions at me. A microphone was shoved under my nose.

"Mrs. Fletcher, was the murdered man a close friend of yours?"

"Not at all. I met him for the first time only recently."

"Mrs. Fletcher, is your next mystery going to be *Murder on the* Done For?"

"No. Of course not."

"How did it feel when the boat sank? Were you afraid?"

"Well, naturally—"

"Jessica, over here. Tell the people what it was like to be stranded with a dead body."

"Sheriff, is Mrs. Fletcher a suspect?"

"Mrs. Fletcher, we understand you're single. Have you dated younger men before?"

"Oh, for heaven's sake."

"Mrs. Fletcher has nothing more to say," Mort barked, opening the door to his marked car parked at the curb. They followed and continued questioning me through the open window on the front passenger side.

Mort started the car, waved away two reporters standing in front of it, and pulled away.

"Bunch of vultures," he muttered.

"I know they're just doing their job," I said, "but what awful questions. I didn't think what happened to me would draw such media interest. I should have known better."

"Combination of a celebrity and a murder," he said. "Gets 'em every time. Where to?"

"Mary Carver's house. That's where the library meeting is taking place."

When we pulled up at the house, Mort turned and said, "Word of advice, Mrs. F?"

"Have I ever turned down good advice from you, Mort?"

"I seem to remember a time or two. What I'm getting at is that you shouldn't put too much stake in what Spencer says. Between all the wine he's consumed over the years, and a brain not as sharp as it once was, he doesn't always make a lot of sense."

"I'll keep that in mind," I said. "Thanks for the lift. Thanks for everything, Mort."

Chapter Seventeen

Mary Carver was arranging stacks of pictures on her black granite kitchen counter when I knocked at her back door. I was early for the Friends of the Library's committee meeting, but I thought it would give me a chance to be alone with Mary and ask her a few questions. One thing I wanted to find out was what the lobstermen planned to do now that they didn't have a broker.

"Oh, Jessica, how wonderful. Come on in. I didn't expect to see you out and about so soon. How're you feelin'?"

"I'm fine, thanks."

"It must've been awful, all alone like that. I would've died of fright."

"Not something I'd care to relive, or even talk about, if you don't mind."

"But you're really all right?"

"A few aches and pains and bad memories, but otherwise I seem to be okay."

"Well, you look well enough. Got some sun, I see. I would've thought you'd be takin' to your bed for a few days to recover."

"I'm not one for moping around," I said. "I would

be bored to tears in no time. I hope you don't mind my barging in on you early like this."

"Not at all. I can use an extra hand here before the others arrive. Gwen Anissina dropped off all these pictures, and I'm trying to sort them out."

"Are they for the children's art exhibition?" I asked.

"Yes, aren't they wonderful? Gwen mounted them all on the same-size boards so they look like they're framed. I'm supposed to bring 'em downtown to the merchants today, and I'm tryin' to decide who gets what."

"Does it matter? They're all charming." I held up a colorful view of the harbor with two boats.

"Not really," she said, "but the store owners who have children in the schools like to hang their own youngsters' artwork in the window. Can't blame them for that. As for the rest, sometimes a drawin' just looks like it should be paired with a particular place. You'd be good at that, I bet."

"In that case, I'll be delighted to help," I said, flipping through one pile of drawings done in crayon that had the young artists' names neatly printed along the top, along with *From Mrs. Weller's Second-grade Class.* I chose one that featured four stick figures standing in front of a house, their oval bodies colored in red. "Here's a family of four in matching sweaters," I said. "I'd give this one to Charles Department Store."

Mary laughed. "See?" she said. "I knew you'd be good at this. I like your logic." She marked the back of the drawing with a small sticky note on which she wrote the store's name.

We reviewed all the pictures and matched them

with the downtown stores. There were more drawings than shops, so some would receive two or even three to hang in their windows as part of the "exhibit." When we finished, Mary put up a pot of coffee for the committee, and I took a seat at her oval table, grateful to sit down. I shook my head. It was still early in the day, but I was feeling tuckered.

"I'm impressed with your organization," she said, patting the top of the stack of pictures as she came around the counter to join me. "I noticed you even put them in store order going down Main Street."

"Just wanted to make it easier for you to distribute them."

"And I appreciate that, Jessica. I surely do. But I'm sure that wasn't the reason for you stopping by so early." She pushed a plate of cookies in my direction.

"You're right," I said, choosing a chocolate-chip in hopes the sugar would boost my energy. "I wanted an opportunity to thank you for making it possible for me to go out on the boat with Levi and Evan."

"You don't have to thank me for that."

"Oh, but I do. Levi told me I owe it all to you," I said, smiling.

"Oh, him," she said, flapping a hand in front of her face. "Have you written the article already?"

"Yes. Fortunately I had most of it completed before my recent adventure."

"Some adventure!" Mary said.

"Anyway, I put the finishing touches on the story this morning and plan to drop it off at the *Gazette* later today."

Mary hesitated. "There's nothin' in it about Henry Pettie, is there?"

"No, of course not. It's not a news story. It's for the special edition Matilda Watson is publishing for the Lobsterfest on Saturday. That's not going to be our regular newspaper. It's more like a promotional piece to publicize the town and its merchants, to show off our positive qualities. The people attending the festival—and certainly those of us organizing it—want to see lively features that encourage people to have a good time."

"But what about that new editor? She likes a juicy story. And there's bound to be a big audience for the paper."

"I can't guarantee what Evelyn Phillips will do, but I doubt she'd fill the festival edition with stories about crime in Cabot Cove. I think she wants the event to be successful as much as we do. And I know Matilda does."

"I hope you're right. This morning's headlines gave me the shivers."

"For good reason," I said. "It's disturbing to think that someone among us is capable of killing another person."

"I would never have believed it of Spencer Durkee. Why, I've known him since I was a kid. Anna was just devastated at the news."

"It's very sad," I said. "But it does seem out of character for him, don't you think?"

"It just shows that you never really know someone. He seems like nothing more than a harmless old geezer, and look what he goes and does. You of all people should be happy he's in custody, Jessica."

I'd been hoping Mary would defend Spencer, would weigh the character of the man she'd known for years against the accusation against him. I was disappointed, but I understood why she quickly accepted the idea—false, in my estimation—that he was guilty. No matter how heinous, a crime solved is much less threatening than one in which the perpetrator is still at large. The arrest of Spencer Durkee for Henry Pettie's murder gave the town a sense of security, of closure. It allowed them to put the incident behind them. That Henry Pettie had not been liked only added to the speed with which his murder could be forgotten. The town was content to forget him and concentrate on the coming festival.

"What are the lobstermen going to do for a broker now that Henry Pettie is gone?" I asked.

"I heard that Linc called into another broker he knows to fill in temporarily," Mary said.

"Where did you hear that?"

"Audrey Williams told me. You can ask her about it when she gets here."

"Do you think the men will start up their own co-op now?"

"Who knows what they'll do? Men are so unpredictable. Evan had been e-mailing with a fellow over in South Bristol to find out how they set up theirs, but when he tried to tell his father about it, Levi wouldn't even listen to him. Now Evan's in a snit. He's even arguing with Abigail." Mary gazed out the window. "I swear, the pair of them are the most cussed men I ever met."

"They don't strike me that way," I said, reaching for a second cookie.

"You all right, Jessica?"

"Yes," I said. "Why do you ask?"

"You look a little pale under that tan."

"No, I'm fine," I said.

"Good. Now, what were we talking about?"

"Cussed men," I said. "You said Evan and Levi were cussed, and I said they didn't strike me that way."

"Well, they are now. Levi's become a fussy old woman of a sudden. Take last night. He— Oh, look, here come the others."

The kitchen door opened and Audrey Williams bustled in with a tote bag in one arm and a quilt in the other. Her eyebrows rose when she saw me, but she said nothing. Behind her came Elsie Fricket in her white plastic cervical collar, which dug into my chest when she gave me a fast hug. The third lady in the group wasn't familiar to me.

"Jessica, you know Audrey and Elsie," Mary said. "This is Sandy Bower. She just came on the committee."

"Hello," I said. "I think we've seen each other at Loretta's beauty shop."

"That's right," Sandy said. "Of course, I know who you are, with all your famous books and all." She placed her hand on my arm and said somberly, "I am so sorry about what you've just been through. How horrible."

"Thank you."

"I always meant to say hello at the beauty parlor but didn't want to disturb you. You know, maybe you were deep in thought plotting your next books."

"I'm afraid that's never the case when I'm under the dryer," I said pleasantly.

"Sandy is Ike Bower's wife," Audrey put in. "You

must've met her husband when you went boatin' with ours."

"That's right," I said.

"Don't imagine you'll want to do that again anytime soon," Audrey said, folding the quilt and leaving it on the counter. "Matilda Watson will be right along," she added. "She asked me to bring her craft project because she had to pick up an ad from Charles Department Store."

"Is she still chasing David for an ad?" Elsie asked. "That nephew of mine better get a pair of roller skates if he wants to get away from her."

"Speaking of nephews, my sister-in-law's boy just got apprenticed to a carpenter down east," Audrey said, settling herself at the table.

"He gave up fishing?"

"Warn't no good to start out, as I hear it."

"Don't blame him with the price of lobsters these days," Sandy said, putting a shopping bag down on the counter. "It's hard to make a living."

Elsie asked the question that was on the tip of my tongue: "Will we have enough lobsters to serve everyone this weekend?"

"Looks like it," Audrey said. "Linc said Nudd's pound is full, and whatever they catch between now and the festival will be gravy. They can hold them till the prices rise if the crowds are small."

"A week ago Henry Pettie indicated there weren't enough lobsters," I said. "Did the numbers change so fast?"

The room grew quiet. After a long pause, Mary said, "He must've exaggerated."

"More likely lied, you mean," Sandy said.

"Let's not speak poorly of the dead," Audrey said.

There was another awkward silence broken by Sandy. "I brought some blueberry muffins," she said brightly. "I hope you ladies don't mind."

"Why would we mind?" I asked.

"You would if you were as tired of blueberries as I am. If any of you ladies want some, come get 'em."

"Why'd you pick 'em if you don't like blueberries?" Audrey asked.

"If I don't, the birds'll get 'em. Ike would kill me. We've got a whole line of bushes. I've been makin' blueberry pancakes, blueberry preserves, blueberry cobbler. Look at this; my fingers are blue." She held up her hands to display stained fingertips.

"Are you selling some of that at the festival?"

"As much as I can get rid of."

"Your leftovers are welcome here," Mary said.

"Why don't you just freeze them?" Audrey asked. "That's what I'd do."

"There's no more room in the freezer. Every piece of Tupperware I own is in there, filled with berries."

"Well, I don't have any bushes, and I'm happy to eat your muffins," Elsie Fricket said. "Mary, hand me a platter and I'll put these out."

The women helped Mary set the table, putting out the plates, cups, and saucers she took out of her cupboard, and filling the sugar bowl and the creamer. From her seat at the table Audrey rearranged the place settings.

We'd just sat down when Matilda Watson knocked on the door and walked in. "Howdy, ladies. Sorry I'm late. Audrey, where'd you put my comforter?"

"You walked right past it. It's on the counter by the door."

Matilda retrieved her quilt and took a chair next to me. She spread the fabric over her lap and fussed with one corner.

"If you're planning to enter that in the crafts show this Saturday, you'd better hurry up and finish it," Elsie said.

"Why do you think I brought it here?" Matilda said, smoothing out the top of the multicolored patchwork. "There's only a little left to do anyway."

"It's very pretty, Matilda," Sandy said. "How long did it take you to make it?"

"Must be at least a year," Elsie said. "Didn't I see you working on this same project for the silent auction for the rectory last Christmas?"

"You did not," Matilda said. "I started this after Easter. A pattern like this is very complicated and involves a lot of delicate work. Not everyone has the skills and patience for it. But I do."

"You're slow at sewing, is what you mean," Elsie said.

"She finished it long ago," Mary said with a twinkle. "She just brought it to show it off."

"I did not!"

But it didn't look to me as if there was anything left to sew. I thought Mary may have pegged her right.

"I can't believe the festival is coming up so soon," Sandy said. "Are we ready?"

"We are if it doesn't rain," Mary said, angling her head so she could peek out her window at the sky. "Forecast is iffy."

"We can move the craft fair into the high school gym if necessary," Elsie said. "Your men can help set it up. They're not lobstering on Saturday, are they?"

"No. They're on one of the floats in the parade," Sandy said.

"Think positive, ladies," Matilda said. "The weather is going to be fine. All our jobs are done. Oh, I almost forgot. Mary, you and I still have to work on the children's art exhibit."

"No need to bother yourself with that, Matilda," Mary replied. "Jessica and I sorted the pictures before you came. We're going to take them into town this afternoon."

"Leave it to you to arrive after the work is done," Elsie said.

"Well, I was doing work of my own," Matilda said.

"And were you successful?" Elsie asked.

"I was," Matilda said, patting her pocket. "I always get my man."

" 'Cept in real life," Elsie said, winking at me. "It's not like you got anything to brag over. That husband of yours is no bargain."

"Maybe not, but he keeps my feet warm in the winter, and he can reach the top shelf of the pantry."

"That's about all Ike's good for, lately," Sandy said. "He's been some ugly since the boat was stove in. But it's gotten worse. Stormed out of the house night before last. Wouldn't tell me where he was going. Yesterday I thought he was goin' to wallop our big one when he sassed him. Had to step between 'em. Never had to do that before."

"Levi, too," Mary said. "Anna and I came home the other evening from watching the pageant rehearsal, and

Levi was cleaning the kitchen, said Anna tracked in dirt on her sneakers. She's always leaving them in the middle of the kitchen floor, just kicks 'em off as she's coming through the door. He says he's like to come near to killin' himself trippin' over them. Says he spent a fortune putting in a new kitchen and the kids are ruining it."

"Linc was broodish last night, too," Audrey said. "He's been very difficult lately."

"Maybe they're in mourning for Pettie," Elsie put in.

"Can't be," Mary said. "We only found out about Pettie this morning, from the newspaper. We didn't know last night."

"I thought the men didn't like Pettie," I said.

"They didn't," Sandy said, darting a look at Audrey.

"Linc got along with him," Audrey said. "Mebbe that's what's buggin' him."

"I just don't understand men at all," Mary said. "I always thought Anna was Levi's favorite, even chided him about it. I've been harping on her to put her things away for months, and he's said nothing. Now he's the disciplinarian. I don't know if I like it or not."

A spirited discussion of their respective children ensued until I took advantage of a momentary break in the conversation to suggest we get down to library business, and the lobster festival that was now breathing down our necks. A half hour later we had ticked off the items on our agenda, and I announced I was leaving. "I'll take these pictures with me," I said to Mary. "I'm heading downtown anyway."

"Not so fast," Mary said. "You're lookin' a little

peaked. Besides, you can't manage all of them without a car. Take these." She pulled off a dozen from the pile of children's art. "Audrey and I will do the rest."

I bade my farewells and was about to leave through the kitchen door when I turned and asked, "Is Spencer Durkee as much of an alcoholic as everyone says he is?"

Sandy laughed. "He certainly is, Jessica. Ike says he don't know how the man's stomach lining has lasted long as it has, with all the wine he consumes. Ask Gordon down at the liquor store. He joked once—and maybe he wasn't jokin'—that Spencer covered his rent every month."

"How sad," I said. "He's so nice."

"Just because he's a drunk doesn't make him a bad person," Audrey said jokingly.

"If he killed Pettie," Mary said, "he most definitely is a bad person." She held the door open for me. "Thanks for all your help, Jessica. Much appreciated. You take care of yourself now."

The door closed behind me, but not before I heard Audrey say, "She doesn't look so bad. What were you fussin' about?"

Chapter Eighteen

I started to walk toward the center of town but didn't get very far. The trials of the day on Spencer's sinking boat were now catching up with me, and I felt woozy and agitated at the same time. My back, legs, and shoulders ached, and a headache had come on while I'd been sitting in Mary's kitchen. It wasn't as though I hadn't expected a delayed reaction. Strain and stress on the body and mind often take a day or two to fully develop, and it was certainly true in this case. I sank down onto a low brick wall in front of a house along the road leading into town and drew deep breaths, looking up at the clouds. The sky was overcast and did not bode well for Saturday's event. But the weather wasn't the cause of my mood, which had grown darker since my triumphant return, despite my protestations that I was fine.

Thankful as I was that I'd come through that miserable business relatively unscathed, and everlastingly grateful to the citizens of Cabot Cove who had expressed concern for my welfare—my letter to the *Gazette* expanded on those sentiments—I was at the same time unexpectedly impatient to put the incident behind me and resume my normal life. The deluge of calls and the interviews by the authorities served only to rake over the cinders an experience I would just as soon forget. What was it about this particular episode that left a sharper mark that so many others had not? It wasn't just the murder that disturbed me—heaven knows I'd been exposed to murder before, and my life had been threatened a few times as well.

I focused on my breathing and tried to relax the tightness in my muscles. Memories and emotions surged through me, each swamping the last like waves on the beach as I tried to analyze why I felt so shaken by this latest scare. Perhaps it was the series of shocks piled one upon the other that had finally overwhelmed my psyche. Finding myself alone at sea, then not quite alone with the discovery of a murder victim. Desperately trying to signal for help and failing. Then struggling to save a corpse when the only security I'd had—Spencer's boat beneath my feet—began to give way and sink below the surface of the sea. The iciness of the water as I hung helpless, prey to the elements and the potential violence of creatures hunting for their next meal. I'd been lucky, yes, that the terrifying fins that approached me belonged to a gentle species, not a voracious shark. But the contemplation of that possibility alone was sufficient to strike terror into my heart, more than any gun that had ever been aimed at my head. The despair that had seized me when I thought my rescuer was flying away was a feeling I never want to repeat. It was perhaps the only time in my life I'd given up, given in to hopelessness.

But I was home now, back in the bosom of my community, alive—and safe. Why did this unease, this sense of vulnerability cling to me? Sitting on the stone wall, I traced my feelings back to their source and found the rough surface that would not be smoothed.

It was the calculated abandonment. That someone who knew me was willing not only to let me die, but to suffer in the process, knowing that the boat would go down and that I would drown far out to sea, where no help could be expected. How chilling that a person could be that cruel. Many murders were the result of passionate emotions—fury, jealousy, lust, obsession, fear. This seemed like such a coldhearted decision. What had motivated my would-be murderer?

Satisfied that I had pinpointed the cause of my discomfort, and rested enough to complete my walk without falling down, I continued into town and stopped in various stores and shops to deliver the pictures drawn by the schoolchildren. My final stop was Kent Liquors, owned by Gordon Kent. He was opening cartons in the back when I entered, setting off harness bells nailed to the top of the door.

Gordon looked up and waved. "Good mornin', Mrs. Fletcher," he said, coming to the counter. "What can I do for you today?"

"How are you, Gordon? I have a couple of things I need, but first of all I brought you a picture for your window."

He held it at arm's length, admiring it. "This is wicked good. Amazing how talented little kids can be. Gives you hope for the future, don't it?"

I agreed.

"Won't be hard for them to do better than this generation. Saw the paper this mornin'. Cabot Cove got a black eye yesterday. Don't know what this is gonna do to attendance at the festival, know what I mean?"

"You're thinking about what happened with Henry Pettie and Spencer Durkee. It's terrible, I agree." I heard the bells over the shop door jingle, indicating that another customer had come in. I turned at the sound, but a series of tall shelves in the middle of the shop kept me from seeing who'd just entered.

"Can't believe it of Spencer," he said. "And I heard about your involvement."

"Just a blur," I said, waving my hand. "Glad it's over."

"You were on Spencer's boat," he said.

I nodded. "But I'd rather not get into that, Gordon." I leaned across the counter and said in a low voice, "I'd like to ask you a question."

"Fire away."

"Is Spencer a hard drinker?" I asked softly.

Gordon drew a deep breath. "Well, wouldn't be right for me to say," he said. "Sort of like doctor–patient confidentiality, I suppose."

"I ask because . . ." I felt light-headed again and gripped the edge of the counter.

"You all right, Mrs. Fletcher?"

"Just need to sit for a minute," I said. He ran to the back and brought a chair for me, onto which I gratefully sank. "Thank you."

"Sure. You were saying?"

I shook my head, trying to collect my thoughts. "I ask about Spencer because I need to know how much he drinks, and what he drinks."

"Sure thing. The sheriff was in asking the same questions. You writin' this up for one of your books?"

"Not right now," I replied.

"Right. Well, I'll tell you what I told the sheriff. I don't believe old Spencer killed anybody," Gordon said.

"Nor do I," I said. "I'm trying to help him."

"Glad to hear that. Sheriff Metzger's sometimes a bit hasty to point a finger."

I didn't respond to his comment about Mort. "Gordon," I said, "Spencer told me he was drinking a special wine the other night. What kind would it have been?"

"Had to be blueberry wine."

"Blueberry?"

"That's right. Always blueberry wine. Never knew him to drink anything else."

"He told me it had a fancy label, and was in an unusually shaped bottle. Do you carry anything like that?"

"You talked with him after he was arrested?"

"Yes."

Gordon rubbed his chin and screwed up his face. "Hmm," he said. "Fancy label and unusual bottle? Doesn't ring a bell for me. Old Spencer's favorite wine is Blacksmith's—at least, when he has the cash. That's not too often. Otherwise, he buys cheaper stuff."

"With fancy labels and unusually shaped bottles?"

Gordon shook his head. "I've seen 'em all, and I wouldn't describe any of 'em like that. But you can take a look at the blueberry wines I have on the shelf over there. I stock different kinds, mostly for the tourists to take back with 'em. You know—Maine, blueberries—Maine, lobsters, that sort of thing."

I walked to the shelf Gordon pointed out. There were only about a half dozen bottles of blueberry wine on it, none that struck me as being unusually shaped.

"How often do you sell blueberry wine?"

"I got some extras in for Saturday, for the tourists. But it's not a big seller with the locals."

"Has anyone bought some this week?"

"Now, let me see," he said, cocking his head. "Nope. Don't think anyone has."

"Spencer claims someone dropped off a bottle on his boat the night of the murder. Might that someone have bought it at a different liquor store?"

"Could be. Mebbe one of them discount stores out on the access highway. Tough competition for me. They buy in bulk and cut prices to the bone."

"But none of them have your charm," I said, standing and patting his shoulder. "Thanks for the education on blueberry wine, and for the chair. Got to be going."

"Sure you feel okay?" he asked, walking me to the door.

"I'm fine," I said. "Just a momentary weak spell. Thanks again."

I realized as I stepped out to the sidewalk that I still hadn't seen who'd entered Gordon's liquor store after me. It was as though whoever it was had deliberately remained behind the shelves in the center of the store to avoid being identified by me. *Why would anyone do that?* I silently asked myself. Probably my imagination. Still, I was curious, and waited outside, pretending to examine something in the window of Charles Department Store two doors down. Less than a minute later, the door to Kent Liquors opened and Alex Paynter exited the shop. His hands were empty— no paper bag. He obviously hadn't made a purchase. He started when he caught sight of me, but quickly pulled on the peak of his cap in acknowledgment and hurried down the street toward his truck. Was it just coincidence that he had been in the liquor store? Or had he followed me inside, hoping to eavesdrop on my conversation? I looked across the way to the village green. The park was strangely empty, but a man was lounging on a park bench, his back to me. I turned toward the shop window, angling my head in hopes I could see him in the reflection of the glass. Would he turn around now that I was looking away? I shook my head. *Don't be so dramatic, Jessica*, I told myself. *Your experience has made you paranoid. Not everyone on the street is shadowing you.*

"You thinking about buying that post-hole digger, or are you just planning to stare at it all day?"

"Oh, for heaven's sake," I said.

David Ranieri stood at my side. "I know our window dressing is a cut above the others on the street," the co-owner of Charles said, "but I can't say I've ever seen a woman show such interest in a post-hole digger."

I forced a smile, and grimaced against a stab of pain in my lower back.

"You okay?" he asked.

"I've been better," I replied.

"Come on inside," he said, extending his elbow for me to hold. "Everybody's happy to see you back after what you went through, but I'm not sure you should be out shopping so soon. Come sit for a spell and I'll get whatever you need, whether it's a post-hole digger or a cup of tea."

I laughed. "I'll take you up on the tea," I said.

"We're trying out a new company from California, Mighty Leaf. They have lovely teas. I'll make you a cup of Ginger Twist, or Mint Mélange, if you prefer."

David escorted me into the store and guided me to

an armchair next to the counter. He disappeared into a back room, and I looked around the store that had anchored Cabot Cove's downtown for decades. My eye went to a pretty blue vase on the counter. It was shaped like a heart, with wilting wildflowers in it, and I thought it would go nicely in my home, on one of my kitchen windowsills.

David returned with a leather-bound book in which little compartments held various tea packets. I selected one, and he went behind the counter to where a carafe of water sat on a hot plate. "I know you're supposed to rinse the pot out with boiling water right before you make the tea," he said, "but I hope you won't mind if I break the rules."

"You don't have to worry about any complaints from this lady."

David brought me a cup and a lovely little green teapot, which he placed on a stool next to the chair. "We always stock distinctive blends of coffees, as you know," he said, "but I thought tea would be a nice change. We're having a special on these this week. See, the infuser is right inside the teapot, so you can drop the leaves in but you won't get them in your cup." He flipped open the stainless-steel lid to show me how it worked.

"Very clever," I said.

"Let this steep a moment and I'll get cream and sugar for you."

"Just lemon if you have it, please," I said.

I heaved a sigh of relief. It had already been a long day, and I still had an appointment to keep with Evelyn Phillips to deliver my story and the letter to the editor. Everything ached from my head to my toes. I was beginning to think Seth had it right: I was a stubborn, hardheaded woman. I should have stayed home to rest, at least for one day. Now I was experiencing the consequences, and wasn't pleased with the results.

"Here you go, Jessica," David said, placing a small saucer holding lemon wedges on the stool next to me.

"I should come here for tea every day," I said, fixing my cup and taking a sip.

"And you'd always be welcome."

"Where are your customers today?" I asked. "It seems very quiet."

"There's a pageant rehearsal at the shore and everyone went down to watch. Half my staff is there. Jim, too." He looked at his watch. "They'll be back in a half hour and business will pick up again. Meanwhile, I can keep you company or leave you alone, your choice."

"I always enjoy your company, David. I've been admiring that pretty vase up there on the counter. I've never seen one like it."

"It's not really a vase," he said, lifting the drooping blooms to reveal the neck. "It's a wine bottle. Too bad about the flowers. Wildflowers don't last very long."

"It's a wine bottle?"

"Yes. Levi Carver brings me a bottle like this every Christmas."

"I've never seen wine in a bottle like that. What kind of wine is it?"

"Homemade blueberry wine."

"And you save the empty bottles?"

"My wife does. The kids brought this one in."

"Your children?"

He laughed. "No. Evan Carver brought these flowers

in for Abigail Brown. I think they're having a lovers' tiff." He laughed.

"I'm sorry, David. Bear with me. I'm a little confused. Did you put the flowers in the bottle?"

"No. The flowers were in the bottle when Evan brought it in. Is there something wrong?"

"I'm afraid I've forgotten an appointment I have." I looked at my watch. "Good heavens, I'm due there right now. I'm sorry to be rude, but I think I'd better be on my way. Anyway, I've taken up enough of your time today. You've been very kind."

"You haven't finished your tea, Jessica."

"It was wonderful. I feel so much better now. Not only did it ease my aching muscles, it cleared my mind. Thank you so much, David. I'll be back to buy some of that special tea. It was delicious."

Chapter Nineteen

I was only a few minutes early for my meeting with Evelyn at the *Gazette*, but when I discovered that she was still at the harbor covering the final preparations for our festival, I was frankly relieved. There was too much pain afflicting my body, and too many thoughts churning around in my mind, to concentrate on much of anything. I left the article and the letter with Evelyn's assistant and limped out of the office, thankful to be off the hook but wondering if I'd be able to manage to walk home.

Lucky for me, I didn't have to ponder that very long. Seth Hazlitt saw me, stopped his car, and got out. He didn't say a word as he came around and opened the passenger door for me, and was silent while I climbed inside and fastened my seat belt. I didn't need words to know what he was thinking. The frown on his brow and the hard line of his mouth said loud and clear that I was in for a tongue-lashing.

"You look like the wreck of the *Hesperus*," he growled once he'd reclaimed the driver's seat. "Any lumper's helper would know they need a few days' rest to recover from what you've been through. And you've been out and about since . . . when? . . . nine this morning?"

"Ten."

"I'll bet you didn't even stop for lunch."

Lunch! I'd forgotten to eat anything since breakfast except for the two cookies I'd had at Mary's.

"If you listened to your body, you'd be home in bed right now."

"Mmm-hmm," I said, closing my eyes and leaning back against the headrest.

"Got yourself a headache, don't you? You had a concussion, Jessica. Rest is the only thing that will heal that."

"I know."

"And with the assault on your body from overexposure in cold ocean water, and Lord knows what else you strained dragging that body out of the cabin, you've got to be hurting bad."

"I am."

"And yet where do I find you? Wandering downtown with no way to get home."

"I was thinking about calling for a taxi if you hadn't shown up."

"Well, at least that shows some common sense."

"You needn't be sarcastic, Seth. I agree with you. Every word you said is true. I am sore and my head aches and I was foolish to press myself so soon after being injured." I knew his scolding stemmed from his concern. I was too drained to argue. Agreeing seemed the only way to head off more reprimands. In any case, I had no excuse. I knew he was right.

Seth grunted but stopped his harangue. "Didn't mean to holler. Well, mebbe I did. I'll drop you home, but I want your promise you'll stay there."

"You have it."

Seth drew up to the front of the house and turned off the engine.

"Looks like you had some visitors."

"Oh, my," I said. A sea of flower arrangements covered the front steps and spilled onto the lawn. The sight of all the flowers, evidence of good wishes from so many friends, lifted my spirits, and for a moment I forgot my aches and pains.

"They're beautiful," I said, wading through the flower gifts to get to the door. "But what am I going to do with all of them?"

Seth leaned down to pluck the gift card from a tall basket filled with fruits and jams. " 'From all your friends at Buckley House Publishing.' And this one says, 'So glad to hear you're safely home. Signed, Harriet Schoolman Bennett.' Who's that?"

"The dean at Schoolman College. I taught there for a semester."

"I remember. Here's one from Levi and Mary Carver. 'Get well soon,' it says."

"How thoughtful," I said, taking the Ball jar from Seth's hands. It was filled with summer roses from Mary's garden.

"The Carvers didn't strike me as the sending-flowers type," Seth said. "I would have thought Mary was good for a casserole."

I opened the door and together we brought in a dozen baskets and vases and arrayed them around the living room and kitchen.

"Looks like a funeral home in here," Seth said, dusting off his hands.

"I love flowers, but this is more than I can handle. Why don't you take some to the nurses at the hospital? Just leave the gift cards so I can write my thank-you notes."

"Think I'll do that," he said. "They'll be much appreciated. Meantime, get yourself something to eat and take a nap, or at least put your feet up and relax."

"I will," I said, "and thank you so much—not just for the ride home, but for everything." I felt my eyes tear up. Seth was such a good friend. How would I ever have managed without him?

"When my friend Jessica Fletcher starts getting sentimental," Seth said, guiding me to a chair, "then I know she's overtired. Get yourself some sleep. I'll be happy to take a couple of these bouquets off your hands."

After Seth left, I listened to the messages on my telephone answering machine. They were all well-wishers, mostly from Cabot Cove, but a few from friends of long standing I'd lost touch with, but who'd read of my recovery in the wire service stories. I would have a lot of thank-you notes to write when things calmed down. One call was surprising. It was from Barnaby Longshoot, who evidently was feeling up to making it. I jotted down all the names and numbers, including his, intending to sit down in my study to begin returning the calls. Instead, I dragged myself to the bedroom and slept for five hours, waking only to have a light supper from the food provided by my generous neighbors before going back to sleep.

I was vaguely aware that the stressful dreams continued, but the sheer number of hours I spent sleeping did a world of good for my body. I awakened the next morning rested and refreshed, still achy, but not nearly as uncomfortable as I'd been the day before.

It was pouring when I went to collect my newspaper. Even though the newsboy had folded the paper into a plastic bag and flung it on my doorstep, it was soaked halfway through, the pages of the front half of the issue stuck together. I opened the newspaper carefully and spread it on my kitchen counter to dry, disappointed that my usual breakfast reading matter was a soggy mess.

Instead, over tea and toast, I tried to pull together what little I knew of the events that had led up to and followed the murder of Henry Pettie.

The broker was not a popular man, and several of the lobstermen—notably Hank Bower, Levi Carver, and Alex Paynter—had talked not only of their dissatisfaction with him, but with their leader, Linc Williams, as well, for supporting Pettie. There may have been others I was not aware of. Linc's nephew Brady Holland, who I was convinced was responsible for having dumped rotten bait on Spencer's boat, was also likely to have been the one who chopped the hole in Hank's lobster boat. Had he acted independently—or was he carrying out his uncle's orders?

According to Linc Williams, Pettie had claimed he was meeting with Spencer Durkee the night the broker was murdered. In the meantime, someone had left a bottle of blueberry wine where Spencer would find it, most likely a homemade bottle of blueberry wine, if my suspicions were correct. Spencer had abandoned his boat and taken his gift down to the beach, where after consuming its contents, he'd fallen asleep and spent the night. Mort didn't believe that story and Spencer was in custody. Without witnesses, would his alibi stand up in court?

I'd had an appointment with Barnaby Longshoot, but a left-handed attacker had lured him away and beaten him. Was it to keep him from talking to me? Or was there another reason?

After the ambulance had taken Barnaby to the hospital, the police had departed, and while I was sitting with Evelyn Phillips in front of Mara's, I'd seen someone—I had thought at the time it was Spencer—carrying something to the *Done For*; I was now fairly confident it was the body of Henry Pettie, which meant he hadn't been killed on the boat. When I came aboard, whoever had dumped Pettie's body in the cabin hid out of sight and then knocked me out. I touched my head where the lump raised by that blow was still tender to the touch. It was on the left side of my head. *My* assailant had been left-handed, too.

The bottle I'd seen at Charles Department Store holding wildflowers kept coming in and out of focus in my thinking. Could it be the same bottle Spencer had taken to the beach? The police hadn't found a bottle where Spencer had been drinking and had fallen asleep, which didn't help his story. Where had that bottle gone? Had someone picked it up to use as a vase? Evan? If so, it meant he'd been at the beach, perhaps at the same time Spencer had been there. If it had been Evan, had he picked up the bottle because he'd appreciated its aesthetic beauty? Or had he taken it for a more pragmatic reason? It was a question I knew I had to find the answer to.

David at Charles Department Store had said that Levi gave him homemade blueberry wine every year, in a bottle of unusual design, and with a striking label.

Another visit to Mary Carver was definitely in order. And a visit to Barnaby, if he was willing.

A knock at the front door interrupted my conjuring. I put down my teacup, tightened the belt of my robe, and went to answer it. Abigail Brown stood on my doorstep, the rain dripping off her slicker.

"Good morning, Mrs. Fletcher. I'm sorry to disturb you so early. May I talk with you a minute?"

"Of course, Abigail. Come in. You're soaked."

Once she was inside, I asked, "Isn't there a rehearsal this morning? From what I've heard, you've been rehearsing night and day."

"I'm not going to the rehearsal."

"Oh? Well, hang up your coat. I've just made a new pot of tea. Would you like some?"

"Sure, but I don't want to trouble you."

"No trouble at all. Come, sit down."

She followed me into the kitchen, her wide eyes taking it all in. "Gee, it looks like a flower shop in here," she said.

"It does a bit, doesn't it?" I surveyed the room. Baskets of colorful blooms—roses, daisies, hydrangea, and myriad other flowers—were perched on every surface.

"You must have a lot of friends, Mrs. Fletcher."

"Yes, and I'm grateful for them."

I poured another cup of tea, set it in front of her with a napkin and a spoon, refilled my own cup, and sat facing the pretty young woman. Her large green eyes had turned apprehensive.

"Too bad about the rain, isn't it?" she said. "They're still planning to hold the parade, but the pageant won't be as nice indoors."

"These things work out," I said. "If everyone coming to the festival is planning to have a good time, they will, whether it's under a tent in the village square, or in the high school gym. Rain won't make a difference."

"My friend Kathy Corr, she's in the pageant, too. She says there won't be any point in getting her hair done if the rain will only mess it up. She's very pretty. I hope she wins." Her voice trailed off.

"I have the feeling, Abigail, that you've decided not to be in the pageant."

Her chin dropped. "I'm not sure," she said glumly. Her hands were fisted in her lap, and she heaved a great sigh. "I . . . I have something to tell you, Mrs. Fletcher, but I'm not sure how to say it."

"Feel free to say anything you wish, Abigail. You obviously have something important on your mind. It's always better to get such things out in the open."

She averted my eyes as she said slowly, "It's about Mr. Durkee."

"Yes? What about him?"

"He . . . he was at the beach, just like he said he was."

I thought for a moment before offering the scenario I'd been considering all morning. "You and Evan saw Spencer Durkee down at the beach, didn't you?"

Her head bobbed up and down.

"Evan brought you flowers in an empty blueberry wine bottle. Did you pick it up at the beach that night?"

"Evan did."

"Do you know why he did?" I asked.

"He did it for me."

"For you?"

"He didn't want people to know we'd been down there that night. You know, the pageant and all, its rules, those silly rules. He thought that if we came forward and said we'd seen Mr. Durkee there, Mrs. Watson might kick me out of the pageant."

"How did you feel about it?" I asked.

"I wanted to tell the police what we'd seen, but Evan told me to stay out of it. He said somebody else would come along who saw Mr. Durkee there."

"You've been arguing about it," I said, thinking back to David's comment about there being a lovers' tiff between them.

She nodded again. Tears appeared on the edges of her eyelids. "We've been fighting for two days," she said. "No one else has come forward, have they?"

I shook my head.

"I read the piece in the paper where they were asking for any witnesses, and I just couldn't keep it quiet anymore. I feel terrible that Mr. Durkee's in jail and it's all my fault." She started to cry in earnest, tears streaming down her cheeks.

"No harm's done yet," I said. "Spencer's had an extra night as Sheriff Metzger's guest, that's all. It isn't the first time."

She dabbed her eyes with the napkin. "You knew we were there, didn't you?"

"No, I didn't, but I started wondering about it this morning. The flowers Evan brought you at Charles Department Store were in a wine bottle. Is that the same bottle Spencer was drinking from?"

"Uh-huh."

"After Spencer Durkee was arrested, didn't it bother Evan that if no one found the bottle, Mr. Durkee's alibi might be compromised and he might be charged with murder?"

"He was thinking of me, Mrs. Fletcher. He was afraid Mr. Durkee might have seen us there."

"And if he had seen you, he might tell someone that you and Evan had been together at the beach after dark."

Another embarrassed nod from her, head hanging low, eyes on the table. "It sounds terrible, I know."

"Yes, it does," I said. "Is a beauty contest that important?"

"When Mrs. Watson read us the pageant rules, I couldn't believe it. We weren't supposed to be seen talking to boys, much less dating them. If she finds out Evan and I were on the beach after dark, she'll throw me out. And she'd probably put it on the front page of her newspaper. My parents would be so embarrassed. I could never look them in the face again. It's not what you think. We weren't doing anything so terrible. We just like to lie on the beach and look at the stars. But no one would believe us if we said that."

"Especially since that was a pretty cloudy night," I said, smiling.

A blush spread over Abigail's cheeks. "We mostly talk," she said.

"But now you realize it was the wrong thing to do."

"We thought we could risk it. We never thought something like this would happen." She drew in a deep breath. "I'd rather drop out now than have Mrs. Watson accuse me of moral turp . . . turpen . . . I can't remember the word she used."

"Turpitude?"

"Yes. That."

"Well, that's one option for you. There may be others," I said, rising and taking my cup and plate to the sink. "Thank you for telling me, Abigail."

She smiled wanly. "You're welcome."

I noticed her hands were still clenched. "Was there something more?" I asked.

"Kind of," she said. "Would you come with me to the sheriff's office? I really don't want to go there alone, and I'm not ready to tell my parents just yet. I'll tell them afterward, I promise, after I tell the police, and after I resign from the pageant. It's just that they're so proud of me." The tears started up again. "And this will be so hard for them. They invited all our relatives to come see me in the pageant, and I know they're going to be heartbroken. And Mr. Ranieri, too. He's been so good to me. They're all going to hate me."

"Maybe not," I said, patting her shoulder. "If I were your parents, I'd be very proud of you. You made an adult decision today, one that has painful consequences for you, but one that is morally, ethically correct. It's the right thing to do for you, and, of course, for Spencer Durkee. You hold your head up, Abigail. You have every reason to be proud. Give me a few minutes to get dressed and we'll go see Sheriff Metzger together."

Chapter Twenty

Mort had a shoe box open on his desk when his deputy, Harold Jenkins, escorted us into the sheriff's office.

"Good morning, Mort. I hope we're not intruding."

"Not at all, ladies. Take a seat. Please excuse me for not standing." He drew out a pair of new shoes from the box and placed them on the floor.

"Did you buy those online?" I asked after Abigail and I had taken seats across from him.

Mort shook his head. "Nope. Maureen picked these up for me at Charles Department Store. I can take them back if they don't fit."

He slid his feet into the new shoes and sat back, a beatific smile on his face. "Ah, much better." He stood, turned in a circle, then sat again, still smiling. "Now, what can I do for you? Must be important for you to come out in this miserable weather."

"This is Abigail Brown," I said. "She has some information I think you'll find interesting."

Abigail related to Mort the same story she'd told me. Having confessed once, she found the retelling of it easier, and was able to keep the tears at bay, although her voice was still full of emotion.

Mort listened carefully and took notes. When she was

finished, he had her repeat her narrative to Deputy Jenkins in the next room. I knew he would compare her first telling to the second one, looking for discrepancies, but I doubted he'd find any. The information she provided him was identical to what she'd told me.

While Abigail gave her statement to Jenkins, I took the opportunity to catch up with Mort on another issue. "Have you gotten back the postmortem on Henry Pettie?" I asked.

"Knew you'd want to know about that eventually," he said. "I have the report right here." He rifled through some papers on his desk and drew out the one he sought. "The toxicological results will take a few weeks, as you know, but the coroner says it looks like Pettie expired from a blow to the head," Mort said, reading from the paper. "'An examination of the skull revealed a single horizontal fissure below the median nuchal line of the occipital bone on the posterior of the cranium.' Back of the head," he said, chopping at his own skull with the side of his hand.

"Must have been a heck of a blow."

"It was enough to kill him, assuming he wasn't poisoned as well. Not likely, I'd say. And you were right: The body was probably moved. There were scuff marks on the back of the heels of his cowboy boots. Likelihood is, he wasn't killed on the *Done For.*"

"I'm not surprised at the scuff marks," I said. "But Pettie liked to put his feet up on his desk, and that could explain them. However, I'm pretty sure I saw the killer carrying his body onto the boat. So I agree. He must have been killed elsewhere."

"Too bad you didn't see who it was toting the body."

"I was way too far away. Besides, it was very dark.

What kind of instrument would make such a horizontal mark?''

"Could be anything," Mort said. "He might not have been standing upright at the time. You didn't see anything on the boat that could have been the murder weapon?"

"No. And I didn't see anything that might have been used to hit me, either."

"The killer probably threw it overboard."

"Together with Pettie's notebook and wallet. His pockets were empty."

"What notebook?"

"Mary Carver told me he kept a record of the money people owed him in a small black notebook. I saw Pettie mark something down in it the day I went fishing with Levi and Evan. It wasn't on his person when I checked the body."

"I wonder how many people owed him money," Mort said.

"Just about everyone, according to Mary."

"Spencer, too?"

"Could be, but I don't know. Does the report indicate time of death?"

"Coroner estimates between seven and midnight."

"That's a pretty wide span," I said.

"The body may have been chilled by the water, so it makes it harder to narrow the time."

"Of course. How foolish of me. I should have realized that."

"You're probably not up to snuff yet, Mrs. F. How are you feeling? I saw the doc yesterday, and he wasn't too happy with your not staying home."

"I am a testament to the curative powers of fourteen hours of sleep," I said. "Not to mention a hot bath. Seth was right: I tried to do too much too soon. But today I'm one hundred percent improved over yesterday."

"You're going to take it easy all the same, though, aren't you?"

"I'm going to follow doctor's orders, and listen to my body."

"Glad to hear it."

Abigail knocked on Mort's door after having given her report to Harold Jenkins, and Mort walked us outside. We stood next to Abigail's car, the rain pelting down on the green umbrella Seth had given me.

Mort raised the collar of his slicker. "I'll need to confirm your story with Evan Carver before I can release old Spencer," he said to Abigail. "But I want you to know that I think you're a very honorable young lady, coming forward to vouch for Durkee even if it might cost you the pageant. I'm sure your parents will be proud of you."

"I told her the same thing," I said.

"I hope you're both right," she said. "I'm going to talk to Gwen Anissina right now. Then I'll go home to tell my folks."

"You do that, dear," I said. "I'm sure Gwen will understand, too."

We waved as Abigail drove off.

"Need a lift somewhere, Mrs. F? The cruiser is right here."

"Ordinarily I'd say no, Mort. I'm only going over to Mary Carver's to see if she needs any last-minute help. But given this foul weather, I wouldn't mind a ride."

"Hop in," he said.

I folded the umbrella and climbed in the passenger seat of the police car.

"Are you going to tell Mrs. Carver about Abigail and Evan on the beach?" he asked.

"No. I think that news is better coming from Evan."

"He's going to have a lot of explaining to do. They tampered with evidence."

"Go easy on him when he comes in to give you his version," I said. "He was only trying to protect Abigail. I don't think they ever expected Spencer would be arrested if the bottle wasn't found."

"I gotta say, Mrs. F, I really thought Spencer did it. But you believed he was innocent, and it looks like you're right. Asking the paper to call for witnesses was a brilliant stroke. Still, Pettie was planning to see him that night. Now we have to figure out who he actually met."

The rain was still coming down when I knocked on Mary's kitchen door and let myself in. Her twelve-year-old daughter was standing at the sink eating a peanut-butter-and-jelly sandwich folded in half. Drips of jam from the open jar, as well as crumbs from a half-eaten loaf of bread spilling out of its packaging, were scattered on the counter, together with a milk carton and an empty glass.

"Hi, Anna," I said. "Is your mother home?"

"She just ran to the store, but she'll be right back. You can wait, if you want."

"Thank you. I think I will." I crossed the room to sit at Mary's oval table, taking care not to step on Anna's sneakers, which she'd left on the floor by the baker's rack.

Anna looked around the kitchen at the mess she'd made. "I better clean this up before Mom gets back, huh?"

"It wouldn't be a bad idea."

"That's what I thought," she said, screwing the lid onto the jam jar and dropping the dirty knife into the dishwasher without rinsing it. "You want some coffee? Mom has some left in the pot."

"No, thank you. I just had breakfast a little while ago," I said. "I understand you've been watching the pageant rehearsals. How are they going?"

"It's going to be awesome. But it sucks that it's raining, don't you think? It would be way cooler if we could be outside."

"The rain may let up tonight. There's still hope for dry weather tomorrow."

Anna put away the bread, jam, and milk, swiped a sponge over the granite countertop, rinsed out the sink, and wiped her mouth with the dishtowel hanging by the window. "There," she said, grinning at me. "Perfect, huh?"

"What about those?" I said, cocking my head at her sneakers.

"Oh, gawd, thanks. She'd kill me if she saw I'd left those there again. My pop almost took a switch to me the other night." Anna flopped onto the floor next to the baker's rack and pulled on the high-tops one at a time, carefully loosening the laces so they wouldn't drag on the ground if she didn't tie them. Finished, she lay on her back and sighed.

"Tough day?" I asked, smiling.

"Yeah. Wow. Everybody's so nervous about the festival. They're fightin' all the time. But rain or not, it's going to be awesome. Really awesome. What do you think?"

"I agree," I said. "A little rain won't make the day any less memorable."

"Mom says all the guesthouses are filling up. I'm really excited."

She rolled to her side to get up. "Hey, what's this?" she said, reaching under the bottom shelf of the rack. She sat up cross-legged and examined the object she'd found. "It's an earring."

My hands automatically reached for my ears, but my earrings were in place. "I've never seen your mother wear earrings," I said.

"She doesn't."

"May I see it?" I asked.

Anna scrambled to her feet and dropped the gold disk into my palm. I turned it over and over, examining the outer surface, where a set of initials had been engraved.

"No, it's not mine," I said, "but I think I know the person it belongs to. May I keep it for a little while?"

"Sure. But let me know if there's a reward for finding it. My friend Emily Corr—she's Katherine's sister—she found a diamond ring in the bathroom at Mara's once, and the lady who claimed it gave her ten whole dollars."

"If there's a reward, I'll be sure to pass it along," I said.

The kitchen door swung open and Mary bustled in, her arms full of packages. "Anna, run to the car and bring in the cake box. Hello, Jessica. Hope I didn't keep you. You wouldn't believe what Sassi's is like this morning. Lines out the door."

"My heavens," I said, relieving Mary of one of her

shopping bags and placing it on the counter. "What's going on?"

"It's the visitors. There's not a room to be found in Cabot Cove. The guesthouses are full, and all the motels and hotels out by the highway are completely sold out. The mayor put out a call asking anyone who can accommodate guests in their spare rooms to sign up at town hall." As Mary talked, she unpacked her groceries. "We have Ginny's old room we can rent out. She and Pete were going to come for the festival, but they can drive over. It's less than an hour. I'm stocking up in case we get called upon."

"Looks like the festival is going to be a big success," I said, handing her a box of cereal from one of the shopping bags.

"Yes, thanks to you."

"Me! Why?"

"All the papers and the TV stations covered the murder, and you being found alive"—Mary imitated an announcer's formal voice—"*only days before the Cabot Cove Lobsterfest.*"

"Oh, my."

"The mayor said the phones haven't stopped ringin' since. I hope Levi won't mind if we rent out Ginny's room. We can use the extra cash. Anyway, I bought a lovely coffee cake for the continental breakfast we're supposed to provide. Do you think it's all right to serve eggs at a continental breakfast?"

"I'm sure any guests of yours will be delighted with your breakfast," I said.

"Mom, can I have one of these cookies?" Anna asked, lifting the corner of a cake box she'd brought in.

"No, those are for visitors. Take one from the cookie jar instead."

"But these have chocolate on the outside."

"You may take one, but if I see you sneaking more, I'll tan your hide."

Anna extracted a long oval cookie with chocolate on both ends and wrapped it carefully in a napkin. "I'm going to share it with Emily. We're meeting at the gym. Okay if I go now?"

"Yes, off with you, but be back early."

"Okay. 'Bye, Mom." She kissed her mother's cheek. " 'Bye, Mrs. Fletcher. Don't forget my reward."

"I'll remember," I said.

"What is that girl going on about?"

"Mary, why did you buy cookies when you've got homemade ones?" I asked.

"There are only a few in the jar," she replied, folding the grocery bags and putting them away. "All the ones in the freezer are for the festival bake sale tomorrow. I won't have time to make a new batch before then. Too much to do." She stopped and took a deep breath. "It's so exciting. I've got coffee. Want some?"

I shook my head.

"Tea?"

"No, but you go ahead."

Mary poured herself a cup of coffee and we sat at her table.

"Are you still on duty for tomorrow?" she asked.

"I was signed up to cover the used book sale," I said, "but the library director left a message saying that in light of the recent incident, they'd gotten a replacement for me."

"That was smart of her. You shouldn't be on your feet so much. But you look a lot better today than yesterday."

"I feel a lot better, too. Thank you for the beautiful roses, by the way. It was so thoughtful. A lovely surprise to come home to."

"That was Levi's idea," she said. "I would've sent you a casserole, but he said you probably had a dozen of them already."

"People have been very generous," I said. I hesitated. Perhaps now wasn't the time to ask about the wine bottle. Everyone was in a holiday mood. The festival was upon us. Why bring up accusations and suspicions? I conducted an internal debate. Should I wait until the Lobsterfest was over to continue my investigation? Who would suffer if I waited a few days? What would be the right thing to do?

"Mary, I have a question for you."

"Yes?"

"I saw a pretty heart-shaped bottle at Charles the other day. David said it was from homemade blueberry wine, and that Levi gives him a bottle every year."

"I know exactly what you saw." She jumped up, pulled out a step stool, climbed on it, and reached the top shelf of the cabinet over the refrigerator. "You mean this, don't you?" she said, coming down and placing a full bottle of blueberry wine in front of me. It was the same shape and color as the bottle with the wildflowers in it, only this one had a label on it with an elaborate drawing of blueberries and glasses intertwined. In calligraphic script, it read CABOT COVE BLUEBERRY WINE, VINTAGE 2004.

"Yes," I said, turning the blue bottle around. "I didn't know Levi made wine."

"He doesn't. We get a couple of these as a gift every year. Levi isn't crazy about the stuff, but he doesn't want to be rude, so he gives it away to someone who might like it." She giggled. "Don't tell."

"Who makes the wine?"

"Ike Bower, Sandy's husband. You met her the other day."

"Yes, of course. The lady with all the blueberries. Her husband makes wine from them and gives it away?"

"Everyone I know has at least one bottle in their pantry. You should have one, too. Take this home and try it. You might like it. Lots of people do."

"You wouldn't mind?"

"No, I've got another bottle, although I thought I had more. Levi must have found another taker."

Mary wrapped up the bottle in a newspaper and put it in a shopping bag for me.

As I was leaving, I asked, "Where is Levi today? Is he out fishing?"

"All the lobstermen are checking the stock at the pound for tomorrow."

"Will he be home later? I'd like to talk to him."

"Actually, he probably won't be home till late. There's a meeting of the executive committee of the lobstermen's association tonight. You want me to tell him you're looking for him?"

"That's not necessary," I said. "I can catch him another time. Thanks for the wine, Mary. I can't wait to taste it."

I stepped outside and was hit in the face by a wet

gust of wind. The rain was coming down even harder, if that were possible. I stepped back into Mary's kitchen.

"I think I need a taxi," I said.

"You want me to drive you?"

"Absolutely not. You've got enough to do today."

"I'll call the cab company," she said, taking the receiver from a wall phone.

A few minutes later, the cab, driven by an elderly man who'd been working for Cabot Cove's largest and busiest taxi company for years, arrived. I ran to it, pulled open the rear door, and tumbled in. "My goodness," I said, "it's a downpour."

"Not fit for man nor beast," he said with a scowl.

I pulled the gold earring from my blouse's breast pocket, and a wave of despair swept over me, as the rain had done. That small, gold disk, with its initials on the surface, had the potential, I knew, to cause a great deal of pain to certain people in my beloved Cabot Cove, and possibly place a damper on the lobster festival that no rain could ever equal.

That I was the one who might be the instigator of this bad news did not sit well with me.

Chapter Twenty-one

I called Seth from home, and asked if he'd like to bring more flowers to the hospital. He had said my kitchen resembled a funeral parlor, and while I was thankful for the thoughtfulness of so many friends, it was not a look I was eager to preserve. Seth had just seen his last patient of the morning, and agreed to drive over and pick up some of the bouquets. I placed baskets of blooms in my bedroom and living room, put Mary's roses on the kitchen table, and even pulled a few blossoms to go in a small bud vase to brighten the bath. That was more than sufficient. Knowing the excess would cheer up the day for patients and nurses alike was a pleasing contemplation.

"You feelin' better, my friend?" Seth asked, while we selected the arrangements he would take with him.

"Yes, much."

"Stayin' home this afternoon?"

"I, ah . . . I'm not sure. I thought I might treat myself to lunch at Mara's."

"Well, that's all right, but don't go getting cocky just because you're feeling better. Takes a long time to get over what you went through."

Dodging raindrops, I helped him load the flowers in his car. Afterward, over a quick cup of tea, I quizzed him on a question that had been bothering me.

"I keep thinking about the murder," I said.

"I imagine that will be on your mind for a while."

"No, not from an emotional point of view—although I can't deny the lingering effects of the shock—but from a practical one."

"What do you mean?"

"I didn't examine the body as carefully as I might have."

"For heaven's sake, Jessica, you were abandoned at sea on a sinking ship. You can't fault yourself for not conducting an autopsy."

"I know that, but hear me out. From what I did see, I don't believe Henry Pettie knew what hit him," I said.

"Why do you say that?"

"There were no defensive marks on his hands or arms."

"Well, if you don't see what's coming, there wouldn't be."

"Exactly. The strike came from behind, and there was only one. Can a single blow to the head be fatal?"

"Ayuh. Blunt-force injury to the back of the skull is more likely to be fatal than one to the front. That's why you're such a lucky lady. That bump you sustained was toward the side."

"I must have turned my head slightly. It's hard to sneak up on a person. I was certainly aware of someone behind me just before I got hit, even though I didn't have time to defend myself."

"That movement of your head may have saved your life. Gave you a painful egg but did relatively little damage to the braincase, a mild concussion, but that will heal—if you rest and let it."

"I'll remember that," I said.

"Be sure you do." He glanced at his watch, rose from the table, carried our cups to the sink, and rinsed them out. "Come along and I'll drop you at Mara's," he said. "Got a meeting at the hospital, and I want to deliver those flowers first."

I grabbed my raincoat, still damp from the morning's deluge, and opened the front door. The sight that greeted us was a surprise. As though someone had flipped a giant switch, the drenching rain of the past hours had suddenly ceased, and shafts of sunlight played off the glistening grass and wet, shiny road. We stepped outside with buoyed spirits. As I stood on my front step, I was able to see a lovely rainbow that arched from a massive cloud down to the eastern horizon.

"What a positive omen for the lobster festival," I said.

"Ayuh, looks like we may get good weather after all."

Mara's was virtually empty when I walked in. The inclement weather had kept people at home, and the change from rain to sunshine had been too sudden to change that in the near term.

"Will you look at that?" Mara said, referring to the sunlight. "The man upstairs is looking out for us."

"Wonderful, isn't it?" I said, settling into a booth by a window. "Clam chowder on the menu today?"

"Certainly is. Just made it. Bowl or a cup?"

"A bowl, please."

I sat back and drew deep breaths. All the tension

of the past week seemed to drain from me, and I enjoyed the resulting feeling of well-being. The sound of the door opening caused me to turn. It was Barnaby Longshoot. He stood just inside the entrance and seemed unsure of where to sit. I could see from my vantage point that he still bore the scars of his beating. The area above his right eye was swollen, the eye itself ringed with a greenish-purple hue, turning yellow, a classic black eye. His lips, too, were still puffy from where a fist had connected.

"Hello, Barnaby," I said, waving. "Join me?"

He hesitated, looking left and right in search of others in the restaurant. I was pleased that he eventually decided to take me up on my offer. He slid into the booth opposite me and managed a painful smile. "I don't look too good," he said, his lips barely moving, the pain from talking evident in his expression.

"Actually," I said, "you don't look that bad, considering the beating you took. I feel terrible about it, Barnaby. You waited here after Mara's closed because I asked to meet with you."

"Wasn't your fault, Mrs. Fletcher."

A few other patrons entered Mara's, but fortunately took seats apart from us. Barnaby seemed visibly anxious that others had arrived, and I knew any productive time with him would be limited. I leaned across the table and asked, "Are you still willing to talk to me, Barnaby, about what's been going on?"

He nodded solemnly. "My mother says you're somebody who can be trusted."

I hadn't expected that answer, and paused to digest it before saying, "Thank you, Barnaby. That's very flattering, and I'll try to live up to your mother's faith in me. Do you know who was responsible for dumping rotten bait on Spencer Durkee's boat?"

Barnaby nodded again.

"Was it Brady Holland?"

Another nod.

"Was he also responsible for the hole in Ike Bower's boat?"

Another nod.

"And was it Brady who attacked you?"

"Yes, ma'am."

"Yet you told Sheriff Metzger it was too dark to see your assailant."

"Didn't want to tell tales outside the association. Linc, he gets real mad when anybody does that. No airing our dirty laundry, he says. What happens here stays here." He smiled. "They say that about Las Vegas. I've never been there. I'd like to go someday."

"I'm sure you will," I said. "But Barnaby, you're not a member of the association. You're not a lobsterman. You can tell the truth about what happened."

His smile turned into a frown.

I leaned even closer as others came into the restaurant. "Barnaby, what do you know about Henry Pettie's murder?"

"I think I'd best be going," he said, sliding to the edge of the bench. "I've got things to do."

"Sure you don't want lunch? My treat."

"No, thank you, ma'am."

"Barnaby, I appreciate your talking to me today, and for telling me the truth about Brady Holland."

"I can do it now."

"Why? Why can you do it now?"

"He doesn't live here anymore."

"Ah."

"But I've got one more thing to say."

"What's that?"

"You be careful. There's bad stuff going on around here."

I watched him grimace as he stood. He placed the index and middle fingers of his right hand to his brow and gave me what I assumed was a form of salute, navigated tables between him and the door, and left just as Mara delivered my chowder.

"Looks like someone wiped up the floor with him," Mara said.

"He took quite a beating, that's for sure," I said.

"I told him to take off a few days and come back for the festival."

"That was nice of you."

I drew in a whiff of the steam coming up from my chowder bowl. "Smells delicious," I said. "How about some fresh bread?"

"Coming up," Mara said, leaving me to enjoy my chowder—and contemplate my next move.

I took the earring from my pocket again and rolled it in my fingers. I'd formulated my own theory of what the earring meant to the murder that had taken place, and the question of who had committed the crime. Whether Mort would agree with me was conjecture. But we needed to talk again. I'd make my case and accept where the chips fell.

Chapter Twenty-two

I went directly from Mara's to Mort's office, and from there home, and used my time to put together what was essentially a presentation, not unlike opening and closing statements used by attorneys in criminal court cases. I was fairly confident that I'd pieced together what had happened to Henry Pettie, and the events following his death. But I was also realistic enough to admit that there were holes in the scenario I'd created, questions that still did not have answers, at least those that would stand up in a court of law.

I ate a light dinner from among the selection of casseroles stacked in my freezer, thanks to my neighbors. Seth called as I was having my meal and asked what my plans were for the evening. I hated to lie to him, but I knew that if I were truthful, he'd be upset and try to dissuade me. So I fudged in my answer. Fortunately, he was pressed for time and didn't question me further. It was better that as few people as possible know of my plans. Mort Metzger was an exception. He needed to know.

The August night had just begun to descend on Cabot Cove as the taxi driver I'd called drove me down to Cabot Cove's dock area. My ultimate destination was Nudd's Bait & Tackle where I assumed the lobstermen's executive committee meeting would be held that evening. But I had the driver drop me off at the opposite end of the dock. I wanted some time in the outdoors before confronting those who would be in attendance. I walked slowly along the dock, the briny sea air clearing my nostrils, and hopefully my mind. The break in the weather had held. It was a lovely, pristine night, warm enough to make a sweater unnecessary, but with low humidity that ensured a minimum of annoying insects. The tourists were out in force, as were townspeople. I stopped to chat with a few friends, and a visiting couple recognized me from photos on my books and asked for an autograph. But my progress toward Nudd's was only slightly impeded, and I arrived at a quarter of eight to see Alex Paynter coming out the door.

"Good evening," I said.

He seemed slightly dismayed at my presence.

"Is this where the meeting is taking place?" I asked.

"Thought so," he replied, "but got it wrong. Tim's stayin' open for the visitors. Our meetin's bein' held down at Henry Pettie's dock, I'm told. Just heading there. You plannin' to stop by?"

"Yes," I said. "I wanted to thank the association and everyone in it for having launched the search for me."

He shrugged. "Just glad you come back safe, Mrs. Fletcher. Terrible thing that happened."

"It certainly was."

"Want a lift over to Pettie's dock? My car's right here."

"Thank you."

During the short drive, I asked whether he'd ever

gotten the part he needed to fix the engine on his lobster boat.

"No, ma'am. Still waiting for it. Had to order it out of Rhode Island. That's the problem with old clunkers like mine. Parts aren't easy to come by."

Linc Williams was about to close the door at Pettie's when we pulled up.

"Mrs. Fletcher," Williams said as I got out of Paynter's car. "What brings you here?"

"I wonder if I could have a few minutes to address your members, Linc. I wanted to officially thank you and the association for having looked for me out on the ocean."

"No thanks needed, Mrs. Fletcher. The least we could do. Besides, this is just an executive committee meetin'. You can come back when the full membership is here."

"I'll do that," I said. "But I'd feel better if you let me express my appreciation now—if you won't mind my taking time from your meeting."

"Sure, that'll be fine," he said, although I sensed he wasn't quite sure whether he meant it or not.

We entered the large office where Henry Pettie had conducted business as the lobstermen's sales broker. Including Linc, a half dozen men were gathered there; with him were Levi Carver, Ike Bower, Alex Paynter, Ben Press, whom I remembered from my first lobstermen's meeting, and Maynard, whose last name I'd never learned. They observed my entrance with a mixture of curiosity and confusion. Some nodded their greetings; others expressed them verbally. Linc invited me to take a chair next to the desk that had been

Pettie's, behind which the association's leader stood, raised his hands for quiet, and said, "Glad you all could make it this evening. Now, Mrs. Fletcher here has something she wants to say to us. I said it was okay, so listen up. I know every one of us is happy that she got to come back to us in one piece." He looked down at me. "Go ahead, Mrs. Fletcher. The floor is yours."

I stood and faced them. "First," I said, "I want you to know how much I appreciate the way you banded together and gave up a precious day of lobstering in order to help organize the search for me out there on the ocean. I can't adequately express how much your concern and actions mean to me."

Ike said, "Only right," and Levi added, "Happy to have helped."

"Well," I said, "I just wanted you to know how much I appreciate what you did."

"Thanks for stopping by, Mrs. Fletcher," Linc said. "We're grateful you're safe and sound." He looked out over the members of his executive committee. "Now, fellas, let's get down to business." He glanced at me; I hadn't sat down, or made a move toward the door.

"You have something else to say, Mrs. Fletcher?"

"As a matter of fact I do," I said. "I'm afraid it has to do with Mr. Pettie."

A sudden, profound silence filled the room, and I took advantage of it before Linc could protest.

"As you all know," I said, "the man who used to occupy these premises was killed not long ago, and I was the victim of an attempted murder." I turned to look at Linc, who'd settled into the swivel desk chair that had been Henry Pettie's. His head was cocked, his eyes narrowed. He said nothing, so I continued.

"I believe I know a great deal now about what happened that night on Spencer Durkee's boat, and the next day out at sea. But I still have some questions that need to be answered. I was hoping you'd help me fill in the missing pieces."

"Seems to me this is a matter for the law, Mrs. Fletcher," said Ike Bower, "for Sheriff Metzger."

"I agree," I said, "and he's fully aware of what I intended to say here this evening." I looked deliberately at Levi Carver, who sat in the first row. "I believe you might be able to fill in some blanks for me, Levi," I said.

"Me? Why me?"

"Because Henry Pettie was killed in your house."

"My house?" He guffawed.

"Mr. Pettie wasn't killed on Spencer's boat, as the newspaper speculated. I saw someone carry his body aboard the *Done For*. He was killed elsewhere and taken to the boat."

"Maybe that's so," Levi said, "but it doesn't mean it happened in my house."

I reached into the pocket of the gray blazer I wore that evening, pulled out the gold earring Anna Carver had found in the kitchen, and held it up, light from a ceiling fixture playing off its shiny surface.

"This is an earring Mr. Pettie wore," I said. "It was found this morning in your kitchen, Levi."

"Lemme see that," he said. I handed the earring to him. Others leaned close to him and shared in his examination of the piece of male jewelry. "That's Pettie's, all right," Ben said.

"Always thought it looked pretty silly on him," commented Alex.

"May I have it back?" I asked, and Levi gave it to me.

Ike Bower loudly cleared his throat and, after a false start, said, "Seems to me the sheriff's got the one responsible. No doubt in my mind that that crazy old coot Spencer Durkee did in Pettie. Open-and-shut case, I say." He said it with little conviction.

"Spencer Durkee didn't kill anyone," I said. "He was set up with a bottle of blueberry wine."

"No doubt about it, old Spencer loves his blueberry wine," Ben offered.

"And all of you knew that," I said. "That's why a bottle was left on his boat on the night in question." I reached down into the large canvas tote bag I'd brought with me and extracted the wine bottle Mary Carver had given me. I'd opened it at home and tasted it—it was good, although a little too sweet for my liking—and poured what was left into a crystal decanter. I held up the empty bottle and said to Ike Bower, "You make a very good blueberry wine, Ike. And from what I understand, you're very generous with your yearly output."

He said nothing.

"So," I said, "whose idea was it to entice Spencer away from his boat that evening by leaving a bottle of this wine on his deck?" I surveyed the room. Discomfort reigned; eyes went to the floor or the ceiling.

I turned to Levi Carver again. "What happened that

night in your kitchen, Levi? Were you there alone with Henry Pettie?"

Linc answered for Levi. He stood, smiled, and said, "Mrs. Fletcher, all this is very interesting, but you're whistling in the dark. Sure, maybe the men didn't like Pettie because his honesty was questionable, but no one here is a murderer."

"Was it an accident then?" I asked, my eyes zeroing in on Levi.

When he failed to respond, I said to him, "If it was an accident, Levi, I suggest you get it on the record. Finding Pettie's earring in your kitchen, and knowing that you owed him a great deal of money, will make you a prime suspect in Sheriff Metzger's eyes."

Levi started to say something, but Linc cut him off. "Don't say anything, Carver. Look, Mrs. Fletcher," he said, "it was nice of you to come here and show your appreciation for what we tried to do to save you. Now, I suggest you leave it at that, take yourself a walk on this nice night, and let us get down to the important business we have on the agenda tonight."

I ignored him and faced Alex Paynter. "It was your lobster boat that came out to meet Spencer's boat and retrieve the man who tried to kill me."

"Hey, wait a minute," he said.

"It was your engine," I said. "I knew when I heard the second boat that night that the sound was familiar. Where I'd heard it before has been plaguing me ever since. It's like a distinctive odor from our past that lingers over the years. You're not able to put a finger on where it was experienced, but it's always with you. That sound. It has been driving me to distraction, but not anymore. It was your boat, Alex. There's no doubt about that. You should have had the engine fixed before you set out on a criminal mission."

"Not me. I was home with my wife. You can ask her."

"I think the sheriff will want to do that."

I'd been throwing out these things in the hope that they would prompt one of the men to break ranks. Just when it seemed that I would be unsuccessful, Ike Bower said, "I didn't put that wine on Spencer's boat."

I raised my eyebrows. "Then who did, Ike?"

He looked to Linc Williams, whose face was now set in stone. Bower sat back and fell silent.

I refocused on Alex Paynter. "You may have been home, Alex, but Maynard, your sternman, was down at the dock on your boat."

Maynard, who'd been sitting in the back, picking through a box of supplies, raised his head. "What are you talkin' about?"

"Yeah, what're you talkin' about?" Alex echoed.

"It's another case of sound triggering memories, Alex. On the day I went out with Levi to research the article I was writing for the *Gazette*, Maynard turned on his—what is it called, a boom box?—and you told him to shut it off. He was playing loud music, a new album by someone he said was his favorite. Although I only heard a snippet of it, I recognized that same tune the night Henry Pettie was killed. It came from the dock where your lobster boat is tied up. I'd say Maynard was there about the same time Brady Holland beat up Barnaby Longshoot. The music was loud. Was that to cover up the beating so no one would hear Barnaby moaning?"

"You're crazy," Maynard yelled.

"Did you take out my boat without my permission?" Alex demanded.

Linc Williams, who hadn't spoken during my presentation, said, "This meeting is adjourned." He slapped his left hand on the desk for emphasis.

"Not so fast," a voice said from the door. Standing in the open doorway was Mort Metzger. He reached behind him and pulled Brady Holland into the room. His deputy, Harold Jenkins, brought up the rear.

"What the hell are you doing here?" Linc barked at his nephew.

"I'll tell you what I'm doing here," Brady responded in a harsh growl. He came to the desk and stood a few feet from his uncle. "I'm not taking the rap for you and these guys." He indicated the others in the room with a flip of his head.

"Shut your mouth, Brady," Linc commanded.

"It was an accident," Levi Carver blurted out. "It was just an accident. I swear."

"Maybe you'd like to tell us about the . . . accident," I said.

"Pettie fell; that's all. Yeah, it was in my kitchen. He came trying to collect money I owed him, but I didn't have it. He got real nasty, real surly, and said he was going to repossess my boat. You know what that would mean, don't you? I'd be out of business. What would my family do without me lobsterin'?"

"So you killed him?" Mort said.

"Hell, no." Levi was now on his feet and facing me and Mort, who'd come to my side. "He shoved me, and I shoved him back, that's all. He tripped."

"Over Anna's sneakers?" I said.

"God help us. Yes! She's always leaving them in the middle of the kitchen floor—and Pettie, he fell backward and hit his head on the edge of our granite counter. Got a square edge. I couldn't believe he was dead, I swear to God. I tried to help him, talked to him, got a dishrag and tried to stop the bleeding. I said prayers that he'd be okay. But he was gone like that."

Levi was nearly in tears, and I felt for him. I had wondered whether Pettie's death had been an accident, not a premeditated murder. These hardworking men in the room, with families of which they were justifiably proud, were not the sort who would plot to kill someone, not unless pushed to the limit. Had Levi been pushed over that line? My answer to myself was no. I believed his account of how Pettie had died that fateful night. But it was evident that a cover-up had taken place, certainly involving Levi, and possibly the others in the room.

"It wasn't my idea," Brady said loudly.

"What wasn't?" I asked.

"Getting rid of the body," he replied. He turned and glared at Linc. "Tell 'em, Linc, how you came to the rescue again, figured out how to dump Pettie and lay the blame on old man Durkee."

Linc addressed his answer to the sheriff. "The kid's a liar and always has been, Sheriff, a foul ball. I didn't tell him nothin'."

Brady turned red with anger, his hands clasped into fists at his sides, his eyes going from person to person. He raised his left arm and pointed his index finger at Linc, inches from his face. "Tell 'em, Unc. Tell 'em how you called me, told me to get rid of Pettie's body. Tell 'em!"

I noticed that the knuckles of his left hand were red and bruised. At least he'd sustained some injury to himself from his brutal attack on Barnaby.

Mort started to say something, but Brady raged on, directing his tirade at Mort. "I get a call from Linc here, who's at Levi's house. There's Pettie dead on the kitchen floor, so who does Levi call? He runs to Uncle Linc, of course. So Linc heads over there, and he and Carver put their heads together to try to figure how to cover up what happened. Only they're not smart enough or gutsy enough to get the job done."

"But you were," I said.

"Damn straight, Mrs. Fletcher."

"What did they tell you to do?"

Brady smirked. "Get rid of the body. That's what Linc here said. Levi, he's in a corner about to bawl. Linc says, 'Get rid of the body,' and says he doesn't care how I do it."

"*You* came up with the plan to take the body out on Spencer Durkee's boat and sink it?"

"That's right." He sounded positively proud.

I looked at Linc. "You told the sheriff that Pettie said he had an appointment that night with Spencer. Did you come up with that after you learned that Brady had used Spencer's lobster boat?"

Linc ignored my question and said to his nephew, "You'd better get yourself a lawyer."

"You, too," Brady said defiantly.

Linc came to where Mort and I stood. He said to Mort, "Nobody murdered anybody, Sheriff. It's like Levi says: It was an accident. Pettie tripped and hit his head on the edge of the kitchen counter. Maybe you can find bloodstains using whatever that stuff is you use to see blood when we can't see it with our eyes."

"Luminol," Mort said.

"Yeah, that's right, Luminol."

"I'll do just that," Mort said.

"Nooo," Levi moaned, holding his head. "I cleaned up the kitchen."

"You'd be surprised what we can find," Mort said, "even when people clean up the scene of the crime."

Levi raised his eyes to Mort's. "It was an accident, Sheriff. That's what happened. I'll take a lie-detector test, anything. You've got to believe me."

"I believe you, Levi," I said. "But there's another crime to be considered."

"What now?" Linc asked.

"The attempt on my life." I locked eyes with Brady. "Getting rid of a body and evidence is bad enough, Brady," I said, "but you assaulted me, intending for me to go down to my death along with Henry Pettie's body. That's attempted murder, young man."

Brady started to swear, but Mort said, "Watch your tongue, Holland."

"I surprised you by coming on board the *Done For*, didn't I? You panicked, hit me, and took me along to where you intended to scuttle the boat and get rid of the body—and me. And Maynard over there was your accomplice."

Brady glared at Maynard. "Why, you—"

"I didn't tell them anything, Brady, I swear."

Brady started to reply to me but didn't seem capable of forming the words. Instead, he pointed at Ike Bower. "He was there, too," he said.

"Were you, Ike?" Mort asked.

"Levi called me first," Ike said, his voice quavering. "I went to his house and saw what had happened. It turned my stomach, seeing Pettie lying there on the floor, blood oozing out of the back of his head. Levi wanted me to help move the body, but I wouldn't do it. I told him to call Linc, said Linc would know what to do. So Linc came over and called Brady. That's all I did, show up. That's all I did."

"That, along with concealing evidence, Ike."

Mort turned to Deputy Jenkins. "Better get another squad car down here. Looks like we've got at least five to bring back to headquarters."

Later, after Brady, Linc, Levi, Ike, and Maynard had been taken away in handcuffs, and Alex and Ben had gone off to notify the wives of the prisoners, I stood outside with Mort.

"I feel terrible for Mary," I said. "She had no idea anything was seriously wrong. She came home that night and found Levi cleaning the kitchen and complaining that the kids were tracking in dirt. She thought he was becoming a disciplinarian, and was confused by his change in behavior."

"Funny she didn't question him about it."

"Yes. She should have." I looked up at Mort. "I believe Pettie's death was an accident," I said.

"Yeah, me, too," Mort said.

"What will happen to them, do you think?"

"I don't know. The judge will hear their stories and maybe he'll let them out on bail."

"What a shame they concocted an elaborate scheme to cover up an accident. You see it all the time, the cover-up being much worse than the crime itself. If only Levi had picked up the phone and called you instead of Linc Williams."

"People do strange things when they're scared, Mrs. F."

"Yes," I said, "like trying to kill me, too, as part of the cover-up."

"Attempted murder. Brady will go away for a long stretch for that. I'm going to argue against bail for him."

"I can't say I'm sorry," I said, wrapping my arms about myself as a sudden chill coursed through my body. Visions of being on Spencer's boat as it was sinking caused me to close my eyes against the memory. "I think I'd like to go home now," I said.

Chapter Twenty-three

"Now, the founder of Rum Row was one Cap'n William S. McCoy."

Spencer Durkee sat on a folding chair outside Nudd's Bait & Tackle, a deep-peaked fishing cap shading his eyes from the brilliant sunshine. A gaggle of children surrounded him, some holding their parents' hands, others dancing in and out of the circle the adults had allowed around the storyteller, more sprawled at his feet. "He was a sharp one, McCoy was. Had this slicked-up boat called the *Tomoka*. British registry it was, and he'd heave to outside the three-mile limit, in international waters."

Anna Carver sat slouched on the dock and squinted up at the old salt. "Why wasn't it American?" she asked. "Wasn't *he* American?"

" 'Cause the guard—the coast guard to you—could stop U.S.-registered ships outside our waters, but they couldn't touch the foreign ones."

"Oh, so he was pretendin' to be British."

Spencer smiled. "Kinda. This was back in 'twenty-three, in Prohibition days, you see. McCoy, he was a teetotaler, didn't touch alcohol hisself, but he knew a lot of people could go for a jug now and then, but the law wouldn't let 'em."

"So he brought up rum from the Caribbean," Anna announced, sitting up.

"Now you let me tell it, missy. You're too young to remember these things."

Anna slouched down again and fiddled with her laces. The day was not shaping up as she'd expected. She knew something was wrong at home, but no one had told her what it was. Her parents had been silent at breakfast on this, the most exciting day ever in Cabot Cove. She couldn't understand it. They'd decided against renting out Ginny's old room for the festival. Well, at least that meant more for her of those special cookies from Sassi's Bakery. But she'd trade all them, even those with the chocolate on both ends, for a smile from her father.

"McCoy was no piker," Spencer said. "He got the best booze from the islands, didn't water it down like some others I could tell you about, and sold it at a fair price. He was an honest man in a dishonest business. Anyway, Cap'n McCoy got so popular, people started askin' for his goods by name. They didn't want just any old booze; they wanted the stuff sold by the cap'n." He leaned over and mussed Anna's curly hair. "So, missy, tell the people what they said when they motored out to the *Tomoka* to buy the booty."

Anna smiled. She straightened her back and sang out, "They said 'Gimme the real McCoy.' "

There was laughter from the crowd, mostly from the parents, but also from children who didn't really understand what was funny.

"Ayuh, that's what they said, all right. And that's where we get that sayin' 'the real McCoy.' It's 'cause'a the honest rumrunner, Cap'n William S. McCoy. You ask Tim Nudd, inside, if you don't believe me. He's got a book on rumrunners off the Maine coast. He might show it to you, if you ask him nice."

His audience gave Spencer a round of applause. He nodded his acknowledgment and sat back to bask in the admiration of the youngsters who lingered nearby while the crowd dispersed.

"How do, Mrs. Fletcher?"

"It's nice to see you, Spencer," I said. "You're a star attraction down here."

He cocked his head toward the door. "Old Tim, he hired me to tell my stories, says if I tell a hot supper of a tale, people will come in and look around the store. Guess it's workin'."

"Clever marketing on his part," I said. I leaned down to tap Anna on the shoulder. "How are you, young lady?"

"Okay, I guess. My pop didn't go on the lobstermen's float this mornin'. Said he wasn't feelin' up to it. Too tired. He walked next to it for a while, though."

"And you were disappointed," I said.

"Yeah, but it was the biggest float in the parade, and everybody clapped and yelled for them."

"The lobstermen deserved all those cheers. They provided the reason for the festival—lobsters. That's why all these people are here in Cabot Cove." I looked around. The docks were chockablock with visitors, and so was the downtown, which I'd passed on my way to the harbor. Shoppers were wandering in and out of Cabot Cove's stores on Main Street, smiles on their faces, their arms filled with packages. The Cabot Cove Lobsterfest was a big success.

"I'm goin' over to watch the pageant now," Anna announced. "My friend Emily's sister, Katherine, is one of the contestants. I don't know whether to root for her or for Abigail, my brother's girlfriend."

"Root for Abigail," Spencer told her, winking at me.

"Okay," she said, skipping off.

In light of the honesty and courage demonstrated by a certain young lady, the judges of the Miss Cabot Cove Lobsterfest beauty pageant, among them my good friend Dr. Seth Hazlitt, had rejected the resignation of Abigail Brown the day before, and ruled instead that she could continue as a contestant. Abigail and her parents were ecstatic. *Gazette* publisher Matilda Watson was not certain it was the right decision, but she said she would bow to the collective wisdom of the judging committee.

Judge Ralph Mackin had left his bed to arraign Mort's prisoners in the middle of the night. Levi Carver and Ike Bower were released on their own recognizance, and told not to leave town. Brady Holland and his sidekick, Maynard, who'd driven Alex Paynter's boat out to pick Brady up and whose last name turned out to be Young, had been remanded over to the county seat to face changes of attempted murder and conspiracy to murder. Bail was denied, and they remained in jail. The judge came down hard on Lincoln Williams, head of the lobstermen's association, who, together with Levi and Ike, faced charges of obstruction of justice. Judge Mackin clapped him in a home-detention ankle bracelet, effectively keeping him from participating in the lobster festival, and lectured him on the moral obligations of leadership.

Two Months Later

Fall arrived in Cabot Cove, and I was firmly ensconced in my house working on a new novel. The fallout from the lobster festival, Henry Pettie's untimely death, and the attempt on my life had pretty much dissipated, although they were still topics of conversations at Mara's, in the beauty parlor, and around water coolers in Cabot Cove businesses. I'd managed to put behind me the terror of that night and day at sea on Spencer Durkee's lobster boat, although an occasional dream about it caused me to awake with a start and wonder for a moment whether I was still on that sinking boat.

I'd just finished a chapter in the book I was writing, and had made myself a celebratory cup of tea in my kitchen, when the phone rang.

"Jessica? It's Jim Shevlin."

"Good morning, Mr. Mayor," I said. "What a nice surprise hearing from you on this lovely autumn day."

"I debated bothering you, knowing you're in the midst of another book. But I'm hosting a dinner the night after next for the key people involved in the festival, sort of a postmortem, and hope you'll join us. I meant to do it sooner, but you know how those things can get away from you. At any rate, I'd really be pleased if you can attend."

I agreed to come, and two nights later joined a large group in a private room at Finch Tavern, one of the town's better restaurants. There were more than a dozen people there, including the mayor with a RE-ELECT SHEVLIN button on his lapel, newspaper owner Matilda Watson, her editor, Evelyn Phillips, wearing a long yellow scarf, Jim and David Ranieri of Charles Department Store, Seth Hazlitt, Sheriff Mort Metzger and his wife, and others who'd played a role in organizing the first annual lobster festival. Two of those attending the dinner surprised me with their presence. Gwen Anissina, who I knew had left town after the festival, was there. So was Linc Williams.

"How wonderful to see you," I told Gwen.

"Same here, Mrs. Fletcher. The mayor called and said he wanted me back to work the festival next year."

"What are you doing now?" I asked.

"I've set up my own consulting firm, promoting festivals, concerts, and other community events. I learned a lot here."

"Sounds like you've taken good advantage of the experience, Gwen. It'll be great to have you back."

I looked across the room in which the predinner cocktail hour was taking place, and saw Linc Williams talking with the mayor. Linc noticed me, excused himself from Jim, and came to me.

"Good evening, Mrs. Fletcher," he said pleasantly.

"How have you been, Linc?" I asked.

"Pretty fair," he replied. "Pretty fair."

The legal ramifications of the decisions made by Linc and the others on the night of Henry Pettie's death were well-known to virtually everyone in town.

"I understand Brady Holland is still in jail awaiting trial," I said.

"Yes, but they let Maynard post bail. He's living home with his parents, hasn't been lobsterin' since the summah."

"How are Levi Carver and Ike Bower doing?" I

asked. I knew the three men had received probation, and agreed to hundreds of hours of community service, in return for pleading guilty to obstruction and promising to testify at Brady's and Maynard's trials.

"They're fine. We've finished painting the community center and cleaned up the grassy area next to the highway leading into town. We start in the school next week. We're teaching an assembly on the life cycle of the lobster."

"I'd like to see that myself."

"I don't know if you've heard, Mrs. Fletcher, but the lobstermen's association has established its own co-op to sell our catch directly to wholesalers."

"That sounds like a sensible move," I said. "I *have* heard what you and your men did for Spencer Durkee."

Because there was no record of monies owed Henry Pettie—Brady having tossed overboard Pettie's infamous little black book in which he recorded those IOUs—the men had come up with an alternative way to pay their debts. The association had voted to buy Spencer a new lobster boat. But the old man informed them that, as he put it, "My lobsterin' days are over." The lobstermen then shifted gears and used the money to purchase a small used houseboat for Spencer, and to secure a spot on the docks for him to moor the craft, and live in it rent-free for the rest of his life. He named it the *Tomoka*.

"Anyway," Linc said, "I also want to thank you for convincing Ms. Watson to hold the story out of the paper until after the festival. Even though I wasn't allowed to ride in the parade, having the float and the approval of the crowd meant a lot to the other lobstermen."

"I'm afraid your thanks are misplaced, Linc," I said. "Matilda Watson called me to get my input about holding the story, and I told her I thought it was a good idea. But she made the decision, not me. As for the lobstermen's float, nothing could take away from honoring the men who give so much to our community."

"Well," Linc said, "we were grateful."

He started to walk away, but I called after him, "By the way, Linc, congratulations on being reelected president of the association."

He grinned. "Between that job, lobstering, and the community service I'm supposed to perform, I'll be a busy beaver for the next year. Glad to see you, Mrs. Fletcher. Sorry Brady's a blood relative after what he tried to do to you. I suppose there can be a rotten apple in every family."

He walked away, replaced at my side by Elsie Fricket. She'd shed her plastic collar and was fit and feeling fine again.

"Looks like it's shaping up to be a beautiful fall season," she said.

"My favorite time of year in Cabot Cove," I said. "I'm always full of energy once the trees start turning. Like the squirrels, I suppose, scurrying around getting ready for winter."

She laughed. "I know what you mean. It's a busy time for our youngsters, too. I was just talking to Betsy Corr recently—remember her?"

"That's Katherine's mother, isn't it? How is she, and how is Katherine?"

"Fine. Fine. Katherine is loving college, she says. She sure was thrilled when she won the pageant. She gushed for days, her mom tells me."

"A lovely girl. They all were. I was glad Abigail was allowed to compete. Coming in second isn't so bad. I understand she's settling in nicely, too, over at Colby College."

"It left Evan Carver with a long face, but he'll get over it. These young people are so impetuous, as though their lives will be over if they don't have everything they want right away."

"Life is fleeting," I said. "But I know what you mean. If their budding romance is meant to be, it'll wait until they've prepared for their adult lives."

The dinner was spirited, and self-congratulatory. The lobster festival had been a huge success, and plans were well under way to repeat it next summer. There was much laughter and good-natured ribbing of one another, all in all a wonderful evening.

Seth drove me home when it was over.

"You look happy, Jessica," he said as we sat in front of my house.

"Why shouldn't I be?" I said. "Life is good. I have true friends. The people in this town are caring. Fall is in the air. The leaves on the trees are beginning to paint a lovely picture. My work is going well. Justice has been done. And . . . well, and I'm alive to appreciate it all. Who could ask for anything more?"

Read on for a preview of the next
Murder, She Wrote book

MARGARITAS AND MURDER

Coming from New American Library
in October 2005

The Buckleys left for San Miguel de Allende before I did. Last-minute additions to my book-signing tour, and an interview on The *Today* Show, which was delayed two days due to a deluge of news coverage following the kidnapping and rescue of a world leader attending a conference in Cozumel, wreaked havoc with my travel schedule.

There were compensations. I had an extra day to shop for a special gift for my hosts. The Buckleys were voracious readers, of course, and I'd seen a lovely pair of bookends in Takashimaya on Fifth Avenue that I thought would appeal to them. In addition, the producer who'd arranged my appearance on *Today* tried to compensate for the inconvenience. Grateful for my "flexibility" regarding the change in plans, she gave me a few extra minutes with Katie Couric, more than originally planned, to talk about my new mystery and the life of a mystery writer. On my way out, she stopped me.

"We don't ordinarily do this," the producer said, handing me a videotape with a picture on the box of all the stars of the show, "but we really appreciate your willingness to stick around New York, especially considering the miserable weather we've been having.

I apologize for the heat and humidity, even though there's nothing we can do about it."

"It was no bother at all to stay in town. Besides, I'm leaving tomorrow for sunny Mexico. I have a feeling the weather's not going to be much different. A little drier, perhaps. Thank you for the tape. What's on it?"

"I thought you might like a souvenir of your interview with Katie."

"How thoughtful," I said. "I'll take it with me on the trip. I don't know if my friends get American television in Mexico. I know they'd enjoy seeing this." I didn't mention that one of those friends was my publisher, who would have more than a passing interest in any publicity that might increase book sales, especially mine.

I was lucky to get a seat on a mid-morning, four-hour flight to Mexico City. School was out and the tourist season had begun, filling planes to all the popular places. Olga and Vaughan had told me they usually took a bus from the Mexican capital to San Miguel, although they complained about its erratic timetable and frequent breakdowns in the air conditioning system.

"Fly to León instead," Olga had suggested. "You'll save hours of wear and tear on the road, and we'll send someone to pick you up." So I booked a connecting flight, and e-mailed the Buckleys my itinerary.

Upon landing in Mexico City, I learned the flight to León would be delayed. "Technical problems," a sympathetic gate agent said, shaking her head sadly. The plane wasn't leaving until that night. Since the bus was no longer an option—my luggage had been checked through to León and there was no way to retrieve it—I resigned myself to the wait.

"Take a taxi to the Zócalo," Vaughan said, when I called to relay the news of yet another delay in my travel plans. "It's a short cab ride, unless there's traffic, maybe twenty or thirty minutes. But make sure you use the official cab stands. Don't take a ride from anyone who approaches you in the terminal. There have been a lot of tourist robberies in those kinds of taxis."

"Thank you," I said. "That's good to know."

"There's a beautiful café on the terrace of the Hotel Majestic. They have wonderful food and a spectacular view. Have a late lunch, relax, stroll around the square."

"Sounds wonderful."

"But if you do that, watch out for pickpockets. If you're wearing any jewelry, take it off and hide it somewhere on your person. And stay away from crowds. Perhaps you shouldn't purchase anything. You don't want to be flashing American money."

"I bought pesos before I left," I said, a little taken aback by all his warnings. "Maybe I should visit the Zona Rosa instead."

"I wouldn't. It's not the elegant neighborhood it once was. It fell into decay about twenty years ago. It's being gentrified all over again, but it's still a shadow of its former self and far too trendy for my liking," he said. "I hear Olga calling me. Listen, Jessica, just hang on to your pocketbook, and have a good time. We'll see you later."

I hung up and wondered if I would be better off simply reading my book in the airport, but quickly discarded that idea. Despite it having been many years since I'd visited Mexico City, I remembered the beautiful architecture, the broad avenues, the wonderful museums, the exotic ruins, and the charming people. It was certainly worth giving the city the benefit of the doubt, I thought, as I joined the lines going through immigration.

The main hall of the Benito Juarez International Airport in Mexico City is an immaculate monument to marble—with sweepers pushing long dry mops across the gleaming floors, every twenty feet it seemed, never allowing so much as a dust mote to land on the colorful stone. It was also jammed with people. The hub not only for flights to anywhere in Mexico but also to a good portion of Latin America, the airport handles more than 20 million passengers annually. It looked to me as if a million of them were there when I exited customs. They were leaning on the ropes that separated the travelers from those who welcomed them, crowding the souvenir shops, clothing stores, coffee bars, and magazine stands, jostling me as I walked the length of the terminal, and lined up outside at the "official" taxi stand, manned by yellow-jacketed staff holding clipboards. I stood in line to buy a ticket and waited in line again until it was my turn to climb into the back of the taxi, a small green car in which the front passenger seat had been removed, presumably to accommodate luggage, which I did not have. I told the driver the name of the hotel on the Zócalo that Vaughan had recommended and leaned back against the cracked leather seat for the ride into town.

"Welcome to Mexico, señora," the driver said. He pronounced it "meh-hee-co."

"Muchas gracias," I said, showing off the little Spanish I knew.

"Do you come for business or pleasure?"

"Definitely pleasure," I replied, smiling.

"You are traveling alone, yes?" He didn't wait for me to answer. "You must be very careful traveling alone in the city," he said. "There are some not nice people—*bandidos*—who will try to take advantage of you."

"So I've been told."

He leaned back in his seat, drew a card from his pocket, and handed it to me over his shoulder without taking his eyes from the road. "If you want someone reliable to take you around, show you all the beautiful and historic places, very cheap, you call me. I am Manuel Dias. I don't let anyone cheat you. I take good care of you. Guaranteed."

"That's very kind of you," I said, "but I'm not staying in Mexico City. In fact, I'm leaving this evening."

He clicked his tongue. "We are sorry to lose you," he said. "Where do you go? Acapulco? Cancun? I have a cousin in Merida. Very good man."

"I'm going to San Miguel de Allende to visit friends. They're sending someone to pick me up in León. My flight leaves this evening—at least I hope it will." It hadn't occurred to me till just then that I might have to stay overnight in Mexico City if the "technical problems" were not resolved and wondered if I should buy an extra toothbrush just in case.

"This is terrible," the driver said.

"What's terrible?"

"I have no one for you in San Miguel. In León, maybe yes. I could find someone to help you, but you don't stay there."

"I appreciate your concern, but I'm sure I'll be just fine. My friends will take good care of me."

"You be careful going to San Miguel," he said, shaking a finger. "The country is no safer than the city."

"I'll remember that," I said, leaning forward and extending my arm. "Since I won't be needing it, here's your card."

"No, Señora. You keep it. You must go back to the airport tonight, yes? I will drive you. That way you'll be safe. Some taxis are not reliable. What time is your flight?"

I told him.

"Give my card to the desk at the hotel. They will call. I will pick you up right away. In Mexico, we are very modern. I have the latest in technology." He held up a cell phone.

"That's a wonderful idea," I said. "I'll do that."

"But to be sure, you tell me what time to be at the hotel, and I will be waiting for you."

With Manuel Dias providing running commentary on the places we passed along our way, we set out for the Zócalo. The roads into the city funneled traffic from the wide boulevards of the outskirts, where he kept a heavy foot on the accelerator, to the clogged narrow streets around the downtown square. He guided us forward in agonizing inches, squeezing through impossible openings, and cutting off myriad vehicles to move ahead. Other drivers shouted at him, furious, and he responded with equal vehemence. I was grateful I didn't understand what was being said, and was convinced that the only reason the angry exchanges of frustrated drivers didn't result in violence was that no one had enough room to open a door. The trip took over an hour, and I calculated how much time I could realistically afford to spend in Mexico City before braving the traffic back to the airport in time for my flight. Manuel let me off on a side street around the corner from the front entrance of the hotel, instructing me to meet him at the same place when I was ready to leave. I had a feeling he wasn't going to move from that spot till I got back.

Vaughan's recommendation was a good one. The rooftop restaurant on the terrace of the Hotel Majestic not only overlooked the bustling Zócalo—reputed to be one of the largest public plazas in the world second only to Moscow's Red Square—but afforded a spectacular vista of the city beyond. The hostess ushered me to an empty table by a stone wall from which, by leaning forward, I could observe the goings-on in the plaza below, or sitting back, rest my gaze on the city beyond it. The hot sun poured down on the terrace, but white umbrellas shaded the tables and a steady breeze made the air comfortable.

I ordered *pollo almendrado,* almond chicken, and a glass of orange juice. While I waited to be served, I peered over the wall and watched a group of youngsters dressed in traditional costumes doing an elaborate dance for a throng that encircled them in the square. The boys wore white pants and shirts with multi-colored bands at their waists; the girls were in white dresses with black aprons, red ribbons trailing from small headpieces fluttered as they twirled around. Even from my perch seven floors above them, I could hear snatches of the music and the steady beat of a drum. A burst of applause greeted the end of their performance. They bowed to the audience, then ran to surround the man who had kept time with the drum, presumably their instructor, before he lined them up, two by two, and led them out of the square.

I opened my shoulder bag, pulled out a guide book I'd bought in New York, and identified other buildings that bordered the Zócalo. To my left was the Metropolitan Cathedral, a jumble of architectural styles that nevertheless resulted in an impressive baroque building with a pair of towers flanking one of several grand entrances. My book said it was begun in the 16th Century to replace a cathedral built by Cortes, and that it incorporates not only stones from the ruins of the Temple of Quetzalcoatl, an Aztec god, but also a wall of skulls of Aztec sacrificial victims. Taking up the entire east side of the plaza was the National Palace, built in the 17th Century and home to government offices and the celebrated murals of Diego Rivera depicting the history of Mexico. I glanced at my watch to see if there would be enough time to view the murals or stop into the cathedral. Maybe if I ate quickly, but it didn't look promising.

All thoughts of having a quiet lunch evaporated a few minutes later when a mariachi band—two trumpets, two guitars, a violin, and a vocalist shaking maracas—stepped onto the terrace. I watched those around me look up happily as the band played the first notes of a song, the spirited music coaxing smiles from even the most serious diners. The waiter brought a basket of bread and kept my glass filled with juice until my chicken was served. I ate and listened to the band members as they threaded their way between the umbrellas to serenade each of the tables, my foot keeping time with the lively beat.

The music helped ease the tension of my hectic last few weeks. It was nice to be on vacation. I love to travel, but book tours can be exhausting—a real "if this is Tuesday, it must be Boston" experience. While I enjoy meeting new people, especially readers, seeing new places and learning about them, it's always a pleasant prospect to contemplate a few weeks with nothing specific to do but sit back and relax. No notes to take, no schedules to meet, no rush to catch another plane. Vaughan and Olga were the perfect hosts. They had a busy life of their own, and insisted I was to use their home as it were mine, and join them—or not—as I wished. They had promised that I wouldn't be in their way. "We'll even ignore you, if that's what you want." Which, of course, wasn't what I wanted at all. What I did want was time. Time to renew our acquaintance. Time to stretch out with a book. Time to take leisurely walks in the charming town. Perhaps some gallery or museum visits, or a concert I could treat them to. Just a peaceful vacation with old friends. It sounded wonderful. But I was in for a rude awakening.